DAY TRIPPERS

Recent Titles by Grace Thompson from Severn House

The Pendragon Island Series

CORNER OF A SMALL TOWN
THE WESTON WOMAN
UNLOCKING THE PAST
MAISIE'S WAY
A SHOP IN THE HIGH STREET
SOPHIE STREET

The Holidays at Home Series

WAIT TILL SUMMER
SWINGBOATS ON THE SAND
WAITING FOR YESTERDAY
DAY TRIPPERS

THE SANDWICH GIRL

DAY TRIPPERS

Grace Thompson

This first world edition published in Great Britain 2002 by
SEVERN HOUSE PUBLISHERS LTD of
9–15 High Street, Sutton, Surrey SM1 1DF.
This first world edition published in the USA 2002 by
SEVERN HOUSE PUBLISHERS INC of
595 Madison Avenue, New York, N.Y. 10022.

British Library Cataloguing in Publication Data

Thompson, Grace
    Day trippers. - (Holidays at Home)
    1. World War, 1939-1945 - Social aspects - Wales - Fiction
    2. Domestic fiction
    I. Title
    823.9'14 [F]

    ISBN 0-7278-5830-0

Typeset by Palimpsest Book Production Ltd.,
Polmont, Stirlingshire, Scotland.
Printed and bound in Great Britain by
MPG Books Ltd., Bodmin, Cornwall.

One

The small railway station was full of people waiting for the eleven o'clock train. Shoppers going into town to hunt for extra food to fill their sparsely stocked pantries in this third year of the war. In South Wales as in other places in the spring of 1942, shortages meant a constant search for extras. Besides the hopeful shoppers there were soldiers, sailors and airmen returning from leave, surrounded by their families, all self-consciously watching for the train, dreading saying goodbye. The uniforms were patches of dullness amid the light coats and dresses worn in defiance of the cold breeze by the many civilians. There were workers making their way to shops and offices, thankful it was a Saturday, a half-day for office girls, and even for the shop assistants there was the relief of knowing tomorrow was free.

Three girls were going on a day trip to St David's Well, a seaside town where only limited restrictions on the beach meant it was still a place to have fun. Most beaches were barred to people, and many were mined against possible invasion, even though the imminent threat of Germans landing had eased, due to the remarkable efforts of the Royal Air Force.

As Delyth Owen and Madge Howells worked in a shop, this Saturday off was a treat, a reward from their boss for the long hours they worked now that two male assistants had been called up. Madge was a widow. At eighteen her young husband had been killed in a convoy – only four months after their wedding – and since then Delyth spent a lot of time with Madge, trying to encourage her to look forward and not give in to unrelenting grief.

Delyth was dark, with neatly styled short hair. She liked make-up and sometimes queued when special items arrived

1

in one of the local shops. Madge rarely bothered, in spite of Delyth's entreaties for her to make the best of herself. Since she had lost her husband, and with him the dreams of a home and children, Madge seemed to go through each day in a hazy indifference.

Another girl waiting for the train that Saturday morning stood apart from the others, as though trying to hide herself and avoid being noticed. Vera Matthews was running away. For the day, at least. She had been meeting a married man and the previous evening his wife had found them, kissing, whispering foolish plans they had no intention of carrying out, and had hit her. That wasn't the worst. She had also threatened to tell Vera's parents, and Vera knew that meant a good walloping from her father, whose hands were the size of ping-pong bats to match his size-twelve feet. Dad was a firm believer in punishment, although he was usually loving and kind – except when he felt one of his girls was in danger of going 'off the rails'. Then, he came down on them hard. Getting themselves talked about or developing a reputation for being less than perfect in their behaviour with boys made him over-anxious, and then Vera and her four sisters would feel the power of his anger and distress.

She knew the day away from her home in Bryn Teg was only delaying the punishment. Tonight, when she went back home, he would be waiting. The stupid thing was, she hadn't done half of what she was accused of; she'd only had a bit of fun. What harm was there in a bit of flirting and a few kisses?

She couldn't stop a smile creeping over her face as she remembered Henry Selby's face when his wife appeared. Pity Mrs Selby had been so spiteful. She ought to have been grateful to be reminded that a man needed looking after. From the shrill voice that had screamed abuse at her last night, she didn't seem the soft and gentle kind. Perhaps she'd be a bit more careful in future and look after her husband so he didn't feel the need to cuddle and kiss others. She ought to thank me, Vera thought smugly.

There was another passenger on the platform heading for a day out in St David's Well. Maldwyn Perkins recognised Delyth and Madge but didn't approach them. His days out were a luxury, a time when he could get away from customers at the flower shop where he worked, and from his stepmother's constant reminders that he ought to leave home and get a place of his own. He was so constantly harassed by Winifred that he dreaded walking into the house he had once considered his home.

If only the Army had taken him, he could have gone away without a moment's regret. Not having to make a decision, or wonder where he would live or what he would do to earn his living, would have made his departure easy, even exciting. But how could she expect him to just leave, find himself a job and a place to live? He pushed the worries from his mind. Today was a rare day off and he was on his own, waiting for the train to take him to his favourite place.

When they got on the train, others eased off their coats and settled to chatter and make plans for their day, but Maldwyn tried to blot them all out. He looked solemn behind his thick, dark-framed glasses, his knees close together, his elbows tight against his sides, his head bent low as he concentrated on a magazine he had bought, and his 'closed-up' attitude discouraged other passengers from trying to make conversation. That suited him. He wasn't in the mood to be friendly. He wanted to be on his own to think.

He had found a seat in a carriage far away from Delyth and Madge. He didn't want to face them and have to talk. He'd hurry out of the station when he arrived and with luck might not even have to wave. They had to change trains half-way through the journey, and Maldwyn ran to where the almost-full train was waiting and managed to find a seat without bumping into Delyth and Madge. There were quite a number of people travelling to St David's Well, many returning with full shopping baskets.

As the train pulled into the small station in St David's Well Bay, Delyth nudged Madge and whispered: 'Look over there by the door. Isn't that Maldwyn Perkins from the florist's shop? In a hurry to get off, isn't he? I wonder if he's meeting someone?'

Madge nodded. 'Go on, speak to him,' she whispered back. 'You know you want to.'

Delyth made no secret of her attraction to the rather taciturn Maldwyn, but as he was at least six years older than herself she did nothing about it. 'He's nice to look at,' she told her friend, 'apart from his heavy glasses, that is. They're so thick they cut you off from what he's thinking, don't they? Anyway, I suspect he's too set in his ways to offer any excitement.' At seventeen, Delyth rated excitement very high on her list of important things. The train emptied gradually and by the time they had reached the terminus there were only a few passengers to alight. Maldwyn wondered how he would escape from the platform without having to acknowledge Delyth and Madge. The train slowed to a stop and the remaining passengers alighted and hurried to where the ticket collector waited. Showing their tickets, the two girls hurried from the station and headed towards the sea.

It was almost midday when they arrived and they were the only ones walking down the sandy slope to the beach; others presumably had more comfortable destinations: homes and roaring fires. Delyth and Madge guessed from the loaded bags most carried that they were returning home with their meagre shopping successes. Most women spent hours searching for extras to break the monotony of the restricted food supplies.

Delyth carried a satchel containing a sketchbook and a selection of pencils, Madge carried a book. They had also brought food and a bottle of Tizer.

'Mad we are, planning to sit on the beach as though it's summer,' Delyth laughed.

'If you want to draw the beach without anyone on it, this is your only chance. Full it'll be, once summer comes,' Madge said, tapping her friend's sketchpad.

They both worked in a shop selling clothes, children's school uniforms as well as suits and dresses, skirts and blouses for women. When Mr Howard had given them this Saturday off as a reward for their hard work and staying after hours several times to help re-dress the windows or deal with the reorganisation of the stock rooms, their automatic choice was the seaside town of St David's Well and the sandy bay their destination. Regular day trippers they were, and this was their favourite place.

4

'Would you like to live here?' Madge asked. 'We were going to settle here after the war, John and me.' Her voice echoed with sadness when she mentioned her sailor husband. 'We were thinking of opening a guesthouse to accommodate summer visitors.'

Ignoring the mention of her friend's dead husband, Delyth shook her head. 'Not for me. Too dull. Now London, that's the place to go. Plenty happening there. Once the war's over, that's where I want to go.'

'If you marry someone local you probably won't even move as far from home as this,' Madge replied, waving an arm around the bay and the headland.

'Someone like Maldwyn Perkins you mean? Fat chance of that!'

'Or someone else we've grown up with. Isn't that what usually happens?'

'Not for me. I like Maldwyn, mind, but I don't want a boring future. The war is horrifying and there's no good can come out of something so dreadful, but it has opened the door and allowed us a peep at what's outside our safe little world, hasn't it?'

'I hope you don't leave, Delyth. I'd be lost if you weren't here.'

'Don't worry,' Delyth laughed. 'You're probably right and all my plans for adventure in the big wide world will fade when I meet the man of my dreams. But it won't be Maldwyn Perkins, that much is certain.' She tried to convince herself she meant it, that Maldwyn wasn't part of her dreams, as she took out her pencils and flipped open the pad. She began to draw: strong, confident strokes marking the shapes and a softer lead filling in the varying depths and facets of the rocks topped with grass and the burgeoning promise of the new season's wild flowers.

Madge watched her friend's efforts for a while then opened her book. Her bookmark was a photograph of her dead husband and she stopped now and then to stare at it, trying to convince herself he was not coming back. As always, she failed. She stared across the empty beach at the incoming tide and pretended he was out there in a small boat, waiting to be found. He was only eighteen. How could he be dead?

Maldwyn Perkins leaned against the sea wall and looked down at the smooth golden sand. The tide was far out – 'Gone to Somerset,' the locals joked. Mal had heard the remark often, and every time the listener laughed as though hearing it for the first time. He wasn't a local but wished he were. He had always lived in the same valley town as Delyth and Madge, and this was his special place, his day out. He came as often as he could to enjoy a few hours of the sea air, envying those who stayed.

His home was Bryn Teg, an hour's journey to the north, a small, friendly valley town to which the coal mines gave life. Behind the house was a stream that ran black from the coal and dust that it collected on its journey to the sea. He'd been happy in the neat little terraced house near the stream, but everything in his life had changed since his mam had died and his father had married Winifred and brought her to live with them. Now, with his father dead and Winifred making the little house hers alone, he no longer felt a part of the place. Particularly since Winifred had told him she would be leaving the house – the house his parents had struggled to buy and maintain – to her niece.

He leaned on the strong sea wall and looked down at the beach and the few people wandering along, stopping occasionally like himself to enjoy the peace of out-of-season St David's Well Bay, and wished he could forget his stepmother and stay here, where he felt anonymous but with a completely illogical sense of belonging.

It was April 1942 and he was aware that among the people gathering for a few hours of simple pleasure there were very few men. If only he had been able to join up. Instead he sold flowers and tried to ignore the insults of those who accused him of avoiding the fight. He shivered as the slightly chill wind blew mites of sand across the promenade in a pattern of swirls, changing and re-forming as he watched.

He saw a couple of men walking down the slope at the end of the promenade and on to the sand, carrying some lengths of metal. He settled to watch, content to be entertained by their efforts, which he soon realised were to set up the base for one of the stalls that would soon be selling beach balls, flags, windmills and balloons, as well as the inevitable buckets and spades.

It would be a couple of weeks yet before the stalls opened for business, but with so many men serving in the forces the stallholders would take advantage of help when it was offered rather than wait for the right time.

He watched as the lengths of metal were fastened together to form the frame of the stall, which later on would be clad in striped or brightly painted canvas; then his eyes wandered, looking for further amusement. He found it in the café high on the cliff path to his right. A voice, shouting angrily, alerted him to the activity near the steep metal steps that led up from the beach.

'Marged! Leave that will you, and help me get this bit of wood in place.'

She was a long way away but her voice was shrill and in the silence of the morning, with the tide so far away, the reply was loud and clear.

'For heaven's sake, Huw. I can't now this minute! You'll have to wait!'

Maldwyn turned and ran towards the steps, his feet sinking into the soft sand at each stride. 'Hang about, I'll come and help you,' he called to a man at the top of a ladder who was banging on the window of the café.

'There you are,' the woman's voice shouted, as though she had personally performed a miracle, 'if the Lord don't come, he sends.'

Maldwyn climbed the metal stairway, his shoes making them ring with every step, smiling at being described as God's messenger.

The man, who introduced himself as Huw Castle, proprietor of Castle's Café, waved vaguely at his wife and said, 'That's Marged,' then explained what he wanted. Maldwyn held a piece of wood in place while Huw fixed it with hot bone-glue and screws. 'Takes a bit of a battering, this place does,' he explained as he climbed in through the café window and invited

7

Maldwyn to do the same. 'Every year we have to start early to get the place ready for the season. There's always a bit of patching needs doing.'

Marged handed them both cups of tea and welshcakes, hot from the bakestone where more were cooking. As always when strangers met, they were soon discussing the war.

'You heard about Malta being awarded the George Cross?' Huw asked.

Maldwyn nodded. 'I don't know how they've coped with the incessant bombing without giving in. What's so remarkable is that it isn't just a handful of brave people, it's the whole island in agreement, refusing to give in, determined to repel the German Army.'

'Heroes every one of 'em,' Huw agreed. 'Dozens of supply ships sunk and them on the brink of starvation and still they won't give in. Them and our Merchant Navy and Royal Navy boys show Hitler why we won't ever be beat and that's a fact,' he added.

'We have a son in the Army,' Marged said, staring at him with undisguised disapproval. 'Our Eynon was only seventeen when he joined up. And our Ronnie was wounded so bad he couldn't go back.'

'Everyone is in the same boat, worrying about our boys,' Huw sighed. 'My brother Bleddyn who works with us has already lost one son, and his Johnny in the thick of it. Terrible worry.'

'In case you're wondering,' Maldwyn said, 'the reason I'm not in the forces is because my eyesight is poor. They reckon I'd be a liability rather than a help,' he said, attempting a joke to cover his embarrassment.

'What do you do? Munitions factory or something?' Huw asked.

When Maldwyn, shame-faced, admitted he worked in a flower shop, Huw burst out laughing. 'Damn me, that's funny. Us sitting here talking about bravery and me selling buckets and spades and you selling flowers. Thank God for our wonderful servicemen and the remarkable Maltese civilians.'

Maldwyn felt ashamed, as always, when he explained about his job. He had started there as a young boy and had felt no desire to do anything different. He had tried to find an occupation that would help the war effort but each time he had been turned down. Huw sensed his embarrassment and tried to comfort him. Marged watched over the welshcakes on the bakestone and said nothing. There was disapproval in the swiftness of her movements as she turned the flat cakes over, and in her eyes as she looked at him from time to time. She glared angrily at her husband too.

Why should this boy be safe, while Ronnie was suffering from a damaged leg and Eynon was out there facing danger every moment of his young life? Eynon had already been captured, and had escaped from a prison camp to return to his unit. Huw's brother had lost one son and the other was in North Africa. How could Huw be so kind to a man of conscription age who sold flowers and make a joke of it?

Maldwyn learned that the Castle family owned other businesses as well, including a fish-and-chip shop/restaurant, run by Huw's brother Bleddyn, and a shop that sold novelty seaside rock and other sweets. 'They're talking about rationing sweets before the summer's out, and a sweet shop hit by rationing would no longer survive here on the beach. Being seasonal, we couldn't cope with the conditions of rationing. We can put leftover buckets and spades away until the next season, but you can't do that with sweets,' Huw explained.

'Sell food instead,' Maldwyn suggested. 'Bacon and pease pudding goes down well,' he added. 'Off-ration food is a sure way to make money.'

Huw looked thoughtful but shook his head. 'I doubt if I'll get a licence. No, it'll have to be a gift shop selling souvenirs and saucy postcards like so many more.'

As Maldwyn thanked them and walked away, Huw shook his head and said, 'There goes an unhappy man.'

'Serve him right, cowardly and useless that he is.'

'No, no, Marged. I don't think he's either of those things. I like him. Pity 'elp us if we condemn people without knowing their story.'

Maldwyn went back to the promenade via the metal steps and across the sand. On the promenade he stopped again and looked down towards the edge of the tide, which was slowly approaching. There were more people about now: mothers with children wrapped up in woollen hats and thick scarves against the chill wind, playing chase with the waves, daring to go close then running back as though followed by a fearsome monster. How many times had he played that same game? Other children, wearing matching hats and coats and with leather leggings that buttoned all the way down the sides to protect their legs from the cold, walked sedately beside prams being pushed by neatly dressed mothers. There were young women dressed unnecessarily smartly for such an outing, giggling at nothing at all, just friends enjoying themselves. He felt a pang of envy. He was twenty-three and there wasn't much laughter in his life, and few people he could call friends.

Poor eyesight had lost him the chance of escaping from home when conscription began and he knew that he lacked the nerve to make a move without an excuse, even though his stepmother hinted that she wanted him to leave. He had to get away. If he could make the break and live in a place like St David's Well, his life would change, he knew it. But leaving everything behind him would take a lot of courage. Like leaping off the highest diving-board without being able to see the water below. He didn't think he could do it.

It wasn't as though he had any useful skills. He worked in a florist, and that wouldn't get him far if he went looking for work. He couldn't find useful war work: with his eyes being less than perfect, the Army were doubtful about his ability. The thought of an accident had made them shake their heads when he had tried. Nonsense really. He needed glasses, so what? There were plenty of servicemen who did. His eyes were hazy at times, slow to focus, that was all, but his failure to be accepted into the Army seemed to mark him down as useless.

Vera spent most of her day on the beach. It wasn't really warm enough for sunbathing and it was too early in the season to swim, so she sat in the shelter of the rocks and read a book, unaware that Delyth and Madge, whom she had known at school, were sitting not far away. She had seen them leaving the train, and had also watched Maldwyn hurrying through the

10

exit on some errand of his own. Vera was a gregarious person and spending a day without company was not something she enjoyed. She snapped the book shut, not having taken in a single word of what she had read, and wandered up to the few shops and cafés that were open for business. Surely she'd find someone to talk to?

She was determined not to go home until late. Perhaps she'd be lucky and her father would be out, either on his fire-watching or at a Home Guard meeting. Pity he was too old for the Army. It would have been nice to be without his disapproving presence for a while. She and her mam and her sisters would manage all right, even though Mam was getting a bit vague and kept telling them she'd never cope without him. She probably only said it to flatter him into thinking he was needed, Vera thought unkindly.

Later, when night had begun to creep in over the town and a cold wind encouraged the last of the walkers to hurry away home, she stood outside the darkened fish-and-chip restaurant called Castle's for a while, wondering what to do to fill the time until she could go home. She determined to wait until at least the nine o'clock train. With luck, by the time she reached home her father would be either out or in bed.

Lights around her were slowly being extinguished as black-out curtains and barricades were put in place for the evening. The café behind her didn't show even a thread of light to let customers know it was open for business. Instead a chalk notice had been hung on a hook near the door announcing that Castle's was 'Frying Tonight'.

A man approached and she moved away.

'Waiting for someone?' he asked.

'No, wondering if I can afford a plate of fish and chips,' she said with a laugh.

'Come on, I'll treat you,' he said, taking her arm and guilding her towards the entrance with its blackout doorway, a tunnel-like addition built to prevent light escaping from inside. She allowed herself to be led. This might be an amusing way of killing time.

Inside, the lights dazzled after the dullness of the evening. She looked up to see who her companion was and saw a soldier little more than her own age. He ordered their food and led her to a corner table where they were served by a pleasant woman they learned was Hetty Castle, the wife of the proprietor, Bleddyn.

The young soldier told her he was stranded between trains and, rather than wait on the station platform, had decided to spend a few hours in St David's Well.

'Have you been here before?' Vera asked.

'No, I don't know this area at all. I'm stationed at Brecon and came to visit a friend.'

'I live about an hour away but I come here often, specially in the summer. It's a great place for a day out.'

'A bit early for a day by the sea?'

'To be honest, I'm keeping away from our dad. I hope to avoid him until he's calmed down a bit or I'll get a wallop.' She laughed, and explained something of her family, making a joke of her father's anxiety about his girls getting into trouble.

'I'm one of three, all boys, and I miss my family a lot. There's always this fear that we won't all meet again, that if I get back one of my brothers won't. It's a feeling of dread that fills every waking moment and gives me nights invaded by terrible dreams.'

In the oasis of a corner table in Castle's Café, they shared confidences, safe in the belief they were unlikely to meet again and, when they went for their trains, they kissed goodbye like lovers.

Maldwyn Perkins strolled around the town. There was a florist in the main street: 'Chapel's Flowers of St David's Well', the sign announced. He went to look in the window to see what they were doing that he could emulate in his own place. A waste of time really, as his boss was always reluctant to accept new ideas. From the clothes shop next door a man came out and after the usual pleasantries said, 'She won't be there much longer. I'll be buying her out any time now. Old, she is, and with no family to help she'll be retiring and I can expand. Smart shop I'll have then, eh? Double-fronted and painted a cheerful yellow.' He held out a hand. 'Elliot's the name, Arnold Elliot.'

Mrs Chapel, a small, plump, rosy-faced lady in her late fifties, came out of the flower-shop door and began washing down the windowsills. Mr Elliot waved and went back to his own premises. Mrs Chapel smiled at Maldwyn, glad of someone to talk to. When Maldwyn told her he worked for a florist she treated him like a long-lost friend. They exchanged commiserations about the difficulties the war had caused to the business, and Maldwyn promised to call next time he came to the town. He was smiling as he stepped out on to the pavement and, turning to give Mrs Chapel one more wave, he bumped into Madge and Delyth.

'Hi yer Maldwyn. Going for the train?' Madge asked.

'Yes, but not yet. I'm after something to eat then I thought I'd walk along the front one more time,' he smiled. 'I always hate having to leave, don't you?'

'Glad to get home, me,' Delyth said. 'I only came to do a bit of sketching.' She offered her book for him to see what she had done.

He lifted his glasses up to his brow, held the pages close to his face and examined her work.

Delyth stared at him. His eyes were a deep velvety brown, surprisingly unfamiliar without the thick, dark frame of the glasses around them. He looked sort of naked, and she felt as though she were prying. She turned away as he dropped the spectacles back into place, and Maldwyn thought she was afraid he might criticise her work. She wasn't exceptional, he thought, but had managed to capture the scene of the men setting up the base of the stall on the sand. On another page she had drawn Huw Castle and himself, fixing the piece of wood around the café window. He told them what had happened, then, after praising her efforts, suggested they all went for fish and chips at the café nearby. 'My treat,' he smiled, 'a reward for a budding artist.'

To Maldwyn's surprise he saw Huw and Marged Castle there as he ushered the girls inside.

'Hello again,' Huw said. Marged just nodded, unable to forget his failure to help the war effort; selling flowers while so many suffered.

They were introduced to Bleddyn and Hetty, then settled

into the corner table that Vera and her soldier had recently vacated. They began to talk about their day out and plan the next. The brief assistance he had given Huw and the friendly conversation with Mrs Chapel at the flower shop had given Maldwyn the feeling of being among friends. He was warmed by the encounters and happier than he'd felt for a long time. He no longer felt the need to be alone, and looked forward to spending the next hour or so with Delyth and Madge, to exchange news of their day out.

'When summer comes we'll be here every Sunday, and most Wednesdays too. With the lighter evenings it'll be worth the trip,' Madge said. 'It's great when the town is full of visitors. Starting in May it gets better and better.'

Delyth agreed. Perhaps Madge was right, and her future lay nearer home than London after all. She looked at Maldwyn, remembering the deep brown eyes behind the formidable glasses. 'Perhaps we can meet again and share a meal. It's fun to talk about what we've done, isn't it, Madge?' she said, looking to her friend for support.

They didn't want to go home and end the day yet, so they caught a bus back to the beach and wandered across the now empty sands. Darkness had fallen, and as there were no lights once blackout time had arrived, they all linked arms and ran through the sand at the edge of the tide, where the brightness of the surf gave some illusion of light.

The shops and houses were all in darkness. A few vehicles passed with partially shaded lights, and the buses too were sparsely lit. Still with arms linked companionably, they went to the railway station a short distance from the beach.

Maldwyn was thinking of how Huw had waved and told him to be sure and call next time he came. Mrs Chapel was on the platform with her baskets filled with paper flowers and twigs. 'I've been to collect some artificial flowers made by a friend,' she explained. 'I'll make some arrangements to sell tomorrow.' While the girls listened with interest, Maldwyn and Mrs Chapel discussed her artificial offerings and her plans for using them. She alighted at the station in the centre of the town and waved enthusiastically as she left. 'Cheerio, then, Maldwyn. Come and see me next time. Don't forget now. You girls an' all, mind. Welcome you'll be.'

As he travelled back to the house he shared with his stepmother, Maldwyn had an even stronger feeling than usual that the place he was leaving was where he truly belonged.

He saw Delyth and Madge to their homes, which were next door to each other, but refused an invitation to go in and have a cup of tea. It was late and he had no desire for further company. He wanted to stay with his dream of living and working in St David's Well.

He hesitated before stepping inside his back door. The house had been his home all his life but he no longer had the right to it. When his mam had died, his father had quickly remarried; with Winifred taking on the running of the house, life had settled down into something near to normal. Nothing much changed, the furniture remained the same, and the meals Winifred cooked were chosen to suit his father. But when his father was killed in a road accident only a month after the blackout regulations came into force, everything from his past life had been stripped away. Out went the furniture, in came new, chosen at the auction rooms in the town. Heavy velvet curtains were replaced by pale cream cotton. Woodwork and wallpaper were stripped and workmen employed to redecorate in more cheerful colours. Even the food changed: puddings were a thing of the past and salads appeared practically every day.

His comfortable double bed had been sold and a small one had taken its place. Most of his childhood possessions had been packed into boxes and put in the cellar: planes and ships he had made, photographs of himself and his parents in formal attire, books that had been attendance rewards from Sunday school. Just one teddy bear remained, and a train set on top of his wardrobe, with the suitcase he had used when they had gone to St David's Well for a holiday. All these things had happened without consultation. The house was no longer his; he had been reduced to being a lodger whose opinion didn't matter.

Once, when he went home to find all his father's books burning on a bonfire in the garden, he complained angrily and she had told him he could move out if he didn't like it.

'How can I do that? It's my home,' he'd replied.

'Not any more it isn't. Your father left the house to me, and after my time it's going to my niece.'

After that shock he accepted everything she did without complaint. He didn't earn enough to move out and find a place of his own. Any money his father had intended to leave him was no longer there for him. Winifred cared for him well but regularly asked him what his plans were for moving on, reminding him his future was not secure, that things had to change.

He stood at the door in the darkness of the April night and wished he didn't have to take the next step that would take him into the kitchen that belonged to a stranger, a stranger who wanted him gone.

'It's only me,' he called as he hung up his coat and trilby. He'd stopped using the familiar and complimentary 'Mam' when she'd told him he no longer belonged.

'Have a good day out?' Winifred called, and he went into the living room where his stepmother sat on a couch listening to the wireless.

He sat beside her and told her some of the events of his day.

'Perhaps I'll come with you next time, Maldwyn. I used to like a day at the seaside.'

'That'll be nice,' he lied. He had no intention of going anywhere with her, not after what she had done. Companionable outings, once a regular pleasure, were now a thing of the past.

'I've made a plate of sandwiches and the kettle's boiling for a cup of cocoa. Sit down and I'll bring it in. We can sit by the fire and enjoy the last of the heat.'

She treated him as generously as always, he had to admit that. Meals and clean clothes when he needed them. When they had eaten their supper, she kissed him and said in Welsh, 'Good-night, angels watch over you,' just as his own mother had done.

He knew she wanted him to leave, find a place of his own,

16

but on the other hand, surely she needed him? She couldn't relish living alone. Perhaps, he thought with dread, she was planning to remarry. Then any connection they'd had would be completely gone and he would have no one at all. On that sombre thought, he slept.

At the other end of town, Vera Matthews went inside and ran to her room. Perhaps if she could avoid her father until the following day his temper might have eased and she would escape the thrashing. She sneaked into the bedroom she shared with her sisters and as they giggled she told them of her adventures, making much more of her meeting with the lonely soldier than had actually happened. The door opened and her father came in. He refused to listen to her denials and smacked her as he would a child, turning her over and hitting her twice on her buttocks, while at the doorway her mother looked on in silence.

There were stifled giggles from her sisters, and heavy breathing from Vera as she defiantly refused to cry. She was full of resentment and a determination to leave her home for ever.

In St David's Well, Marged and Huw stayed to help Bleddyn and Hetty to clear up after the restaurant closed. Hetty made a tray of tea and they sat down for an unofficial business meeting.

'With the season starting in a few weeks, we're desperate short of help,' Huw began. 'With the boys gone to fight, and our Beth married and running the market café, she can't be expected to give us more than an hour or two now and then.'

'Your Lilly?' Hetty suggested.

'Useless, as usual,' Huw snapped. 'Never was one for work, our Lilly, and being married and having a little girl she has all the excuses she needs for doing nothing at all to help the family.'

For once Marged didn't spring to their daughter's defence. She was still smarting from the shock of Lilly, an unmarried mother of a little girl, marrying Sam Edwards, a man the same age as her father, without telling anyone what she planned.

They made a list of those available to help on the beach stalls and cafés, noting the hours they might be free from school or other occupations.

'It's looking a bit thin,' Bleddyn sighed. 'I almost asked that young chap who helped you with the window if he wanted a job! Dragging people from the streets we'll be, if the labour shortage gets any worse.'

'The one selling flowers instead of doing war work? We don't want the likes of him working here,' Marged said sharply.

'If he can count and is honest, I'd take him tomorrow,' Bleddyn said grimly. 'Selling flowers might be trivial but there's no sense in being a dead hero either.'

They were silent for a moment, aware of Bleddyn's reference to his son Taff, who had been killed the previous year.

Delyth and Madge had been friends all their lives. They had started school only a term apart, when Madge's parents moved into the house next door, and had rarely quarrelled. They had no brothers or sisters and their closeness was valuable to them both. Madge's parents worked as caretakers at the local school and Delyth's father had been a policeman. He had died several years before and her mother was comforted by an 'uncle' Trev.

Delyth's father had left behind several sketchbooks filled with his interpretations of local scenery. This was the reason she tried to follow him and fill books with her own efforts. She knew she wasn't good enough but had to do it as a sort of link with her childhood, when she had so often sat beside him, watching his pictures come to life.

Everyone told Madge how lucky she was having two devoted parents, with her father being too old for conscription, but in fact Betty and Geoffrey Davies hadn't let the birth of their daughter interfere with their life at any time. She often thought she might as well have been an orphan for all the interest they took in her. During her childhood they had filled their days with the school and the local gardening club and the darts team and many other activities, leaving Madge in the care of Nora Owen, Delyth's mother. She often remarked to Delyth that she had been nothing more than a slight interruption in her parents' lives.

Although Madge had married, she hadn't left home. She and John had decided to stay with her parents and gather the possessions they would need ready for the home they would build once the war ended. Memories of her husband seemed to tie her to the house, with its echoes of the short time they'd had together. She knew she depended on Delyth more than she should, and wondered whether she would ever be able to cope without her, or would retreat into a shell of loneliness. Most of their plans were suggested by Delyth, so when the latest was spoken, she was shocked into making a decision.

'What about us joining the Army or something, Madge?' Delyth asked the day after their trip to St David's Well Bay. 'It's time we did something. In fact it's a miracle we haven't been called up before this. Almost eighteen we are.'

'The Army? I don't fancy that. Couldn't we go into the factories? The pay's better than we get in the shop.'

'That's local. Leaving home is the key. Factory work won't take us away from home, will it? Don't you want to get away?'

'Well, no, not really. I want to stay where we were happy, John and me.'

'Stuck here for ever, you'll be, if you don't make a move now. Come on, let's think about it, make plans before we're told where to go and what to do, is it?'

'I'd quite like to live in St David's Well, wouldn't you?'

'Hardly adventurous, moving to a town an hour's journey away from home!'

'Let's go there again next Wednesday and see what work there is. Talk to people, find out what's going on. There has to be some war work, with employers looking out for beautiful young women like us,' she joked.

April had turned into May before they went and, although the weather hadn't improved dramatically, in the small seaside resort summer had arrived. It was as though someone had pressed a switch and the town had come to life. The month of May heralded the start of the summer season and everyone involved with the organisation of Holidays at Home was determined to make it succeed.

With the war raging on without a sign of an end, the government encouraged every town and village to offer entertainments to keep people from travelling during the holiday period. Transport was needed for the armed forces, their equipment and stores, and there were restrictions on the movements of many commodities that weren't considered absolutely necessary.

The café high above the beach in St David's Well opened at the same time as the stalls on the sands sprang up like mushrooms almost overnight, offering whatever the owners could find to sell. Home-made windmills painted in gaudy colours whizzed around alongside the last of the factory-produced ones. Bathing costumes were now available only with clothing coupons since clothes-rationing had begun in June 1941, but the few still in stock would be cautiously offered to interested customers 'under the counter' – a phrase increasingly used for illegal transactions.

As well as the activities on the beach, the town itself developed an atmosphere of gaiety to entice the people to stay in the town and ignore the temptations offered by other, faraway places. At the same time, the town council ignored the other side of the plans, to reduce the numbers of people travelling, and did its best to coax people from other towns to visit. They wanted their own people to stay but saw nothing wrong with expecting other places to part with their citizens for a day or a weekend or a week to enjoy what St David's Well had to offer. 'Following the plan to the letter but not entering the spirit of it' was how Huw put it.

'Cheating, more like,' Marged smiled as they watched the crowd emerging from the station and heading for the beach one Sunday morning. She and Huw were in the van, having been back to their house in Sidney Street for fresh supplies. With an unexpectedly mild weekend after a few days of rain, the crowds were greater than they expected, and at home, Marged's sister Audrey had been making scones and mixing the ingredients for welshcakes ready for Marged to cook on the premises, offering tempting smells to whet the appetites of their customers.

The café was full, with Bleddyn and Hetty struggling to cope, and at once Huw went to the counter to serve while Marged began unpacking scones and filling them with the thin jam and artificial cream that were all they could get, and turning on the heat under the bakestone ready to cook the welshcakes.

There was the usual lull before lunch and they managed to sit and drink a cup of tea and eat a sandwich. Beth, Marged and Huw's daughter, arrived at twelve to help and she busied herself preparing trays for the few who considered it warm enough to eat on the beach. Beth ran the market café, and as her husband, Peter, was in the forces, she came to help her parents and Uncle Bleddyn whenever she was free.

Maldwyn, Delyth and Madge were among Beth's first lunchtime customers. Once more they had met on the train, being unaware of their joint plan to make the half-day trip.

'Hello again, you three,' Huw smiled. Marged greeted the girls but only nodded at Maldwyn. He sensed her continued disapproval and guessed the reason.

'Looking for war work we are,' Delyth said. 'Are there any factories around the town where we can apply? Got to be good wages, mind, we'll have lodgings to pay.'

Huw wrote down the names and addresses of a few places where they might apply and, ignoring the beach and its rowdy activities with regret, they went to seek out employment that would be classed as war work. Maldwyn wished them luck but didn't go with them.

'Why aren't you looking for something similar?' Marged asked, her voice harsh with criticism.

'I know I'll be turned down,' he said, his voice tight with embarrassment. 'I've tried seventeen times and been told the same thing. Everybody thinks I'll have an accident and be more nuisance than help.' Without waiting for further comment, he left the café and hurried out across the headland.

'Now see what you've done!' Huw grumbled. 'We might have found ourselves a bit of help there, if you hadn't been so disapproving! You don't need perfect eyesight to count out a few coppers of change, do you? I can do it with my eyes shut! Poor boy was sick with shame.'

Marged went to the window and looked out across the green grass that led across the hill and down to the next bay. Throwing off her apron, she hurried out to try to find Maldwyn.

He was sitting in a hollow sheltered by bushes that were bent over against the constant wind from the sea, where she guessed he would be. It was where everyone sheltered when they wanted the view and not the cold breezes.

'Want a job?' she asked briskly. She wasn't going to apologise, it wasn't the thing to do if she were to become his employer.

'I might.'

'We need help desperate. Looking after the rides, taking the money, helping sometimes on the stalls selling the usual necessities for a day on the beach, whatever we can find. Interested?'

'I don't know. I'll have to—' He was about to say, 'I'll have to ask Mam,' when he realised how stupid that would sound. 'I'll be needing lodgings. If I can find a place to live I'll come and talk to you, OK?'

'OK,' Marged said. 'Now if you like you can come back and have a cup of tea and a welshcake, no charge. Call it staff perks.'

Vera Matthews wasn't in St David's Well that day. She was at home, trying various make-up tricks to disguise her bruised face. The previous night, after being refused permission to go to a local dance at a nearby RAF camp, she had slipped out through a window and gone anyway. Her father was waiting for her when she reached home and went in through the door her sisters had promised to open for her. The slap and the ensuing argument had ended with her father saying she had to behave or leave. She didn't think the choice would be a difficult one to make.

Delyth and Madge were unlucky with their quest for work. The small town had been designated a holiday area, with no plans to build factories, which had been sited in places convenient to roads and railways that would allow the goods to be moved quickly to their destinations. The town boasted few buildings suitable for converting into factories apart from those already used to store food for the Army, so there was very little employment that could be justified with the name of war work.

They reached home that night, having listened to Maldwyn telling them of his promise of work on the beach, despondent and resigned to staying at home for the duration of the war and probably for the rest of their lives.

'Let's go further afield and try for work in one of the larger towns,' Delyth suggested. 'Desperate I am to get away from home. Mam and Uncle Trev mooning about like two lovesick schoolkids and me feeling more and more that I'm in the way.'

There were letters waiting for them telling them that unless they found suitable occupations beforehand, they had to report to the local machine-parts packing sheds in three weeks and sign on there for work.

'Damn it all, Madge,' Delyth sighed. 'We might have left it too late.'

Madge touched her husband's photograph and tried not to show her relief.

Two

A mong hundreds of day trippers heading for St David's Well one Wednesday afternoon, Delyth, Madge and Vera were on their way to enjoy a day of sunshine, sea and sands as promised by the holiday posters on the railway stations.

Delyth and Madge chattered happily about how they would spend their few hours of freedom. Vera sat silent and alone. She was attempting to hide another bruised face: her father had seen her being escorted home by a young airman. She had seen the friends at the station but, being tired of inventing stories to explain her injuries, she avoided them. Maldwyn hadn't appeared and she was disappointed. She wouldn't have minded explaining to him, and having his sympathy pouring over her like a soothing stream. She desperately needed a friend at the moment.

She waited until the train emptied at the terminus and watched everyone push their way through the exit, laughing and making plans. When the platform was clear, she went out. Offering her ticket, she pulled her dark hair as far as she could over her face but the damage caused by her father's hand didn't escape the sharp-eyed ticket collector.

'What happened to you, love? You could do with a piece of steak on that.'

'If I had a steak I'd eat it!' she snapped, snatching back her ticket.

A few people waiting outside the station looked at her with curiosity. Red-faced, angry with the ticket collector for bringing the embarrassing sight to their notice, she hurried towards the exit. Wearing a red swagger-style coat, tapping on very high heels, she carried a medium-sized suitcase and a couple of small bags. In haste, she pushed her way clumsily

24

through the entrance as she struggled with the weight and awkwardness of them. Almost running down the sandy slope to the promenade, she quickly found a place in the rocks on the left-hand side of the sandy bay, gathered her possessions around her and settled to work out what to do next.

In the town centre three local girls, Eirlys, Beth and Hannah, sat together, sewing and knitting, making gifts to sell in their shop. Eirlys had been given a rare afternoon off, having stayed in the office until nine o'clock the previous evening, working out some of the entertainments the town was planning for the summer to attract visitors.

Marged and Huw Castle's daughter, Beth, had the half-day off as every Wednesday the market closed at one o'clock. With Peter away and her father-in-law busy on his smallholding, she was glad of something to fill the time and offer company. She was working on a colourful pair of mittens made from oddments of wool given to her by Eirlys.

Hannah Castle, Bleddyn and Hetty's daughter-in-law, was using the sewing machine, making a skirt from what had once been a smart pair of cricketing trousers, the quality material creating an attractive garment under her skilled hands. Beside her, a dress small enough for a baby was awaiting the finishing touches.

Two of the three girls had received letters. Beth had heard from Peter. He was training men and women to be dropped behind enemy lines to organise escape routes, but she told few people what he was involved in; careless talk cost lives, as the posters constantly warned them. One of the lives could be Peter's, so she usually said nothing more than that Peter was in an office doing some of the boring but necessary form-filling needed for administration purposes.

Hannah told the others that her letter from Johnny said little more than that he was well and safe, the stilted sentences offering little clue to his whereabouts except that he was in the desert.

Beth told her friends that Peter had been to a concert where a famous comedian had performed. 'I also had a letter from Freddy Clements,' she added. She and Freddy had once been engaged, until he made it clear he found Shirley Downs more fun. 'I think I might go and show it to Shirley Downs; I think they still keep in touch.'

Eirlys finished what she was doing, stood up and reached for her jacket. 'If you'll put the kettle on, I'll go to the baker's and see if there are any cakes left; I'm feeling peckish.'

'Not fancying anything like kippers and jam, are you?' Beth teased, knowing that Eirlys was carrying a child.

'Be careful or that's what I'll bring back for you – or worse!'

When a customer came into the shop, Beth put the knitting aside, smiled and went to attend to the young woman and her little girl. The customer invited her three-year-old to choose from a basket filled with hand-knitted dolls. The variety offered kept the little girl busy for quite a while before she decided on a doll in traditional Welsh costume. Watching them, Beth had an idea. Instead of continuing with the knitting, she reached for a scrap of paper and a pencil and asked Hannah, 'What do you think of a dolls' tea party as an event in August?'

Hannah put down the baby dress on which she was embroidering hearts and daisies and said, 'My two girls would love it, and I suppose Josie and Marie are fairly average. When do you think it could be held? And where? There's always the weather to contend with.'

'Eirlys will sort it all out. She did a brilliant job last year, didn't she?' Eirlys, in her role as organiser of the summer entertainments, was always looking for fresh activities that would involve a lot of people, and they both knew the suggestion would please her.

They discussed the idea for a while, Beth rapidly filling a page with their ideas. Eirlys would be delighted, and they watched the door between their note-making, waiting for her return with their snack. The suggestions continued to flow.

'Best-dressed-doll competition,' Hannah offered.

'Prettiest face?' Beth wondered.

'Most patriotic?'

'Smallest? Largest?'

It was almost five, and the shop was so quiet as they sat thinking about further possibilities that when Eirlys and Ken burst in, arguing loudly, they both gasped in surprise and looked to Eirlys for an explanation.

'Ken promised to take the boys to the pictures. They've been ready for hours and then he tells them he has to go to Cardiff and interview someone for some concert!'

'There is a war on, you know!' Ken retorted.

Hannah and Beth stared from one to the other and back again as the argument raged on. 'I'll make that tea, shall I?' Hannah went to the back of the shop, where a single gas ring provided their only means of heating water. She hated arguments of any kind and she didn't want to get involved in this one.

Ken had a job to do and it was a complicated one, arranging concert parties and dances to entertain the troops and raise money for the Red Cross parcels for prisoners of war and other worthy causes. Hannah guessed that Eirlys was aware that his absences from home were often without a valid reason, but couldn't face the fact that Ken Ward just didn't like living with Eirlys and her father, plus three demanding boys who had come as evacuees and stayed. Stanley was thirteen, Harold was eleven and the lugubrious little Percival was almost nine.

The three young Londoners had been through many changes and suffered miseries of poverty and neglect, which Eirlys and her father had determined they would forget. They wanted the rest of their childhood to be happy. For Ken, the presence of the boys just added to the miseries of being married to the wrong woman.

Hannah handed a cup of tea to Eirlys and offered one to Ken. He shook his head angrily and after a brief apology he left. Eirlys burst noisily into tears.

Hannah and Beth said very little, knowing that saying the wrong thing was a strong possibility. Hannah felt particularly sad. Eirlys had once been engaged to marry her own husband, Johnny Castle, and she constantly had pangs of guilt over the fact that she and Johnny were so happy and Eirlys and Ken clearly were not. She often wondered whether Johnny would have settled happily for a lifetime with Eirlys if they had married before she and Johnny had met, or whether, as for Ken, it would have been a sad acceptance of second-best.

She was relieved when a late customer came in and she was able to put aside her worries. When she went home she would take out Johnny's letters and re-read them all, and reassure herself that Johnny loved her and their marriage had been honourable and guilt-free.

Beth had none of the hang-ups suffered by Hannah. She had no regrets or guilt about ending her engagement to Freddy Clements when he had clearly preferred Shirley. Marriage to Peter had brought her great happiness. She encouraged Eirlys to talk, wiped away her tears and finally persuaded her to go home and take the boys to the pictures herself. 'Best to accept that Ken's heart isn't in it where the boys are concerned,' she advised. 'And why should it be? Most people start married life being a couple. He married you and not the whole tribe! The boys are evacuees who are being fostered by your father. Nothing to do with him.' She glanced at Hannah, who was washing teacups, and whispered, 'Those two were an exception, mind. Johnny loves Hannah's girls like they're his own. But it doesn't always happen so neatly. Give Ken a thought in all this.'

'We shouldn't have married until we could get a place of our own. Now, with the baby coming, I feel trapped.'

'I think that feeling is experienced by women in the happiest of marriages. A child means you can't change your mind if you want to, and really Eirlys, deep down, you don't want to leave Ken, do you?'

'Perhaps not. But I think he wants to leave me.'

Waves of guilt flooded over Hannah. She and Johnny had built their happiness on the misery of another. Superstition made her shiver. She hoped Johnny didn't have to die to punish her. Beth touched her shoulder as they watched Eirlys hurrying away from the shop.

'I hope you don't feel responsible for Eirlys's unhappiness, Hannah. We can't wave a magic wand and make everyone happy. Some people never achieve it, no matter what happens to them. I have the saddest of feelings that that's true of Eirlys.'

'She doesn't deserve to be so unhappy.'

'A marriage needs you to put everything into it, heart and

soul. Eirlys didn't treat Cousin Johnny as the most important thing in her life. He's so lucky to have married you.'

Marriage seemed an impossible dream for Vera Matthews. Her father slapping her for allowing a neighbour to put an arm around her and kiss her cheek, and being caught by the man's wife, had led to another wallop. Then, when a local teacher called on her parents to tell them to keep their daughter away from his wife and stop encouraging her to go to dances and pick up men, no one would listen to her protestations of innocence. She had seen the teacher's wife at several dances and they had walked home together on two occasions. If there had been men walking the woman home on other nights Vera knew nothing about it, but no one would believe her.

Dance halls, with their cheerful decor, sparkling lights and lively music, plus the fun of dancing with fascinating strangers, were magnets for bored young women. When war had been declared Vera had been a schoolgirl, and the only people she knew were people she had always known. Now, three years on, she had glimpsed a wider world and found it impossible to be restrained by the boundaries of home as she once had.

Her mother had remained silent when her father had given her an hour to pack up and leave home. Optimistically, she delayed taking a case down from the top of the wardrobe to fill it with what little she owned; instead she watched her father, glancing at the clock, convinced that when the sixty minutes had passed he would relent. He did not, and with only ten minutes left she had grabbed what she could from the bedroom she shared with her sisters and fled, just in front of her father's flaying belt.

Now, sitting in a sheltered crevice in the rocks with the sound of children playing and music from the roundabouts a cacophony blotting out everything else, she felt the same foolish confidence as she had waiting for the hour to pass, telling herself she didn't need to make a decision, that something would happen and this nightmare would end. She shivered, chilled by the situation rather than the temperature, and pulled her smart red swagger coat around her, trying not to crease it.

Situations like this didn't happen to people like her. Her mam would come and find her; her father had followed her and was only trying to teach her a lesson. The woman had owned up and admitted she had lied. She pictured her mam crying when they found her. But what if they didn't? Perhaps a handsome young man would find her and rescue her from disaster? Perhaps Maldwyn would appear like a bespectacled handsome prince and make everything right. Time passed and nothing happened at all.

Beth lived with her father-in-law Bernard Gregory on a small-holding outside the town. Peter rarely came home on leave. Besides days spent working at the café in the town's market, in every spare moment she made gifts to sell in the shop she had opened in partnership with Hannah and Eirlys. She also helped her parents in Castle's Café when they were in need. Time had to be filled; only that way would the lonely weeks pass, the war come to its end and the men return home. Time was an enemy to be defeated by activity, any activity that would make her forget the fear that froze her heart every time she stopped to wonder where Peter was and what he was having to face.

Until this summer she had always worked on the sands, and like the rest of her family had found work for the winter when the beach activities ended. The winter of 1941–2 found her running the market café, and she had decided to stay there until Janet Copp returned. Beth had always loved working on the sands, and as a member of the Castle family it had been presumed she would continue to do so, but this year, with real regret, she had decided not to support the family firm. She had promised Janet she would stay and take care of the business for her until the war ended. When that would be, she had no idea. The war seemed set to go on for ever.

For Peter, the war had been even longer than for most as he had spent many months in France and Germany long before the conflict had begun, setting up contacts which he later used to provide a rescue route for escaped prisoners and others who found themselves on the wrong side of the front line.

During 1938–9 he had made many trips to the now enemy-occupied continent, facing certain death if he had been captured. He had suffered deprivation, starvation and sickness and on one occasion had returned to her more like a skeleton than the man she had married, but she didn't plead with him to give up on what she knew was a desperately important part of the conflict. Peter, so unassuming and mild, regularly risked his life so others could be saved, and he would never deviate from his determination to continue with his activities, until either peace or his death intervened. She never asked about his work but was relieved to know that, for the moment at least, Peter was in this country, training others to do what he had done for so long.

Everyone was fully occupied for most of the daylight hours and beyond. Most of the men not serving in the forces belonged to the Home Guard and, on a rota system, also spent some hours each week fire-watching. Wardens patrolled the streets looking out for the smallest chink of light escaping between incorrectly drawn blackout curtains.

There were few who weren't engaged in fund-raising of one kind or another. Women collected rags, metal, paper and anything else that could be reused to save valuable resources. Any waste food was collected to feed pigs. And there was the knitting. Women's hands were rarely at rest. They would answer the door to a visitor without putting down the socks, gloves or scarves they were making to distribute among Army, Navy and Air Force personnel. Children in school were taught to knit simple garments in khaki, Navy or Air Force-blue wool, though knitting and sewing lessons consisted mainly of making old from new. 'Make Do and Mend' was the advice offered on posters and on leaflets sent to every household.

When Beth wasn't knitting for the gift shop she was making items for the forces. In rare quiet moments at work she picked up the needles and clicked away, joining other helpers from the market stalls in their efforts to fill boxes with garments for the Women's Voluntary Service to send where there was a need of them.

One Sunday afternoon, while her father-in-law was at the beach with his string of donkeys, giving rides to children, she went to the shop, where she had arranged to meet Hannah and Eirlys.

She greeted Hannah affectionately, leaning over to kiss her and admire the neat smocking she was working on, across the front of a child's dress. Hannah earned her living making clothes, but when Beth asked who the pretty cream dress was for, Hannah whispered, 'Hush,' and nodded in the direction of their friend.

Beth settled down to sew some of the toys Eirlys had cut from remnants of coats and skirts that she had used to make rugs. The supply of unwanted coats had once been unlimited, and Eirlys had begun a business making and selling rugs that seemed set to thrive, but now, with clothing rationed and everyone making do, the supply was dwindling. Good garments were no longer discarded.

Nothing was wasted and the pieces unsuitable for her rugs were cut and sewn into soft toys for children. It was the talented Hannah who made the patterns and did the finishing touches, adding whimsical features that appealed to customers.

The three girls worked companionably together, each doing what she enjoyed most, between them keeping the windows and shelves of their small lock-up shop filled with their work.

Although the shop door had its CLOSED sign in place, they heard a knock. Hannah looked up with a ready smile, expecting to see her father-in-law Bleddyn Castle with her two daughters to remind her it was time for tea, but a strange young woman stood there, peering through the glass, with a hand above her eyes to help her see inside. Hannah put down her sewing, went to open the door and explained that the shop was closed.

'Sorry I am to disturb you, but I wondered whether you knew of any jobs going. You being in business, like, I thought you might know of someone needing help.'

Hannah turned to Beth. 'Do you think they need anyone on the beach?' she queried.

'They are short-handed, but they won't want just anyone,' Beth replied.

The young woman stepped inside and looked from one to the

other, sensing the decision about to be made. 'Good worker, I am. Not afraid of hard work or long hours.'

'I don't know,' Beth said hesitantly. There was something decidedly bold about the young woman. She had an air about her that hinted of trouble. She was what the local people described as 'fit', an expression that suggested someone who could look after herself and would brook no argument.

'Why not let your mam and dad and Uncle Bleddyn decide?' Hannah whispered back. After a nod of agreement from Hannah, Beth wrote down her parents' address in Sidney Street and suggested to the stranger that she might call about seven that evening.

'I'm Vera Matthews.' The newcomer held out a hand solemnly. 'But if anyone asks about me you've never heard of me. Right?'

Beth looked at her suspiciously. 'Are you in any trouble? If so I don't think—'

'Not trouble, just a bit of a quarrel with my family. You know how it is. They might come looking for me.'

Without giving them a chance to change their minds about her talking to Mr and Mrs Huw Castle, she thanked them and hurried out.

Beth called in to her parents' house before cycling home, to tell them what she had done. 'I don't think she'll be suitable, Mam,' she explained. 'Something about a bit of trouble with her family.'

'Don't worry. If we take her on I'll keep a sharp eye on her, love,' Marged assured her.

Vera Matthews was smiling when she left the Castles' home with the promise of a job. She would work really hard for the first week, to impress them; after that she could let her enthusiasm slide a bit. Now she had to find somewhere to sleep. The last two nights on the beach, with everything from her assorted bags covering her, had been far from pleasant.

She had left home with less than four pounds in her Post Office account, plus a few National Savings stamps. If only she'd had some warning, some hint that things were coming to a head, she could have prepared properly. She regretted the time she had sat looking at the clock and waiting for her father to change his mind. She could have used that hour more productively.

If she'd known about nights sleeping on the beach, a couple of blankets would have been a better idea than her dippers and the frilly underwear she had brought so her sisters wouldn't have them!

Vera's suitcase had been packed in such haste, she doubted whether any of the stuff she had brought would be of any use. It was still at the railway station in the left-luggage office. Hiding the rest of the things she had brought in the rocks, she walked up and collected it, then wandered along the row of houses offering accommodation. Unfortunately, with the holiday season getting under way, the cost was higher than she'd expected. After a momentary lowering of spirits she shrugged, hid the case and bags in the rocks where she had spent the previous nights, and went to where some railway carriages gave a promise of shelter. She didn't look around to see if she was being watched. Appearing confident and walking purposefully was a way of avoiding suspicion.

The first carriage door she tried wasn't locked, and from the look of the dusty floor it was not in regular use. She would be safe here for a week, until her first wage packet made it possible to find a room. Food wouldn't be a problem: she was sure to find all she needed during her hours at the café, and if she missed her bedtime drink that wouldn't ruin her life. It was only for a week.

She collected her belongings and cautiously returned to the railway carriage. To her relief she was not seen. The area was deserted.

The following day, Beth's parents came into the market café and told her the young woman had been employed as an assistant in their beach café.

'Only on a week's trial, mind,' Marged said. 'I don't know her or any of her family and I don't like employing complete strangers. She's from away,' she explained, waving an arm vaguely and frowning as though that fact alone was sufficient to make her suspicious.

34

'Getting very daring, you and Dad,' Beth laughed as she handed them both a cup of tea. 'First Maldwyn Perkins and now this Vera Matthews. Look out, Mam, you'll be employing men from the moon before we know where we are!'

'As long as they can count,' Marged grinned. 'We've had quite a job getting staff this summer. You running the market café instead of helping in ours, our Ronnie injured and with a market stall around the corner from you, our Eynon in the Army and our Lilly – well, she's useless.'

'Not that she's ever been any different!' Huw muttered. 'I'll go and tell Bleddyn and Hetty,' he offered, and set off for his brother's house in Brook Lane. When he got there he was surprised to see Bleddyn and Hetty standing near the back door but making no attempt to go in. They warned him to be quiet and together they went into the kitchen, from where they could hear Shirley singing along to a gramophone record, her voice strong and melodious, the tapping of a stick her accompaniment.

'She'll do,' Huw said emotionally, and Hetty nodded proudly.

'Yes, our Shirley's got guts all right. She'll do.'

Maldwyn Perkins was nervous at leaving home. The promise of a job had been alarmingly easy. He had imagined it would take weeks before he found something that would pay enough for him to survive alone and that he would enjoy. Then there was the accommodation. That too had been quickly managed.

He had found a room in a quiet part of the town, about thirty minutes' walk from the beach. His landlady promised breakfast and an evening meal in return for his ration book and a pound a week. He wouldn't have much left from his wages, but he didn't think he would need it. Living in St David's Well town and working in St David's Well Bay, he would have all he wanted – except a family. He thought of his familiar bedroom with its dark furniture and memorabilia of his childhood: the teddy sitting in the Lloyd Loom chair, the train set on top of the wardrobe with a cricket bat he had rarely used, and the compendium of games that had bored him but that he had played to please his father.

He tightened the strap on his suitcase angrily. It just wasn't fair. His job in the florist's hadn't been exciting, but he had been content. Living at home and being looked after as he'd always been, he had seen no reason to change anything.

They went to the railway station, struggling with the suitcase and three other bags beside a rucksack in which his stepmother had packed food and drink for a journey that wouldn't last more than an hour. An exhibition of her guilty conscience, he decided, as she pushed another bar of Cadbury's chocolate in beside the biscuits and cake.

They travelled to the railway station in silence, neither knowing what to say. After packing the last of his cases into the railway carriage, he jumped down and hesitantly gave Winifred Perkins a hug. 'You've got my address if you need me for anything,' he said. 'Anything at all, mind.' Please, write and tell me you need me to come home, he pleaded silently as he forced a smile and jumped back into the train. Surely she would relent and beg him to come back? Her smile was stiff and false but it didn't waver as she waved him off.

Yet she was crying as she handed in her platform ticket and began to walk home. It was the hardest thing she had ever done, but she'd promised his father that she would make him leave, do something positive towards his future before he settled too comfortably into premature middle age.

His real mother had been over-protective once it had been revealed that his sight was not good. It was natural, but not the best way of dealing with a problem. He had to be independent, and leaving the safety of his home was the first step. One day he would find out she had been untruthful when she had told him she was leaving the house – his house – to her niece. She hoped he would forgive her.

Maldwyn woke the next morning and was at once confused. He couldn't understand why the window was in the wrong place. There was the unlikely sound of traffic: horses and carts and a few cars, bicycle bells ringing impatiently and errand boys already up and about, whistling as they went about their daily journeys. At home in Bryn Teg, it had been the sound of heavy boots marching past the house as men went to the pit to begin their shift that had always been the first recognisable noise on waking.

For a moment or two he lay there wondering what had happened, but then realisation dawned and he felt his spirits lowering as he remembered that this was the first day of his new life, a life miles from home and completely on his own. He went over his arrival at his lodgings and the daunting list of dos and don'ts with which he had been presented; the reminder that breakfast was eight thirty, even on Sundays, unless he was prepared to manage without; and the strange bedroom with its view of roofs and chimneys instead of fields and hedges.

He glanced at the clock on the table beside the white-counterpaned bed – seven thirty. Best he didn't close his eyes, he was too afraid of over-sleeping. He tried to remember where the bathroom was. It would be embarrassing to walk into his landlady's bedroom by mistake! He'd never had a bathroom. At home they had dragged the tin bath off the coalhouse wall and filled it with hot water from the washing boiler. He wondered whether he'd be expected to wash in cold water. No one to bring up a kettle full of hot water this morning, he thought sadly.

To his surprise he was wrong about that. There was a loud knock on his door and Mrs Prosser came in with a steaming saucepan. 'Hot water for washing and shaving,' she announced. 'Please to bring the saucepan back and put it in the kitchen.' As Maldwyn stuttered his thanks, embarrassed at having a strange woman in his bedroom and him in his vest, she added, 'Baths on Fridays. The geyser isn't to be used except on Fridays. Right?'

'Right,' he agreed.

When he reached the café high above the sands at half-past nine that morning, he was surprised to see the counters already filled with food and the oven sending out appetising smells of cakes cooking.

'Sorry I'm late,' he apologised. 'I'd have been here before but Mrs Prosser insists on breakfast at eight thirty on the dot,' he said.

'Old trick that is,' Marged laughed. 'Too late for anyone

working, so she gets out of cooking it. She doesn't cut the price of your lodgings, mind, I'll bet.'

'I'll give breakfast a miss tomorrow and be here to help you set up,' he said.

'You do that, and we'll find you something to eat,' Huw promised. 'Only a bit of toast, mind, and maybe an egg now and then, when there's time.'

Maldwyn was being shown the routine of the rides when Vera Matthews arrived to start work. Marged had told her to arrive at ten on her first morning, giving the others the chance to get everything under way. Maldwyn and Vera greeted each other hesitantly, both wondering what had brought the other to St David's Well beach. There was no time for questions, though. The first customers were wandering into the café for coffees, teas and toast, and Vera quickly saw what was needed and helped Marged deal with the simple orders.

At eleven thirty the chips were blanched, that is, cooked under a lower than usual heat so they did not brown. Then as the lunch orders got under way they were quickly reheated a few at a time in very hot fat and browned to an attractive finish. Vera served while Marged cooked and a young girl called Myrtle helped serve and took the money.

Myrtle and Marged worked quickly, experience giving them the ability to deal with several things at once, and Vera tried hard to keep up with the speed at which they dealt with the queues that grew and eased and then grew again. The tables were set and reset as families came and ate and went back to the beach. The neat gingham tablecloths were smoothed, and soiled ones replaced when necessary.

The floor was soon covered in sand. Children came barefoot and wearing swimming costumes, or dippers as they were usually called, and mothers took towels from their shoulders as they sat them at a table, shaking them unthinkingly before packing them away.

Myrtle's sister Maude, on holiday from her factory canteen, dealt with orders for the beach. Trays were set with teapots, china and plates of sandwiches which were taken down to the sand, a small deposit taken on the promised return of the tray and its contents.

Stopping occasionally to watch the activities, Vera marvelled at the amount of food that was cooked, served and eaten, and the calm way the industrious team organised their time so none was wasted, and even managed to smile and offer a pleasant comment or two. By three o'clock she was exhausted.

'Thank goodness that's over. I'm dead on my feet,' she sighed, flopping into a chair half-way through clearing a table.

'Over?' Marged laughed. 'We've got the teatime rush yet!'

They managed to drink a cup of tea and eat a thick slice of bread covered with sandwich spread between customers. Vera hid a welshcake in her handbag for later in case she wasn't offered anything more, but she needn't have bothered. Once the last rush of teatime customers had stopped, they began to clear away. A greaseproof-paper-wrapped package was handed to her and Marged told her she could go. 'Take these sandwiches and cakes for your supper in case your landlady doesn't feed you proper. I'll let you off the cleaning as Maude and Myrtle are here to help. Tomorrow I'll need you, mind.'

'I'll be here at eight,' Vera promised, wondering how she was going to wake in time. One thing she hadn't brought from home was a clock.

Maldwyn hadn't enjoyed his day. He lacked the ability of Huw and Bleddyn to banter with the customers on the swingboats and helter-skelter, and the children on the roundabout scared him with their curious, unselfconscious stares. He looked up at the café, where someone was closing a window, and wondered how Vera Matthews had managed or whether, like himself, she was already thinking of looking for a less hectic way of earning money.

On the following day, because of the long hours, both Vera and Maldwyn were given a few hours off during the morning. Bleddyn and Hetty came to relieve them and they set off together towards the town.

'Where are you going?' Vera asked and, shame-faced, Maldwyn confessed that he was going to look for a different job.

'Me too, when I've had a chance to look around this boring town,' Vera surprised him by stating.

'Boring? I love it here, always have. I like the atmosphere of the seaside holiday town. It's the job I don't like. Children stare so, don't they? And the young girls embarrass me.'

'Make fun of your thick glasses, do they?' Vera asked cheekily. 'I probably did the same at their age.' She laughed. 'They are a bit heavy, mind.' He smiled ruefully. 'Join in the teasing; make them see you don't mind. They'll go away thinking you're one hell of a lad.'

'Perhaps I'll get some lighter frames when I have enough money.'

'Good idea, those are . . .' Lost for words, she said, 'Yuck!'

'I hadn't thought of it before. I've always worn horn rims like these.'

'What are you doing here in St David's Well?' she asked, and he tried not to tell her, but her insistent questioning dragged out the whole story of what he saw as his stepmother's betrayal.

'Betrayal? Now there's a big word,' she said, laughing at him again. 'Perhaps she was making you stand on your own two feet?'

They were still together when Maldwyn reached the flower shop.

'I worked in a flower shop before I came here,' he said. 'I thought of asking Mrs Chapel for a job.'

'Flowers, eh? There's me thinking you were an adventurer just back from the jungle,' she teased. She saw his hesitation, and sensed his wish to go in alone, but she was amused by the stuttered goodbyes and the apologetic air so, ignoring the hint that she should leave, she went in with him.

'Hello again. Aren't you the young man who works in a flower shop?' Mrs Chapel smiled. 'You've brought your girlfriend this time, I see.'

Before he could refute the assumption, Vera stepped forward and introduced herself. 'I'm Vera. I work in Castle's Café over on the beach.'

'I'm working on the sand with the stalls and rides, but I

40

don't think I'm going to like it,' Maldwyn said, trying to turn so he blocked Vera from Mrs Chapel's view.

Vera was having none of it. She slid around and said, 'Better with flowers than dealing with rowdy kids. It's what he does, see. Arranges flowers, isn't it, Maldwyn?'

'Mrs Chapel knows what I do,' he said stiffly, trying again to block her from his conversation with the proprietor.

'So, have you got a job for him?' Vera went on relentlessly, ignoring Maldwyn's frown, mischief shining in her hazel eyes.

'What about you, Maldwyn, is it really what you want? Don't you fancy trying something different now you've broken away from home?'

'I liked what I did and I didn't want to leave.'

'His mam threw him out, see,' Vera said, amused at the uncomfortable expression on Maldwyn's face. 'Wicked stepmother,' she further confided with a laugh.

'Mind the shop for me for a few minutes, will you, Vera?' Mrs Chapel beckoned for Maldwyn to follow her and led him through a curtained doorway into the room behind the shop. The room was obviously were she worked and was filled with wreaths in various stages of completion and other flower-arrangement forms, plus buckets and vases, rolls of green wire and shelves laden with more pots, containers and paper-wrapped dried flowers, all in a careless muddle.

'Now, without the parrot on your shoulder, why did you come to see me?'

'Vera's right, I would like a job. I didn't need her to talk for me,' he said, trying to look offended but then, catching the quizzical look on Mrs Chapel's face, he laughed. 'Hell of a girl, isn't she?'

The two young people hurried to the bus stop and made their way back to the beach, reaching the café still laughing at the news that Maldwyn was going to hand in his notice after only one day, and stood meekly as Marged told them off for being fifteen minutes late.

They were late leaving that evening, guilty at being late for the lunchtime session and subdued at the telling-off Marged had given Maldwyn for finding another job after only one day.

Every dish and pan had been scoured and every surface wiped clean. The floors were swept free of sand and dropped food, and washed carefully.

'You going straight back to your digs?' Vera asked.

'I ought to, or I'll miss supper as well as breakfast.'

'Forget it. I heard today of a pub where they sell pork sandwiches. Illegal it'll be for sure, and more fat than lean, but let's give it a try.' Without waiting for an answer she took his arm and dragged him towards the bus stop. She couldn't go back to the railway carriage too early. Better to wait until there were fewer people around. She had been lucky yesterday not to have been seen when she first went there.

They ate their supper, which was better than they expected, and, strolling along the back lanes, Maldwyn asked, 'Where do you live?'

'I'll show you if you like,' she promised. 'What about the pictures first?'

'Not tonight, I'm a bit tired. Tomorrow?'

'Tomorrow's fine. We can go back to my lodgings after, just so you know where to find me. In case you get a bit lonely without your cruel stepmam,' she teased.

'And my teddy and my three-wheeler bike with a bell,' he added with mock seriousness.

The following evening they left the café together. Maldwyn had helped Huw with a bit of repair work after closing the rides and stalls on the sands, and they both carried a package of leftover food given to them by Marged. They were discussing what film they would see when Vera suddenly left him, ran back down the slope to the beach and disappeared among the people slowly making their way up to the promenade.

Maldwyn looked for her, leaning on the thick stone wall and peering down at the straggle of women and children in the hope of seeing Vera's red coat. A voice called and he turned to see Delyth and Madge pushing their way towards him.

'Hello, wasn't that Vera Matthews you were with just now?' Delyth asked.

'No, she's er—' He remembered her warning about her family looking for her and stuttered, 'I've never seen her before. She works – um – somewhere in another town,' he ended stupidly. He pointed to Castle's Café on the cliff path above the beach. 'I'm working up there in Castle's Café. Nice, eh?'

'Sure of that are you?' Madge asked suspiciously. 'Looked to me like you and Vera Matthews are friends, and she's missing from home.'

They told him about the girl from their home town who had been accused of 'carrying on' with a married man and had left after being threatened by the man's father-in-law.

'You're mistaken,' he said, shaking his head. 'Vera Matthews, you say? Never heard of her. I'm off to the pictures. On my own.' He glanced again to Castle's Café where, climbing the steps to the doorway, was a figure in a red coat.

It was much later when he met Vera, having got rid of Delyth and Madge, and they made their way to the picture house.

'Who were those girls you were talking to?' Vera asked innocently as she offered him a sweet. 'Friends of yours?'

'Delyth Owen and Madge Howells. They know you, said you were missing from home.'

Vera gave a low chuckle and in the darkness of the cinema he felt her hair touch his face as she shook her head. 'Never heard of 'em. They're mixing me up with someone else, aren't they?'

'Glad to hear it. She's a bad un from what they told me. Carrying on with a married man and being chased out of town by the man's father-in-law.'

Vera began to giggle. 'Sounds like a better story than this film we've just paid a shilling and threepence to see. What a laugh, eh?'

They watched the film to the end but didn't stay for the programme to move through the second feature and the news to the repeat of the main film and on to the point where they had entered.

'Let's go,' Vera said. 'Come and see my lodgings. I think you'll be impressed.'

When they went out it was raining. 'Oh fiddle, no umbrella,' Vera groaned.

'Where's your mackintosh?' he asked. He offered her a share

of his raincoat. 'I've never seen you carrying one, yet rain has threatened all day.'

She couldn't explain that in the haste of her exit she hadn't had time to pick it up.

'Boring old thing it was. I threw it out and haven't bothered to get a new one.' She grimaced. Clothing coupons! She had forgotten to bring them! 'Got any clothing coupons to spare?' she asked. 'I need plenty for a raincoat and I haven't even got one.'

They caught a bus for part of the way, Maldwyn offering the fare and Vera telling the conductor where they were going. Then they made their way on foot around the large open area where railway engines and carriages were awaiting repair. Puzzled but not particularly anxious, presuming this was a short-cut to houses close to the next bay, Maldwyn followed her, protecting her from the worst of the downpour. When she stopped at one of the carriages and jumped in he stood staring at her in disbelief.

'Get in quick, before we're seen,' she hissed, and grabbing hold of his lapel she hauled him inside, pulled him against her and kissed him.

'Either shut your mouth or relax, Maldwyn. It's like kissing the top of an eggcup!'

He looked down at her tempting face and could only stutter in reply. Laughing, she pushed him gently out of the carriage door and waved until he was out of sight. The carriage was quite comfortable with its well-upholstered seat and there was even a mirror on one wall. Food in plenty from the café, Maldwyn for company until she found better. With a regular wage life could be very good. Although she'd be able to afford a room once she'd worked for a couple of weeks, she thought she might stay for a while. She wasn't doing any harm and no one would worry about an abandoned railway carriage.

Maldwyn hurried away from the railway sidings, doubled up, trying to stay in the shadows although the night was dark. He was afraid of being seen and guiding someone to where Vera was living. What nerve the girl had. Sneaking into a place like that, where she had no right to be, that was something he would never be able to do. He wondered whether he could

44

help her find somewhere safer, then asked himself if she would want him to. Vera was not the dependent type. She was the sort to go out and get what she wanted. If only he were the same, he might not be living alone, far from home, in a house where the landlady didn't want him, only his money and his ration book.

As he went inside, he heard her call, 'That you, Mr Perkins? Sorry but you're too late for supper.' Which only confirmed his morbid thoughts. He was ungraciously allowed to make himself a cup of cocoa before going to bed, where he dreamed about Vera Matthews with her tantalising lips and mischievous eyes.

Three

The following day, Maldwyn felt very aware of Vera. Every time they met during their working hours he smiled and tried to think of something interesting to say, but failed miserably. He waited for her while she and Marged dealt with the last-minute floor-cleaning and saw Marged hand Vera a package which he guessed contained food.

They walked down the path together and Vera said, 'Pictures again, is it? I've got enough food for you not to need to go home for your supper.'

They weren't the only ones eating their tea in the picture house, and the rustle of paper continued for a while before the audience settled to enjoy the film. At nine o'clock they left and, again without discussion, Maldwyn went with her to the railway sidings and entered her unusual accommodation.

She reached up and kissed him as soon as the door was closed, and he lost himself in the thrill of it. When Vera finally released him from their kiss, Maldwyn sank down on to the carriage seat and, smiling, she sat down to face him. Trying to calm his racing heart, he looked away from her tempting lips and the wickedly amused expression in her hazel eyes. Turning away, knowing his face was as revealing to her as a thousand words, he asked, 'Vera, what are you doing here?'

She relaxed into the seat and stared out of the grimy window. 'I had to find somewhere to sleep and I didn't have the money for lodgings.'

'I mean, what are you doing in St David's Well?'

'Long story,' she sighed.

'We've got all night.'

Now she admitted to being the girl Delyth and Madge had told him about. 'It wasn't true about the schoolteacher, mind.

46

I did meet our boring neighbour once or twice but we only kissed and cuddled. Nothing wrong with that, is there? Then I was thrown out of the house when my father was told I had been friendly towards one of my neighbours while his wife was doing a night shift at the munitions factory.'

'And were you? Seeing him? Was it true?' Looking across the darkening compartment, he wanted, oh so badly, for her to say it was a nonsense. He wanted to be the first person she had kissed, to be told that she was pure and perfect and had been waiting for him to find her.

'It was true.' She stared at him, unblinking, as though daring him to criticise her. 'I wasn't the one to start it. Pestered me he did, and it wouldn't have been anything more than a five-minute wonder if his wife's father hadn't got to hear about it. He told my father and, well, my father agreed with him and presumed the very worst.'

'What *was* the worst?' Maldwyn was so still, so locked in agony, he didn't think his muscles would obey him when he tried to move. 'Tell me, Vera.'

'I flirted, and kissed him, and talked a bit of nonsense. We didn't do anything worse. Dad wouldn't listen, he believed everything I was accused of.'

'There was more?'

'I walked home a few times from the dance with the wife of a schoolteacher. They accused me of leading her into trouble. She walked home now and then with a man she knew and Dad wouldn't believe I hadn't persuaded her. He wouldn't believe me, Maldwyn. That's so hurtful. Then he gave me an hour to get out of the house. I've often been here as a day tripper. First as a child with Mam and Dad and my sisters, then on my own or with friends. It seemed a friendly town and, well, that's it. Here I am.'

'Surely he didn't mean it? What father would do that, throw his daughter out of the house!'

'Perhaps he didn't. Perhaps he thought I'd apologise as I had so many times before when there was nothing to apologise for! But I was angry and I wanted to frighten him. He was always threatening me with a beating, always suspicious.' She grinned then, her face lit like a child's, and added, 'Fun it was, with him next door. I enjoyed being told I was beautiful. Not that I believed it, mind, but it was fun to be told.'

'You are beautiful. Perhaps that's why your dad worried so much.'

'Am I, Maldwyn? Beautiful?'

Maldwyn looked away. He was feeling uncomfortable being in the small compartment with the lovely Vera, like swimming out of his depth, unable to touch the security of the bottom with his feet.

'What about your sisters?' he managed to ask. 'Don't they support you?'

'No, they stick together and treat me like – like a tart. And I pretend, just to shock them, say things so they believe it. It's all a game really,' she said sadly.

'And you're planning to go on living here in St David's Well? Aren't you afraid being on your own?'

'A bit.'

He gestured around the small carriage and asked, 'What about if you're caught?'

'What can anyone do except throw me out?'

'It's wartime. You could be arrested.'

'I'm all right. A comfortable place to sleep, and breakfast for free when I get to Castle's Café. Not a bad life – for a while. Until I get some wages anyway. I'll tell you this for nothing: if I do fall foul of the law I'll make sure everyone knows that I was thrown out by my own father. If I can get my story in the papers I will. There, doesn't that tell you how wicked I am?' She was finding it hard to control her tears and when Maldwyn spoke soothingly she allowed them to fall. 'It was a bit of fun, that's all, knowing men find me attractive. Life can be very boring. Some of my friends are in the forces or with the Naafi and I'm stuck at home with a dad who's determined to stop me having any fun.'

'I'll find you a place to stay, somewhere comfortable,' he promised.

'I'll stay here until I'm discovered.'

'But what if you're put in prison?'

'You'll visit me, won't you, Maldwyn?'

Another kiss disturbed him and he didn't want to leave her

48

there, but she insisted, and when he hesitated outside she shooed him away impatiently. 'Go, quick! Before you're seen and give me away!'

As he hurried away Maldwyn was upset, but his anger was not directed at Vera's father, whom he didn't know, but at Winifred, his stepmother. If she were more reasonable, he could have taken Vera back home and looked after her.

Days passed, and Vera's unconventional home remained safe from discovery. She settled in happily to work with Marged, enjoying the atmosphere and the pleasant work of feeding the day trippers. Any intention of finding some better employment faded as the summer season filled her with the excitement of serving the lively crowds that poured into Castle's each day. She quickly began to feel like a local, a part of the reception committee keen to ensure the visitors enjoyed their stay. Maldwyn, on the other hand, couldn't wait to leave the beach and start work with Mrs Chapel.

During their few hours off from the café, Maldwyn took Vera on walks. They explored places they hadn't previously discovered, and found a small rocky bay not far from the popular main sandy beach, which they called their own. There they could sit undisturbed and talk and learn about each other. Marged often unwittingly supplied a cake or a sandwich which they would enjoy, pretending they were far away on some distant shore where they were safe and free from families and their accompanying problems.

Few people came to 'their' bay, which was known as New Bay from the story that it had been formed by men removing the reddish rock, first to retrieve the iron ore and more recently to build some of the smart houses above. People stopped sometimes to look down, but most were discouraged from joining them by the precipitous and undefined path leading down to where they sat.

One Wednesday afternoon when they had been given two hours off, they heard someone call, and looked up to see Delyth and Madge. They shouted for the girls to wait and clambered up to the road to join them.

'I knew it was you the other day,' Delyth accused Vera.

'Why did you pretend it wasn't?' Madge asked.

'Please,' Vera begged, 'don't tell our dad you've seen me.' She didn't explain but the girls curiously agreed, deciding that it was not their business to interfere. Delyth showed them her sketchbook, with a drawing of the two of them sitting on the rocks staring out to sea.

The four of them walked back to Castle's Café, the three girls chattering happily and Maldwyn walking beside them, smiling at the unexpected friendships he had made since leaving home. Leaving Delyth and Madge on the sand at the bottom of the metal steps, to lean on the craggy rocks and enjoy what was a warm, pleasant afternoon, Vera went up to deal with the busy couple of hours serving teas, Maldwyn down to relieve Bleddyn on the sands below taking money for rides.

After a while Huw gave him the takings to carry up to Marged and, seeing Vera taking cakes out of the oven and Marged calling for more plates, he stayed to help. Marged came into the kitchen where he was washing dishes and Vera was piling the hot cakes on to serving plates. They were laughing over some observation Vera was making about one of the more difficult customers.

'Haven't changed your mind, have you?' Marged asked. 'You're still going to leave us and work in that flower shop?'

It was at moments like this, with Vera working beside him and fresh memories making his heart sing, that he was tempted to change his mind. With undisguised regret he shook his head. 'Sorry, but I'm better suited to a back room arranging flowers than a beach full of rowdy children.'

Later Delyth and Madge came up and bought a tray of tea, which Vera took down to the sands, the three girls enjoying a brief moment of chat before Marged, her voice shrill and easily heard over the sounds of the beach, yelled from the top of the steps for Vera to go back to the kitchen.

A few days later, three other girls who had also been surprised to find themselves friends were spending a Saturday afternoon in their shop. Eirlys had left her father looking after the three evacuees and, having prepared a meal for the evening and written to her husband, she had come to spend the rest of the day with Hannah making gifts and serving customers. Beth would join them after closing the market café at four o'clock.

The shop was not very busy, but Christmas had depleted their stock and they had been making use of these quieter months to replenish the shelves, ready for what they hoped would be a busy summer. St David's Well was usually full of visitors and day trippers from May until September, the population doubling in size when the miners' week closed mines and factories. Since the war had changed the pattern of many years and the closing down didn't happen, the season was spread more evenly, and pleas by government for the population to stay at home for their holidays seemed to have made no difference. The crowds still flocked in their thousands to the friendly inhabitants and golden sands of St David's Well Bay.

As always the three young women discussed the letters they had received from absent husbands. Hannah told them that Johnny was still in North Africa and that two brief letters had arrived that week. Beth heard regularly from Peter as he was not overseas, and she eagerly waited for his next leave. Eirlys said nothing. Ken was away from home a lot but rarely wrote to tell her where he was, what he was doing or even that he missed her.

Ken was resentful about Eirlys's job. He should be able to keep her, and it was shaming that he could not. That she was successful seemed a slight on his abilities. It was a large part of Eirlys's work during the summer to arrange entertainment for the town's Holidays at Home programme. As Ken ran concerts and dances he initially expected her to need his help with her plans, but found she managed well on her own. Unfortunately, he worked more and more with Janet Copp, who owned the market café now run by Beth.

With Shirley Downs, Janet had sung and danced a little when she wasn't running the café. Gradually, partly because of his estrangement from Eirlys and her work, they began to feel more than friendship.

His love for Janet Copp had almost ended his marriage, but

51

knowing that Eirlys was expecting their child had convinced him that his duty, if not his love, was with his wife. When Janet had left the town and joined the Naafi service, Ken had promised himself that he would stay faithful to his wife, but his resolve was weak: they had made contact again and the affair was once more a large part of his life.

Ken grieved for what he had lost. Eirlys and he had a partnership that was damaged, and with Janet in his life, even with the forthcoming child there seemed little chance of it mending. Eirlys tried to pretend, but he was aware that she knew she couldn't depend on the birth of their child to magic everything right. Both were uneasy with each other, aware that their relationship was second-best.

There were many times when he could have come home but did not, happier to stay with a friend and invent an excuse of needing to work on arrangements for the next concert party, holding auditions, planning programmes, making transport arrangements, booking halls or promising a performance in one camp or another. It sounded impressive, but Ken knew he could deal with it all and still spend days at home during most weeks.

Knowing he could have been with Janet was a constant ache. If only Eirlys wasn't expecting their child, their disastrous mistake could have been rectified. The marriage should never have happened. He believed that Eirlys regretted the marriage as much as he. What a mess.

Sitting in the bedroom of a friend, he wrote to Janet to arrange a meeting to discuss her appearance in a singalong he planned at a factory near where she was stationed. Two days later he had her reply agreeing to meet him. He then wrote a brief note to Eirlys, explaining that he might not be able to come home the following week as promised. He told her with false regret that he had to go to Scotland with a party of actors who were to perform one of Shakespeare's plays. He threw down the pen, wondering why they were telling lies to each other. He couldn't write any more. He just signed it 'Your loving husband, Ken'. Another lie, he thought, as he licked and stuck the envelope. At least they had stopped adding a row of kisses along the bottom.

Eirlys had the letter in her pocket and sadly she showed it to Hannah and Beth.

'Hardly a romantic letter from a husband whom I rarely see, is it?' she said with a forced laugh. She doubted whether either Beth or Hannah could show anyone the letters they received from their husbands. They would be personal, full of loving affection and dreams of a wonderful future.

'Some men are embarrassed at showing their feelings, specially on paper,' Hannah said softly. 'They're afraid of it being seen by someone else who might perhaps make fun of them.'

'He doesn't love me,' Eirlys said, her voice matter-of-fact, her eyes moist with unshed tears. When the others began to protest and to offer argument, she shook her head. 'I know that if it weren't for my little friend here,' she patted her swelling belly, 'I know he'd have left me. There. Are you shocked? I'd be one more addition to the statistics of mistaken marriages. "Marry in haste, repent at leisure," isn't that what everyone says?'

Beth didn't know what to say. She and Peter were so happy, even though they were separated for most of the time. Their love was a strong thread holding them close however far apart they were.

Hannah stood up, put an arm around Eirlys and said, 'Thank you for telling us, Eirlys. We can help now we know. I don't know how at the moment, but we can listen when you want to talk, and laugh or cry with you. Friends we are and we care about you, we really do.'

The three girls settled back to their respective jobs, Hannah sewing the ears on yet another stuffed rabbit, Beth neatening the edges of a doll's cot eiderdown, and Eirlys fixing the backing on a pretty bedroom rug. Beth began to sing, and Hannah smiled and tried to join in, but Eirlys seemed lost in her thoughts.

'What have the boys been up to lately?' Hannah asked, knowing that to talk about the three former evacuees was a certain way to make her smile.

'They're helping Dad on his allotment,' Eirlys told them, but even thinking about Stanley, Harold and Percival Love didn't work the magic for her today.

53

She walked home at six o'clock, wishing for the first time that this baby had not happened. She felt a superstitious guilt at the thought, but knew she meant it. Without the baby she doubted whether she and Ken would still be together. What was so noble about two people being unhappy, she thought sadly, staying together when duty and doing the right thing were so painful? Ken's brief note was in her pocket and she tore it up and let the wind take the pieces where it would.

Delyth and Madge had heard no more about their leaving the shop and finding war work but they knew that it could happen at any time.

'I think we should look for work in St David's Well again. It might be our last chance of getting away from home,' Delyth said.

Unaware that Vera had done the same thing, they went into the gift shop, on their next day trip, and asked if the owners knew of any jobs for which they might apply. At once Beth and Hannah offered their help, and as they discussed the possibilities over cups of tea, the promise of friendship developed.

Maldwyn's first day at the flower shop was enjoyable. His nimble fingers designed displays from the dried flowers Mrs Chapel had in stock and he redressed the rather formal window with a summer display that delighted his employer.

'Natural talent you've got, young Maldwyn,' she said when they stood outside the shop admiring the attractive window.

'I've been learning since I was fourteen,' he said. 'You can't help getting better after all those years.'

'It's forty years for me and you're far cleverer. Don't put yourself down, there's plenty of others more than willing to do that.'

They were about to close when a man came running up, pleading with them to stay open a little longer. 'I need flowers real desperate,' he told them. 'I forgot my wife's birthday.'

There weren't many flowers left, but Maldwyn prepared a bunch of marigolds and cornflowers with some stems of goldenrod to fill it up and handed it to the grateful man.

He took the money and noted the transaction neatly in the book.

Mrs Chapel smiled at him. 'I think in a week or so I can leave you in charge and go to visit my sister,' she told him. 'Years it is since I've had a little holiday.'

'I'll be pleased to help, and you needn't worry about my closing at lunchtime either. I can get something sent over from the café.'

He was whistling as he brushed the floor and washed down the pavement outside.

'Big mistake coming to work for Mrs Chapel,' Arnold Elliot called. 'Your job won't last long. But I might have something for you when I extend.'

'I hope she stays for many years yet,' Maldwyn said, glancing through the doorway to see whether Mrs Chapel had heard the gloomy prediction.

'Don't take any notice of Arnold,' she told him when he had closed the door. 'He's been talking about extending ever since I've known him and he still hasn't persuaded me to move. It would take more than he offered to get me out of this place.'

'Good on you,' Maldwyn smiled.

The following Sunday he and Vera went up on the cliffs, where a flat area of grass seemed a pleasant place to sit. The plateau was half-way between the top of the headland and the shoreline below. There was no beach, just a few rocks that were exposed at low tide. They wriggled towards the edge and looked down at the rocky shore below them. A long way below.

'Gosh!' Vera exclaimed. 'Falling down there would give you a headache!'

They heard shouting, and for a moment they presumed the remarks were for someone else. Then they realised the voice came from a man below them in a small fishing boat.

'Get back, you fools! You're sitting on an overhang and it's likely to collapse!' Still they didn't grasp what he was saying and they waved cheerfully. With hands around his mouth to increase the sound the man repeated his warning and at last they realised and crawled back from the edge.

They heard laughter and, turning, saw they had been joined

55

by Delyth and Madge. Standing a few yards away, Delyth swiftly drew the scene and followed it with another showing the couple flying through the air and down towards the rocks.

'Lot of fuss about nothing,' Vera said. It wasn't until later when they were walking back to St David's Well Bay that they looked back at the place where they had been sitting and saw that the turf actually overhung the edge by a few feet and they had been in real danger of falling.

'We'll keep away from there in future!' Maldwyn said, hugging her. 'I don't want to lose you.'

Delyth was saddened by the growing affection between Maldwyn and Vera. She remembered his dark, deep brown eyes and grieved silently for what might have been.

They had asked at various places where they thought they might have found work, but Delyth's heart was no longer in the idea. Maldwyn had been a strong reason for her decision to move to the town.

Maldwyn sent cards and letters regularly to his stepmother and received a letter from her every Friday. Sometimes she sent a postal order for two shillings for him to go to the pictures. Although her words were cheerful he sensed an underlying sadness; she mentioned the visitors she had, and there seemed very few. He thought often about going home, but the need for Winifred was less than when he had first left. Would she tell him to come back? Would he want to? He was practically running the flower shop and that was something his previous boss would never have allowed. Then there was Vera, and Delyth and Madge, and the Castle family at the café. He had more friends than he'd ever had and he knew he didn't want to give up on this new life. Yet he did have a responsibility to Winifred. If she was unhappy, he had to at least go home and see what he could do to help. Perhaps she was ill? That was the decider.

'I'm going home on Wednesday,' he told Vera. 'I've been away long enough to risk seeing my stepmother without the danger of feeling homesick.' To his surprise she said she would go with him.

'To see your family you mean?'

'I think they'll be able to forgive me by now,' she said sarcastically. 'Considering I didn't do anything except tease Mr Henry Selby, the silly old fool!'

It was a morning in early June when they caught the train for Bryn Teg, and the weather was behaving impeccably. The sun shone and gave colour to the houses and fields they passed, the ever-changing view lightening Maldwyn's heart unexpectedly as he recognised familiar places. Surely he hadn't been away long enough to feel this excitement at coming home?

As the train approached their station even the dark, mountainous slagheaps had a beauty of their own, the sun giving them a greenish sheen broken by patches of brighter green where grasses and a few wild flowers had begun to colonise.

The village streets were peopled with shoppers, the school-yards reminiscent of a Brueghel painting. Balls bounced against walls and were thrown and kicked and argued over by small children. Others played chase, skittering through other games and causing minor battles. Skipping in its many forms, whip-and-top and chanting games he recognised and still knew by heart. He was years away in age but only moments in memory.

As Maldwyn's excitement grew, Vera's spirits dropped. Was she really brave enough to walk into her home and say, 'Hi yer Mam,' as though nothing had happened? What if Dad was there? How would she greet him? Would she take one look at his furious face and make a run for it? Or was she strong enough now to face him and dare him to take his belt off, and threaten to call the police if he did? When she was in St David's Well she had been confident. She had lain on her comfortable seat in the railway carriage she called home and imagined how boldly she would walk in and face them all.

Over the past few days she had lived and relived the scene as she stepped into the kitchen and stared them down. Her mother would see how she had changed, and her sisters too would see she was no longer the falsely confident child fearing her father's anger. She was independent, and no longer needed his support. She was strong now and could say goodbye to the days when she had to conform to standards set by Mam and Dad. Now, as the train slowed to a squealing stop, her confidence seeped away like the steam from the engine that had brought her here. The fire in her eyes dulled and she knew that coming home had returned her to being a child again.

Maldwyn walked her to her door then left, arranging to meet her when it was time for their train back to St David's Well. She took a few deep breaths, listening to the argument going on inside between her sisters. No sound of Dad, she thought with relief. Pushing open the door, she walked resolutely through.

The first person she saw was her father and her heart began to bump painfully in her chest. To her surprise he smiled and said, 'Home again is it? And about time too. Auntie Kitty fed up with you is she?'

'Auntie Kitty? I haven't been near her.'

Her mother, who had been washing towels in the sink, turned around and stared at her husband. 'There, I told you we should have looked for her.'

Vera sank into a chair and stared at them. 'You mean you didn't look for me?'

'I thought— Damn it girl, you always go to Auntie Kitty's when you flounce out of here and you've done that enough times!' her father defended.

It was true. Whenever she and her father had clashed she had always run to be comforted by his sister Kitty, who never seemed to be too busy to spend time with her. As soon as she could walk she had regularly made her way to her auntie's in the cottage on the hill where there were chickens and cats and a sheepdog and, on occasions, other animals as well, which she looked after for other people.

'You didn't go and find out if I was there?' Vera felt tears well up. She had imagined her parents worrying about her, and causing them concern was the reason she hadn't written. She had wanted Dad to feel shame at his treatment of her, make him see how unreasonable he had been.

'I wanted to go, Vera, but your dad thought it best to leave you alone till you felt ready to say sorry,' her mother whispered, wringing out a towel and shaking it to straighten it. Her face was serene, and Vera knew she wasn't really aware of what was being said. Accepting the cup of tea her sister Netta offered, she wondered with rising irritation when one of them would be interested enough to ask where she *had* been.

'Are you staying home now?' her father asked gruffly.

'No, I'm not staying with a family which cares so little, and I'm certainly not going to apologise for doing nothing at all!'

'Will you have a bit of cake with your tea?' her mother asked politely, continuing to deal with the washing.

Vera shook her head. 'Best I don't stay, Mam. I have a train to catch.'

'A train?' Her mother frowned.

At last she's going to ask me where I've been, Vera thought, wondering how much she would tell them all.

'Time for a bite to eat?' her mother asked, dashing her hope of a belated show of interest.

'Next time, Mam,' she replied, standing to leave.

'Yes, you must come again. We miss you, Vera, love.'

Sadness overwhelmed Vera and she hugged her tiny, vague mother and nodded towards her father. So much for the welcome of the prodigal, she thought bitterly.

'Where are you going then, if you aren't with Auntie Kitty?' her father asked.

At last! But the question was too late. She hid her disappointment, the hurt showing only in the tightness of her jaw. 'I've got a job and a temporary address. I might write when I get something permanent,' she said casually. As she hugged her sisters, her mother took the towels she had washed, rinsed and put to dry back in the water and began washing them all over again.

'You can stay if you want to,' her father said.

She was tempted, not by a need to be home and a part of her family, but by knowing she ought to be there to help her mother. She was the oldest daughter and had a duty to support the rest. But she had only to think of sharing a bedroom with her four sisters, and recall the fight for the kitchen sink and some precious privacy for washing herself, to mentally flee from the idea of returning.

The doctor's surgery was open and she went in and sat to await her turn. The doctor was sympathetic when she asked if there was any help available for her mother, and he explained that he visited her as often as he could.

'The trouble is your father,' he said.

'Surprise, surprise! When is the trouble not my father?'

'He refuses to accept that there is a problem and won't take advice.'

'Surprise again!' She looked away from the doctor and asked, 'Would it help my mother if I stay? I find my father impossible to live with and I've moved away. I feel guilty, wondering if my staying would be best for her.' She held her breath as she waited for his reply. Please make it easy for me to go, she prayed.

'You have four sisters and they all do what they can and, to be truthful, there isn't much anyone can do. There are tablets, which I'm told your father throws on the fire, and apart from making sure she is safe from danger, doing everything you can to prevent accidents, all we have left is a home for the elderly and the, er – the sick.' He hesitated to say the 'mentally ill'. Mr Matthews was almost certainly not the only one to refuse to accept that evaluation. 'Your father won't agree to that either.'

'I think he'd consider sending her away as his failure.'

'Where are you living?' he asked.

'I've got a job in a beach café in St David's Well. I'm enjoying it. I've made new friends and I'm happy. But if you think I should come back home, then I will.'

'Stay where you're happy, Miss Matthews. Your staying will only add to the list of miserable and frustrated people. I wish you well.' He smiled and stood up, dismissing her.

'You won't tell Dad or my sisters where I am?' she asked. 'I'll keep in touch, mind, but I want to decide when.'

There were hours to wait before meeting Maldwyn for the journey home, and she wished they hadn't agreed to travel together. She didn't want to stay any longer. She needed someone to tease and to laugh with, someone to make her forget her contempt for herself. She wondered what Maldwyn was doing and whether his homecoming had been more pleasant than her own.

*   *   *

Maldwyn had pushed open the back door and called to Winifred. He no longer called her Mam, as in the early days of her marriage to his father, and unable to decide on an alternative he called, 'Hi there, it's me, Maldwyn.'

'"Hi there", indeed. You sound like one of those American soldiers. Nice boys they are mind, so friendly, and such manners you'd never believe!' she chattered as she came forward and hugged him and took the bag he was carrying, adding, 'There's lovely it is to see you, Maldwyn. Is this the washing I asked you to bring?'

Embarrassed, tearful, unable to cope with the first few moments, Winifred was glad she had the clothes to deal with. Giving him a cup of tea and a few biscuits, she busied herself in the small back kitchen and soon had the washing sorted. The whites were put on to boil and the rest were soaking in the big galvanised bath brought in from the garden.

She had saved what food she could and set out the table with a spread worthy of Christmas Day. After they had eaten, replete and glad to be home, Maldwyn flopped into the large, overstuffed couch and felt happiness pouring over him like a ray of warm sunshine.

They didn't do much besides talk, eat, and drink tea. At four o'clock, while the washing blew cheerfully on the clothes-line in the garden, they went for a walk. They went first to see the owner of the flower shop where Maldwyn had worked, and, to please his stepmother, to the cemetery to put flowers on his parents' graves. Then they went to sit awhile in the park.

There were no shops open, it being a half-day closing, but they found a café and Maldwyn treated Winifred to yet more tea and a slice of fruit cake, with mysterious contents they failed to identify. Walking back through the park, they saw Delyth, who was filling the pages of her sketchbook with drawings of children at play. He introduced her to his stepmother, who admired the girl's work profusely and made her blush.

Near a bench a few yards away, two people were standing close together and obviously quarrelling. The man's demeanour appeared calm but the girl was waving her arms and stamping her foot in her determination to be the winner of the argument. From their distance the words couldn't be heard but the attitude and position of the two figures left them in no doubt that the meeting was far from joyous. Maldwyn was amused to see that Delyth was hastily sketching the two figures, glancing at the couple then at her pad as she tried to capture the scene. 'Careful, Delyth, you could get in trouble here. They might be married, and not to each other!' he warned jokingly.

Delyth continued to draw, catching the anger as the woman raised a hand to strike the man, who held her hand and leaned forward to talk soothingly to her. Then the girl's shoulders sagged, her head moved back as she straightened up and she fell silent. Moments later they walked away, arms around each other, her head on his shoulder, unaware of the audience they had attracted.

Maldwyn left Delyth, who told them she had seen Vera sitting on the station platform reading a book.

'Don't tell me *she's* home again. Vera Matthews! Trouble, that girl is, carrying on something wicked,' Winifred said, unaware of the startled expression on Maldwyn's face. 'Not that I could have done what her father did and send her away from home without a thought for her safety, whatever she'd done.'

'Specially as she might not have been at fault!' Maldwyn retorted, his lips tight with anger. 'She's seventeen years old; the neighbour is almost forty. Who do you think was to blame? Eh?'

'The man, without a doubt,' Winifred said apologetically.

The momentary anger faded and they said their goodbyes with sadness. In some childish, petulant corner of his mind, Maldwyn wanted Winifred to ask him to come back home, only so he could tell her no, that his new life was a happy one. She didn't, and he was relieved and a little ashamed at his unkindness.

With the freshly ironed washing in his bag, he thanked Winifred and set off to meet Vera to travel home. He asked her why she had been sitting on the station reading that afternoon, instead of being home with her family.

'What family?' she said with a sigh. Maldwyn didn't ask questions. Better to wait until she was ready to tell him. She went into a shop doorway to wipe away her tears on the pretext of combing her hair and adding powder to her nose.

They were on the road approaching the station when, hearing a voice calling, Maldwyn turned to see Delyth running towards him. 'Will you look out for work for Madge and me,' she began, but her voice was drowned out by the sound of an engine. They saw a lorry coming towards them quite fast. They didn't take much notice at first, although the engine sound might have warned them of its increasing speed. The pavement was narrow, with privet hedges growing over the low wall and impeding their progress, so they were near the edge of the pavement when they realised that the lorry was crossing the road and coming straight for them.

It mounted the pavement and grew larger, the sound becoming more terrifying until their heads seemed filled with the noise and the image of its approach. In the shop doorway, Vera froze. Maldwyn reacted firstly by throwing down his bag. Then he lifted Delyth up and pushed her over the wall and through the dense hedge.

With engine screaming, the lorry careered on, narrowly avoiding a collision with an oncoming car before disappearing around the corner. Vera and Delyth were shaking, Delyth wailing almost silently. The occupants of the house ran out, first to complain about the damage to their hedge, then, on being told what had happened, to comfort them with hot, sweet tea and kind words.

Maldwyn's bag had burst open; its contents were spread over the road and had already been run over by the lorry and a postal van. The clothes so lovingly laundered by Winifred were ruined. Leaving it to be picked up later, Maldwyn walked Delyth home.

They were all subdued when they reached the small terraced house. The apparently deliberate attack had frightened them, and even though Maldwyn insisted it had been someone fooling about, or at the very worst mistaking them for someone else, Delyth wouldn't be comforted.

When they finally reached St David's Well, Maldwyn knew he had once again missed supper so they stopped in the town at Bleddyn Castle's fish-and-chip shop and walked towards the railway sidings as they ate them. Hardly looking up, their feet took them to where the carriage was parked, and it wasn't until they were within yards of it that they realised it was no longer there.

'My clothes! My suitcase, it's all gone!' Vera sobbed. 'What am I going to do? My ration book! The clothing coupons you gave me! Everything!'

'Come back with me. I'll smuggle you into my room while the landlady's in the kitchen. It'll be all right,' Maldwyn soothed, holding her tight. 'Whatever happens, I'll look after you. I'll take good care of you, I promise,' he told her, determined to make her feel less afraid. 'For tonight, the best thing is to get you somewhere warm and safe. Don't worry. I'll make sure you're all right.' They stood for a long time between the rails, hugging each other, Vera's sobs subsiding as Maldwyn described how comfortable his bed would be while he slept by the side of the wash-stand with a jug for a pillow. He succeeded in making her laugh at last and he happily added to the nonsense as he wiped away her tears. 'I'll stuff it with socks to make it nice and soft.'

Voices called, whistles blew and they looked up to see three men running, jumping the rails, heading towards them. Carelessly grabbing his battered bag, he took Vera's hand and they ran. Clothes, stained with tyre tracks, fell as they ran, leaving a trail of neatly folded but filthy garments in their wake. They outran the men and hid, panting, laughing, behind a line of trucks until they were gone.

They went into Maldwyn's lodging house without being seen, and he spent a very uncomfortable night curled up in a corner, while Vera slept peacefully in his bed. In the morning, very early, Maldwyn went down and stood at the bottom of the stairs ready to beckon when it was safe for Vera to leave. He quietly opened the door to a morning dark with rain. She was leaning over the stairs, looking down and awaiting his signal, when a firm hand touched her shoulder. The face of the landlady showed no inclination to listen to explanations.

'I'll give you five minutes to get out of here,' she said,

glaring down at Maldwyn. 'This is a respectable house and there's no room in it for the likes of you!'

He ran up, intending to plead, but she slapped his ration book into his hand and insisted that the week's rent was due. As they collected their few possessions, the only sound was the woman's impatient breathing and the rain. It was coming down relentlessly and with no sign of ever stopping. Looking at the useless paper carrier bags Mrs Prosser had provided, he began to ask, 'D'you think I could borrow a bag or two—' A glare was the only reply.

They stood in the porch outside the swiftly closed door and he looked gloomily at Vera. 'And there's me thinking I can look after you. I can't even look after myself!'

Her response to that was peals of laughter and, carrying the assorted luggage, they went down the road, apparently oblivious of the downpour, singing, 'It ain't gonna rain no more no more, it ain't gonna rain no more.'

Four

M aldwyn struggled to gather together his clothes and books and tuck them into the suitcase that was already over-full. He looked up at Vera and began to apologise, but quickly realised she was again laughing. It was still early and Maldwyn offered to go the beach café with Vera to explain the reason for her arriving in such an untidy state. 'I'll put a note in through the flower-shop door,' he said. 'Mrs Chapel will understand. Thank goodness she goes to the early-morning market, not me.'

'I can't serve in a café in this state,' Vera complained, trying to brush wet strands of hair from her eyes as the rain continued relentlessly.

'Perhaps Mrs Castle will let you wash and clean up before you start work?'

'What's the point if I have to put wet clothes back on? Oh, Maldwyn, what will I do? I'll have to go back home. I've lost my clothes and I don't have any money or clothing coupons to get more.'

'If you go to the council offices and explain, you might get some more,' he comforted. 'You can't be the first person to lose everything like this.'

'Very convincing I'll be, won't I? When I tell them I've been sleeping illegally like some tramp, trespassing on railway property, d'you think they'll want to help me?'

'I would,' Maldwyn said, looking at her admiringly. 'If I saw someone like you in trouble I'd break every rule in the book.'

They went to the bus stop, as it was nearer than the station and they had so much to carry. They stood, self-consciously aware of how bedraggled they looked, feeling more and more

uncomfortable in their wet and crumpled clothes. On impulse
Vera asked Maldwyn for half a crown, dashed into a chemist's
shop and came out with a small lipstick. Handing him his
change, she applied the colour to her lips and declared herself
one hundred per cent improved. 'If only I could comb my hair
I'd be ready to face anyone.' Struggling with his assorted and
inadequately packed load, Maldwyn managed to put his hand
into a pocket and retrieve a comb. A few seconds later, Vera
smiled at him and gave a sigh of relief.

'You're amazing,' Maldwyn said admiringly. Her eyes were
shining, her face with its addition of lipstick bright and fresh,
and the rain had added a sheen to her hair, which framed her
face, emphasising her loveliness. 'Just amazing.'

With their excess baggage they took up extra seats on the
bus, receiving disapproving looks from people forced to stand,
until they reached the sandy beach and alighted. They were
so wet they were oblivious of the continuing downpour and
walked without haste to the café.

'Sorry we're a bit early—'

'We're in a spot of trouble—'

'What on earth—? Where's your mac? Where's your
umbrella?' Marged demanded, reaching for a couple of
towels and handing them to the apologetic pair.

'I've lost all my clothes, everything,' Vera began. Then
she looked to Maldwyn to tell Marged the rest.

'Vera's been sleeping in a railway carriage, just until she
could find a room she could afford. Last night when we got
back, it had gone, with all of her things. So I took her back
to my lodgings and smuggled her in.' He looked at Marged's
face, anxious to see how she was taking it. 'Nothing wrong,
mind, I slept on the floor,' he added quickly as Marged's
lips began to curl. 'Then, this morning, before she could get
out, we were seen, and – well, now we're both homeless.'

Marged stared at them for a long moment then, from the
kitchen, deep booming laughter was heard. She joined in as
both Huw and Bleddyn appeared.

'It isn't funny,' Maldwyn complained huffily, which only
made the laughter double in volume.

'You'd better go back to Sidney Street and clean yourselves

67

up,' Marged said, handing them her door key. 'Knock on my sister Audrey's door and she'll give you some clothes. There's bound to be something that will fit.' She scribbled a note to her sister and saw the couple on their way.

'Hang about,' Huw said, 'I'll take you in the van.'

'And you'd better take the morning to look for somewhere to stay,' Marged called.

Audrey ran a bath in her house for Vera, and Huw did the same in his house a few doors away for Maldwyn. On the way back to the café, Huw called to tell Mrs Chapel that her assistant would be later than intended. He was unable to resist telling the whole story, with much exaggeration.

Once they were warm and dry in borrowed clothes they took a huge black umbrella, which Audrey said was normally only used for funerals, and went looking for accommodation. It was June, the season was beginning to build up and there were no vacancies. All the spare rooms were occupied or booked in advance for the summer visitors that were flocking into the small town.

'Just for a couple of weeks before your visitors start coming,' Maldwyn pleaded on their seventh try.

'Sorry I am, but I can't risk it. You might make a fuss about leaving when the time comes. Or you might make a mess after I've got it all clean and ready for my visitors.' Even by promising to do little more than breathe in the rooms, they couldn't persuade any of the landladies to help. They had to accept that there was little chance of finding a place until October.

Disconsolately they made their way back to the beach, trying at every likely house on the way. 'What will we do, Maldwyn?' Vera sighed. 'I don't want to give up and go home. Perhaps we can sneak into another unused railway carriage, eh?'

'Find anything?' Huw asked when they went into the crowded café, where he and Marged were serving a long queue of holidaymakers escaping from the rain.

'We've tried everywhere, but the rooms are either full or ready for visitors.'

Marged looked at them sympathetically. Vera looked ready to drop just where she stood, and fall asleep on her floor.

'Come with me after the café closes and I'll take you to see Mrs Denver. She doesn't normally let rooms but she might if I ask her.'

Maldwyn left Vera at the café and went to make his apologies to Mrs Chapel. His employer was both sympathetic and impressed. 'Good on you, Maldwyn, for looking after that poor girl. You couldn't have left her on her own without a place to stay. What you should have done, mind, was tell your landlady. She'd have helped if you hadn't tried to cheat on her.'

'Perhaps.'

'What's happening now?'

'Vera is working, and when the café closes we'll go to see someone who Mrs Castle thinks might help us.' He took off his mac and reached for an overall. 'Until then I'll do what I can to clear out the back room and rearrange the last of the flowers.'

'Not a tidy worker, am I?' Mrs Chapel laughed.

Maldwyn began collecting the half-empty buckets and other containers and clearing up the remnants of wreath- and flower-arrangement-making, cut stems, pieces of wire. When the shop was quiet, Mrs Chapel had busied herself making the evergreen-covered forms ready for wreaths and the floor was cluttered with pieces of fir-tree branches interspersed with yet more pieces of green wire. His movements were automatic as he restored order in the cluttered and overfilled room, his mind with Vera.

'Thanks, Maldwyn,' Mrs Chapel said when he had finished and she stood to admire the now orderly space. 'I know you hate working in a muddle, but I seem to attract mess, don't I? I stand there and it just sort of happens,' she laughed.

'You are wonderful with flowers and I wish I had your talent. I've learned more since I've been with you than in all the years I worked in Bryn Teg,' he said shyly. 'So it's me who should be thanking you. A bit of clearing up is a small price.'

She looked at him and smiled. What luck it had been for him to call in and ask for a job. She hoped he didn't plan to leave and go back home. Working alone was something she would no longer enjoy.

*   *   *

69

That evening, when the café was closed, Vera and Maldwyn met at Marged and Huw's home in Sidney Street and enjoyed a meal of vegetable soup and crisp fresh bread. Nothing had ever tasted better, Vera told them. It was seven when a weary Vera and an anxious Maldwyn knocked on the door of Mrs Denver. Huw waited in the van and they left Marged to do the talking. They quickly found themselves invited out of the rain and into a tiny living room that was made even smaller by the over-large furniture. It was chilly and dark with the rainclouds still low over the town.

Marged explained briefly what had happened and Mrs Denver nodded at almost every sentence, longing for Marged to come to the point so she could agree to what was almost certainly going to be the question.

'Of course they can stay,' she beamed, her rosy face with its bright blue eyes a picture of delight. 'They'll have a bit of sorting to do mind.'

'We don't mind that,' Maldwyn said at once, standing up and shaking the woman's hand.

The stairs were without carpet or even linoleum, but they were well scrubbed and smelled sweetly clean. The bedrooms were a shock. The two rooms they were shown were full of furniture, which had obviously been pushed in and discarded with no attempt at arranging it. A quick assessment, once Mrs Denver had increased the light by opening the curtains to their full extent, showed that everything they would need was there; the place just needed 'a bit of sorting', as Mrs Denver casually put it.

'You'd better stay with Huw and me tonight and come back tomorrow to get it ready,' Marged said.

'Thank you Mrs Denver, we'll be pleased to take the rooms and we'll try not to cause you any extra work,' Vera said.

'And please don't try to shift any of this stuff yourself,' Maldwyn said firmly. 'I'll go into the shop tomorrow morning and ask Mrs Chapel for the afternoon off. I'll have the place straight in no time.'

'So that's where I've seen you! I go into the flower shop to buy a bunch for my Philip's memorial,' Mrs Denver said, pointing to the vase of flowers in front of a fan of photographs showing a baby, then a child in various stages and ending with a photograph of a handsome young man in Army uniform. Facing the array of photographs, on the other side of the shelf, was a picture of a small baby in the arms of a young woman. 'That's my Phil,' she said, tapping the photograph of the man in uniform, glancing at Marged. 'No grave, see, him being lost in battle.'

'And the baby?' Vera asked politely.

'My granddaughter. Beautiful she is, and so smart you'd never believe.'

'And she's our granddaughter too,' Marged said sharply. 'The mother is our daughter, Lilly.'

On the way back to Sidney Street, Marged and Huw explained that although Lilly was now married the child was not her husband's. 'Mrs Denver's son, Phil, was the father,' Marged explained harshly. 'Best you know so the gossips don't get their fun telling you.'

'We wouldn't criticise,' Maldwyn said uncomfortably. 'Mrs Denver seems a nice lady. Fond of your granddaughter.'

'She didn't criticise either. She wasn't in a position to criticise! She never married Philip's father. So don't make it three in a row, right? Behave yourselves. Being under the same roof doesn't mean you have an excuse for any hanky-panky.'

Vera blushed and Maldwyn's imagination took flight.

Delyth told Madge about the lorry being driven towards her, and Madge tried to make light of it. 'Drunk he was, for sure,' she said.

'No, it was deliberate. I should have told the police, but they'd probably do what you're doing, pretend I'm making a fuss over nothing.'

'Sorry, Delyth.'

'The driver aimed the lorry right at me, and if Maldwyn hadn't thought quickly, well, I wouldn't be here trying to convince you, would I?'

Delyth was afraid to go out at night, insisting on staying at home, listening to the wireless or reading. On most evenings

71

Madge kept her company. Even walking home from the shop, she was nervous and glad Madge was there. She still started every time an engine revved loudly, and crossing the road was never a casual race against approaching traffic but a cautiously executed move.

'Let's go to St David's Well after work on Saturday,' Madge suggested. 'If the lorry driver is from around here, you'll feel safe there.'

'In this weather?' Delyth was searching for an excuse not to move from the house all weekend.

'We could go to the pictures. Your mam'll meet us at the station if we're home late.'

'It's a long way to go to the pictures,' Delyth said, unconvinced.

'Better than getting into the habit of being a prisoner in your own home.' She could see her friend was weakening and added, 'Less chance of an accident so far from home, eh?'

Delyth finally agreed, and when they told their kindly boss, he said they could leave early. 'I'll ask my wife to come and help for the last couple of hours,' he promised, and they jigged about like children at the thought of an extra treat as day trippers heading for their favourite beach.

Two days later the rooms were ready, and Maldwyn and Vera moved into their new accommodation. The small front room with its dark, heavy furniture was given to them as a sitting room and they immediately felt at home. Mrs Denver fussed over them happily and did everything she could to make them comfortable.

Maldwyn's first task was to write to tell Winifred his new address. Vera wrote to her parents but did not include that basic information.

On Saturday evening Maldwyn suggested the pictures, and they were settled into their seats when they heard their names hissed and turned to see, a few rows behind them, Delyth and Madge.

Madge threw them a toffee each and the audience moved irritably as the search for them disturbed their concentration. Delyth appeared outwardly to have fully recovered, and it was

72

only Madge who heard the extent of her fearful imaginings. She had made light of it when she told her mother and 'Uncle' Trev. When her mother had wanted to inform the police she had refused. 'The driver probably got his sleeve caught in the steering wheel,' she had laughed, pooh-poohing the idea as a waste of police time. But at night, and other times when she was alone, the image of that lorry increasing its speed and being deliberately aimed at her brought fear that almost amounted to panic. If she weren't careful she'd allow fear to take hold and would become afraid to go out. As always, Madge was right.

When they returned from their Saturday outing they sat in Delyth's front room and talked.

'I try to tell myself it was an accident, that it wasn't intended, but the driver was looking at me; he knew what he was doing. If it hadn't been for Maldwyn's quick action, I—' A great shudder ran through her. Madge let her talk. 'Why should anyone want to harm me?'

'No one! You have to believe it was unintentional, Delyth,' Madge urged. 'He was drunk, or perhaps he was an injured soldier thinking he was back in the battlefield aiming his Army lorry at a German gunner. It has happened. Mental images can make a man do strange things.' Her voice dropped a little as she said, 'There's poor Vera's mother as an example of illness being in the mind, poor dab, and it's harder for others to accept than a broken leg, or – or a boil on your bum.' Her ruse succeeded and she saw Delyth smile.

'You're right, the man was looking at me and seeing Hitler.' She pulled a length of hair across to imitate a moustache and put a hand straight out in front of her as a Nazi salute and said, in a high voice, 'He vill be punished!'

'Let's cheer ourselves up and go to St David's Well again tomorrow,' Madge suggested. 'I can afford the fare, and we'll take a picnic and go up on the cliffs. Nice up there in the sun.'

'What sun?' Delyth laughed. 'It hasn't stopped raining for days!'

'It'll be fine tomorrow. You'll see. There's bound to be something interesting for you to draw.'

73

'What's the point? I'll never get to art school, why go on kidding myself?'

'Oh, poor thing you! We are a little misery today, aren't we? Come on, Delyth, you know it takes perseverance to get anywhere, specially now with the war and everything. You have a talent and you should use it.'

'If Dad had lived there might have been a chance, but can you imagine "Uncle" Trev supporting me while I study?' She looked at Madge's doubtful expression and said, 'No, neither can I!'

'Go on with your drawings though. They're a wonderful record of our lives. We'll value them when we're old and cranky.'

'A record of our youth and how it was wasted!'

'Shall we get some chips?' Madge knew that Delyth had to face the dark streets sometime. 'Come on, Del, I'm sinking for something tasty!'

They walked along the pavement and Madge tried to be casual as she made sure she walked nearest to the road. She felt almost as scared as Delyth with the public houses closed and few people around, but she talked and made jokes and tried to appear relaxed.

When they got back with the savoury packages, Delyth admitted to feeling as though she had run a five-mile race, and Madge felt little better herself.

The suggestion of arranging a dolls' picnic pleased Eirlys and was quickly arranged. Posters went up and all they had to do was hope for a fine day. Hannah quickly made patriotic clothes in red, white and blue for Josie and Marie's favourite dolls, and Beth filled the window with some they had made to sell.

The park was the venue and they asked Mrs Chapel to be the judge. She and Maldwyn dressed the judge's table with flowers and Mrs Chapel made an enormous doll out of paper flowers, twigs and flowerpots. Eirlys was constantly amazed at the way everyone contributed when there was a need. People were so busy but, when asked, they managed to find time to help.

*   *   *

74

Maldwyn had settled into a very happy routine. Mrs Denver provided breakfast at a time convenient to his hours, except on the mornings he was up specially early to go to the market with Mrs Chapel to buy their stock. Mrs Chapel was teaching him the trade in a way his previous boss had not, and he was enjoying it enormously. He soon learned to choose what he knew they could sell quickly and with a reasonable profit.

He had been taught the basic rules and was talented at displaying flowers and making a bunch into a bouquet. It was the business side he appreciated being taught, and also being allowed to experiment with ideas of his own. Mrs Chapel left the window for him to fill and he had added a few carefully arranged displays in buckets outside the doorway to attract the attention of passers-by.

One morning, as they were on their way to market, he asked, 'Have you ever thought of opening up the back room and extending the range of what you sell?'

'What good would that do? All I can buy, we can sell. We don't have a lot of choice. Since the war started everything has changed.'

'A lot of flower shops sell fruit as well as flowers. They go together well. And fruit makes an attractive display.'

Mrs Chapel shook her head. 'You have to be careful with fruit. It can kill off flowers in no time.'

'I know we'll have to keep them separate, that the acid in apples can harm flowers, but so can putting tulips and daffodils in the same vase, and we manage not to do that. We could try, couldn't we?'

Mrs Chapel looked up at him and smiled. 'Very persuasive you are, young Maldwyn. Pity 'elp that girlfriend of yours, once you start using your pretty words.'

'Not a girlfriend, Mrs Chapel. Just a friend.' He tried to talk brightly so she wouldn't guess his disappointment. With all the opportunities they were given, he hadn't managed more than a chaste kiss on Vera's cheek since she had started sharing lodgings with him at Mrs Denver's. Earlier kisses, filled with passion and promise, were forgotten and Vera treated him almost with indifference. Hopes that had

75

blossomed during their moments in that railway carriage had been dashed.

Sunday found Delyth and Madge on the train to St David's Well with a crowd of lively travellers intent on having a day of fun. It was impossible for Delyth not to become as enthusiastic as the rest as she and Madge stepped off the train and took a deep breath to savour the sea air with its harmonious blend of seaweed, warm sand and the stronger infusion from the chip shops.

It was ten thirty and Delyth's first thought was of food. 'I know we've got a picnic, and we're a bit short of money, but we can afford a cup of tea and a cake, can't we? We could go to the café on the cliffs as we're going that way. The Castle family are very friendly and it would be a nice start to the day.' She didn't add that she hoped Maldwyn would be there. She knew he sometimes called for Vera to spend her off-duty hours with him. Amiably, Madge agreed.

Everyone seemed to have the same idea. There were queues at every café they passed, and looking up at where Marged, Huw, Beth and Vera were serving teas, coffees and snacks they doubted if things were any different there. People were coming down the metal steps to the beach carrying trays of teas. So instead of going to Castle's they caught the bus into the town.

The gift shop was closed, being Sunday, but inside they saw Hannah with her two little girls. They could hear Hannah singing, Josie and Marie's voices a thin echo as they learned the words. 'This old man, he played eight, he played knick-knack on my gate.' There was laughter as one of the girls sang 'plate'. On the strength of their previous visit, Delyth and Madge leaned towards the letterbox and joined in the chorus: 'Knick-knack, paddy-whack, give a dog a bone . . .'

Still laughing, Hannah opened the door and invited them inside.

There was a kettle filled ready on the single gas ring and Hannah lit the flame, warning the girls to stay away from the shelf on which it stood.

'Beth is working at the café with her parents, but Eirlys will be calling in soon. We can all have a cup of tea.' She reached for the tea caddy and spooned tea leaves into the pot, which she put near the kettle to warm.

When there was a knock at the door, she smiled. 'That will be Eirlys,' she said as she opened it. But it was Ken instead.

'I'm looking for Eirlys. Is she here?' he asked as he walked in.

'Not yet. Would you like a cup of tea while you wait?' Hannah introduced him to Delyth and Madge, who stared at him, trying to remember where they had seen him before. It was Delyth who remembered. When Hannah was behind the screen attending to the tea, she dug around in her shoulder bag and retrieved her almost full sketchpad. Flipping through the pages, she held it out to Ken.

'I thought I remembered you. We saw you in Coronation Park back home. Quarrelling you were, but you made it up quick enough.'

Ken looked at the drawing and fear curled in his stomach. It was him and Janet Copp. There were no features shown, but the clothes and the situation beside the three-sided summerhouse where they had met in Coronation Park left him in no doubt. The sketch of the surroundings was as clear as a photograph. Of all the places to meet they had chosen the park where this young girl had been casually practising figure-drawing! Or perhaps not so casual, he thought, suspicion and fear filling his head with ugly thoughts.

When he turned to look at her, Delyth was smiling, about to offer it to him as a memento of that afternoon, but to her surprise he snatched the book and demanded, 'What d'you want? What are you playing at?'

'I don't want anything!' she protested. 'I wasn't trying to sell it, if that's what you think. I thought you might like it, to remind you of a day when you quarrelled, then kissed and made up.' Her voice softened as she added, 'One day you'll look back on it and laugh.' She took the book back from him and turned a page to show him another picture of the same

77

couple walking off arm in arm, heads almost level and close together.

Abandoning the offer of tea, Ken left, asking Hannah to tell Eirlys he wouldn't be home until later. If Hannah had heard the strange reaction to the drawing she said nothing and, embarrassed but not knowing why, Delyth and Madge remained silent.

The next time there was a knock at the door, they were introduced to Ken's wife and at once they realised why he had been so suspicious. Eirlys was several inches shorter than the woman in the sketch.

Seeing the pad open on a shelf, and before Delyth could stop her, Eirlys picked it up and admired Delyth's skill. She turned the pages, studying each drawing with interest before returning to the page on which Delyth had depicted Ken and a mystery woman. She clearly did not recognise her husband as the man in the drawing.

'You're very observant, Delyth. I can see that these two are quarrelling although their faces aren't clear. I hadn't realised how the way we stand, the position of people's bodies, the movement of an arm, can give so much away. I'll have to be careful in case someone like you sees something in me I don't want known.'

'Oh, it was just two people in our local park. I'm trying to concentrate on figure-drawing, learning to quickly sketch the relevant lines and increase the speed at which I draw. Although I do like to take memories of a scene back home sometimes.'

'You're very good,' Eirlys said, handing the pad back. 'You ought to be at art school; I'm sure you have the talent.'

'Talent isn't enough,' Delyth sighed. 'I don't have anyone to support me. My father is dead and my mam thinks my scribbling is just an idle waste of time. Poor me, eh?' She hastily stuffed the pad into her shoulder bag.

Ken cancelled his plans for the morning and walked home, his strides revealing his anger. Had that girl been following him? Would she ask for money not to tell Eirlys about his meetings with Janet Copp? What should he do to stop her?

78

Threaten her? Warn her that the police don't approve of blackmail?

He went into the house where his father-in-law, Morgan, was cleaning shoes, and the three boys were playing a game of draughts which was slightly revised to their own rules. The counters were horses, and when the counters were crowned with another, they were horses and riders and were noisily galloped back to the corral. Too many cowboy films, he thought irritably, telling them to be quiet.

'Hello, Ken. We didn't expect you back till later. Eirlys said—'

'I changed my plans. That is all right, is it?' Ken snapped. Then he apologised. 'Sorry, I've had a bad morning. Two acts I depended on for next week's concert in Newport have let me down. Then there's the singer I hoped to take to record *Worker's Playtime*, who's sick. I'll have to leave tonight and try and find replacements.'

'Oh, that's a shame. I'm taking the boys to see a football match in the park, and Eirlys was cooking you something special, as you'll have a rare evening on your own.'

'Oh.' Guilty at his meeting with Janet, alarmed at the drawings of them together and aware that he spent hardly any time with his wife, he agreed to change his plans again and stay until the following morning. 'As it's special, d'you think Mr Gregory would sell me some flowers?'

Morgan smiled. 'Eirlys would be pleased. You can borrow my bike if you like.'

The evening wasn't a success. The meal consisted of roast potatoes and very little else. The slice of mutton Eirlys had saved from the lunchtime joint enjoyed by the three boys and her father was hardly visible it was so small, whilst the home-made custard was boring even with her attempt at dressing it with fruit and a pattern of heated jam. She thought it was disappointment that gave Ken his irritable mood, but in fact he hardly tasted the food. Try as he might, he didn't want to be there. He wanted to be with Janet.

Eirlys wished he would go out and allow her to tackle the pile of ironing waiting for her. There were three school uniforms urgently needing to be dealt with ready for the morning, as well as her father's limited supply of shirts. The evening together was so rare, she felt unable to leave Ken and it irked her.

At ten o'clock, when Morgan and the boys burst in, they were sitting at opposite sides of the room, the wireless playing softly, Ken slouched and stealing glances at the clock, Eirlys tense, doing the same, still wishing she could get on with the ironing.

The boys began shouting before they came in, excitedly telling Eirlys about the football game, which had been invaded by a couple of toddlers who had escaped from their mothers. Eirlys hugged them; Ken stared at them glassily, pretending to be interested, then went to bed. Eirlys gave the boys a snack and settled them into bed, then began to deal with the clothes for the next day.

'Better put some more coal on the fire, Dadda; these clothes will need to air for the morning.'

'Did you enjoy your evening?' Morgan asked as he unfolded the clothes-horse and placed it near the fire.

'Lovely,' she lied.

Apart from her red coat and a skirt and blouse, Vera had nothing to wear, and she was too proud to go home and explain to her sisters what had happened. Besides, they couldn't help so what was the point? Their childish clothes would have been unsuitable for her, they wouldn't have had coupons or money to spare to give her, and Dad wouldn't offer anything more than criticism, threats and a demand for her to come home.

There were times when she thought that eventually she would have to go back. There was growing guilt over her mother's inability to cope, concern about her father trying to support an ailing wife and even, on rare occasions, a desire to see her sisters. Selfish I am, she told herself. She told Maldwyn how she felt about her lack of clothes but not about her feelings of guilt. 'Here I am with no clothes, no money to buy any, and no coupons either, so even if I found a five-pound note lying on the ground I'd still be in this mess.'

It was Marged again who helped. At first she lent her own clothes, but knew they were an embarrassment to the smart young woman; and she explained the situation to Hannah.

'I've got ten clothing coupons to spare and I've offered her an advance on her wages. Can you do anything for her?'

Hannah forgot about the clothing coupons and went around the second-hand clothes shops. They were doing a busy trade, buying from some of the better houses and reselling to people like herself who were proficient at sewing. She bought dance dresses and unpicked them, using the full skirts to make blouses and summer skirts, following Vera's instructions as to style. There was a black-market outlet for parachute silk, which made lovely underwear, and within a few weeks Vera had a wardrobe to be proud of.

She enjoyed being admired by men. It was definitely a case of 'Look but don't touch', but her confidence was heightened by the admiring glances she received. So the necklines were sometimes altered to reveal a little more than Hannah had intended and skirts shortened more than government demands for reasons of economy. She had the knack of making the more ordinary outfit into something to turn heads. Maldwyn walked beside her proudly, and hoped fervently that none of her admirers would turn hers and cause her to leave him.

At the flower shop, Maldwyn finally persuaded Mrs Chapel to remove the walls on either side of the back room's doorway, extending the shop and making room to sell fruit. The cellar could be cleared of the clutter of many years' disuse, and could be both workroom and storage area, replacing the space lost upstairs.

'All right in the summer, when there are apples and pears and even a few peaches, but there isn't much about during the winter. What will we do then?' Mrs Chapel had asked. 'More expense with a bigger shop to keep warm – or suffer chilblains from the cold. And a long way to walk to the cellar to collect what we need. And what about working down there out of sight of the shop, eh? That isn't such a good idea, leaving the place unattended.'

'There would still be room for some stock, to replenish the displays as we sell. Let's try it for a couple of months. The market usually has something extra we can buy if we have the room,' Maldwyn pleaded. He wanted to earn his wages by working harder. The shop was very quiet on some days and he felt he owed Mrs Chapel more than he was giving. And so it was decided.

Mrs Chapel lived in a flat above the shop and she agreed to leave Maldwyn to deal with the work of taking the door down and getting a builder to remove some of the wall on either side while she was away visiting her sister. Mondays were quiet, so they would close until Tuesday, by which time the work should be far enough advanced to reopen for business.

Excitedly Maldwyn told Vera of the plans. 'Just as well you're busy,' she said. 'I'll be working all Saturday and Sunday to make up for the time I've had off moving into Mrs Denver's and seeing Hannah about my clothes.'

'You'll be able to manage pictures on Saturday?'

'I don't think so. I've promised to help with a bit of extra cleaning. You wouldn't believe how fussy Mrs Castle is.'

After a great deal of persuasion, the builders came on Sunday morning, after being reminded that there was a war on and everyone had to forget previous restrictions on working on the Sabbath. What flower-selling had to do with the war effort, Maldwyn would have been unable to say. Fortunately he wasn't asked.

The two men arrived at eight as promised and Maldwyn worked with them, labouring, fetching and carrying, clearing up in his orderly way as they worked. With a wheelbarrow he trundled the rubble and old bricks through the garden and on to the builders' lorry parked in the lane behind.

Arnold Elliot came in and complained about the noise and told Maldwyn they were wasting their time trying to improve their business. 'The place'll be mine before long anyway, so you're only doing all this to save me the bother.' Maldwyn smiled and asked him politely to move in case the wheelbarrow accidentally tipped its load over his feet.

The cellar was full of unwanted rubbish. He gradually emptied it, carting load after load up and on to the lorry parked in the lane. He disturbed mice, spiders and an assortment of beetles and found some damaged vases and pots, which gave him an idea. Apart from one or two of them, everything went on the lorry and by four o'clock, when the men were finishing plastering the new doorway arch, he had cleared the garden too. Among the shrubs which they used occasionally for foliage were broken toys, watering cans and other abandoned items and, once cleared, he saw that the place could be made into a pleasant area for Mrs Chapel to enjoy on summer evenings. At five o'clock, stiff, filthy dirty and exhausted, he paid the men for their work.

He looked with pleasure at the new frame the carpenter, Sammy Richards, had fixed around the now wide access to the second part of the shop. He hoped the extra business would justify the expense.

He went down to the cellar and gave it one more wash with a mop and soapy water. He thought he heard someone in the shop and tutted impatiently. Surely no one would expect to be served at this time on a Sunday afternoon?

He moved quietly up the steps, as he wore soft shoes and always trod lightly. He heard something fall and, alarmed, he stopped to listen. There was silence for a few moments and he smiled at himself. He was being foolish; it was probably nothing more worrying than a cat walking in to investigate. But, only partially reassured, he picked up a tall slim vase as a weapon before continuing up the stairs. The shop was empty but the door was wide open and he knew he had closed it although he hadn't bothered to turn the key. He stepped outside and looked around but there was no one near. It must have been a cat.

When he went inside again and closed the door, a man moved out of a doorway a few shops further on and walked quickly away. Maldwyn looked around and realised something was missing. It was an ornate picture frame he sometimes used for a window display. 'Strange cat!' he muttered to himself.

He locked up and as he was leaving he saw the picture frame in a doorway of a shop further along the road. Was it Arnold Elliot playing tricks? Mystified, but too tired to ponder long, he put it in the shop and went back to Mrs Denver's to wash and change his clothes. He didn't eat, apart from a piece of toast spread with Marmite: he was too weary. Rather than sit around, he decided that he would sit in the park to kill a couple of hours then leave in time to meet Vera when she finished work. They might treat themselves to supper at Bleddyn's fish-and-chip café in the town. She was sure to be hungry, even if he was not.

Delyth and Madge were on their favourite part of the cliffs that day. They had brought a picnic and planned to go back home on the nine o'clock train as the rain had ceased, the day was warm and the holiday mood of the town hard to leave.

Standing near the edge where Vera and Maldwyn had been warned of danger, Delyth leaned over to look at the beach far below. A small boat went past, and she lay on the springy turf and drew it. The engine *phut-phutted* calmly in the summer air, sounding relaxed and adding pleasantly to the lazy mood of the afternoon. She noticed that there was a mast that had been broken and was no taller than the man who stood beside it. There was something in the boat, a mound barely distinguishable from the brown of the seat and its shadow.

Her sketchbook was almost filled and she took out a new one. Two other small boats passed; these had no engines but were quietly rowed. She saw the men lift the gleaming oars from the water before dropping something over the side. Round floats revealed their position. Lobster pots, she guessed. She captured the tranquil scene on paper before lying back and enjoying the last of the sun.

Later they sat up, ate some of their food and discussed how they would spend the rest of the evening.

'Let's stay here,' Madge said. 'We're only twenty minutes' walk from the station and we've enough food for a snack before we leave.' She settled back against the rocks, behind which a rugged path led up to a headland before snaking down to the next cove, called St Paul's Bay. She picked up her book with the photograph of John as a bookmark and read for a while, but the day was peaceful, the air silky and warm, the sound of the waves far below soporific, and she closed her eyes against the bright sun and let daydreams take her.

Delyth walked along and looked down on St Paul's Bay and the small recess at beach level, hardly big enough to be called a cave but which a few of the more foolhardy local children dared each other to enter when the tide was low.

She stood, leaning against the sun-warmed rocks, and drew what she could see, strong, confident strokes marking the shape of the rocks and the sea below. The cave at one side of the drawing looked dark and mysterious and, simply for fun, she depicted two figures standing in its shadowed entrance.

'What are you doing?' a voice demanded.

'What business is it of yours?' she shouted back, frightened and angry. A man stood there, a man she recognised as Ken Ward.

'Who is it?' Madge called, and the stranger turned away and disappeared behind the rocks.

'Nothing, go back to sleep,' Delyth said, her voice calm but her heart racing. She wanted to run, to get away from this place where an angry push would send her down to almost certain death. She looked towards Madge. She was so content today, better than she'd been since the news of her husband's death had torn her apart. How could she spoil it for her by a return to the fanciful fear that someone was trying to kill her?

Logic told her that Ken had been as startled by seeing her there as she had been by his sudden appearance. He was afraid she was going to pester him. That must be it; he was misled by what was only a coincidence, that was all, she insisted, and persuaded Madge to close her eyes again as the man disappeared up the path towards the headland.

Putting the now filled sketchbook in their picnic bag, she picked up the new one and in cartoon form drew Madge sleeping, with grass grown around her as though she had been there for a long time, and another of a seagull perched on their picnic bag.

Determined to face her own demons, she walked back to the place from where she could look down on St Paul's Bay and drew the scene again. This time she drew a solitary man, looking up at her, his face no more than a blank space but the droop of the shoulders and general demeanour giving an air of menace.

When the sun began to sink and the gentle breeze to cool,

Madge woke up, stretched luxuriously and declared herself starving. She didn't worry when there was no reply. She sleepily reached over to the bag, then looked around her. There was no sign of Delyth. Only her new sketchpad lay on the grass, marking the place where she had stood. When Madge picked it up she saw that all the recent drawings had been torn out.

Five

A t first Madge presumed that her friend was hiding and preparing to jump out and startle her. She crept slowly around the bushes and rocks on the narrow strip of land between the drop to the beach and the rise of the rocky cliff, prepared to laugh. There was no sign of Delyth. She called a few times, her voice hardening as she began to think the joke had gone on long enough. Irritation swelled to anger. Then, as minutes passed and there was nothing but silence, she began to be alarmed.

She called with more urgency and crawled as close as she dared to the edge, trying to look down to where the tide was rushing in. The tumble of rocks that passed as a beach was about to vanish below the turbulent water.

Surely Delyth hadn't fallen? Cautiously she searched as close to the edge as she felt safe, her heart racing, but to her relief there was no sign of freshly broken turf. She looked again at the few places where her friend could find concealment and her fear increased. The air around her seemed to crackle with danger. She turned sharply once or twice, convinced that someone was behind her, about to strike. Still calling, a pitiful wail in her voice, she stood against the wall of rock, her back pressed against it as a form of protection.

She was undecided whether to wait, in the hope Delyth would reappear as suddenly as she had vanished, or run to find help. Her fear increased as she realised that, if Delyth had fallen, then she must be seriously injured: she had heard no sound, no call for help.

Facing her fear, she told herself she had to go down the precarious path to the disappearing beach below and look for

Delyth before the tide came too far in for her to be able to find her. There wasn't much time: the inexorable swell of the water would soon obliterate the narrow beach completely and rise high enough to cover an unconscious person, she thought with a shiver of fear.

Leaving everything behind except Delyth's coat, which she thought she might need, she went behind the rock and began to make her way down the dangerous route to the sea. She had reached half-way when she paused for a moment. The coat was an encumbrance and she pushed it between some rocks. Before starting down again, she called Delyth's name, although with little hope. To her unspeakable relief, she heard Delyth call back.

'Down here, Madge! Quick, I'm at the edge of the cave.'

Slithering, careless of the danger, Madge made haste down the rest of the way and saw her friend with her foot stuck in a crevice in the rocks.

Typically in moments of relief after fear, Madge began remonstrating with Delyth for not calling before. 'I've been calling and listening. Why didn't you shout, let me know where you were?'

'I was trying to get my foot out. I didn't want you to try coming down to help and for both of us to get stuck! But now I'm frightened, the water's coming up so fast.'

With the tide around them rising against their legs, both girls struggled to free Delyth's foot from the grip of the rock. Minutes passed in frantic tugging and pulling and all the time the water rose around them.

'We're going to die,' Delyth sobbed.

'Don't be melodramatic!' Madge snapped. 'Even at its highest the water won't reach our faces.' She was far from convinced of the truth of her confident statement but there was no chance for them if Delyth gave up and stopped trying.

Although it was summer, their hands began to feel stiff with the coldness of the water. The waves hit them repeatedly, playfully wetting them as they came in with a rush of foam, and showering them as they bounced off the rocks as they departed. Soon they were completely soaked and Madge had to crouch with the water covering her face as she bent down and tried to ease her fingers around the recalcitrant shoe. Delyth was groaning and shaking with shock, fear, the chill of the water and the growing conviction that she would die. The shivers became an ululating moan.

'Stop that!' Madge shouted. 'When I say, "Now," I want you to grab your leg and pull back. Both together, ready – NOW.'

Whether it was desperation giving them added strength, or Madge getting a better grip around the front of Delyth's foot, their combined effort released her and sent them both falling heavily into the foaming waves. The deeper water made walking difficult and they struggled towards the point where they had clambered down. Their muscles were weak from their efforts and they stopped several times as they climbed back to the path. Eventually they stood panting, high above the relentless tide, soaking and bleeding, but safe.

'Look what you've done to my hands,' Madge said, showing her cut hands and broken nails.

Delyth was trembling uncontrollably. 'What about my back and my legs and my foot?' she said, before they both burst into noisy tears.

They had towels and bathers with them and a spare jumper, so they dried themselves and dressed in everything they had, wrapping their towels around their waists to walk down the path and along the promenade to the railway station, their coats around their shoulders and buttoned under their chins, worn as cloaks.

It was not until they were sitting on the train, still trembling at the shock of the near-fatal accident, that Madge asked Delyth what she had been doing in such a dangerous place.

'It was that man, Ken, the one I sketched in the park with the woman who wasn't his wife.'

'What are you talking about? How could Ken, or anyone else with any sense, be down there with the tide coming in? You didn't hit your head as well as jam your foot, did you?'

'He pulled me behind the rock and demanded the drawings I'd done in the park. He was afraid we'd tell that wife of his, poor dab. Eirlys she is, remember? The girl who works in the handicraft shop? I showed him the new book I was using and he snatched it and threw it down to the bay. I told him the used sketchbook was in the bag near where you were sleeping and he made me promise not to tell anyone about seeing him there that day.'

'As if we would!'

'I think he expected me to ask for money but I didn't even think of it. I promised to tear them up in little pieces so long as he'd go away and leave me alone. I was real scared, Madge.'

'I saw your book with the pages torn out.'

'He took the other one. He wouldn't trust my promises and made me go and get it without waking you. He tore out the two sketches I'd done and stuffed them in his pocket, then threw the book over the edge of the cliff.'

'All this was going on with me lying prostrate and helpless? I'll never sleep in the sun ever again!' She shuddered at her vulnerability.

'Then,' Delyth went on, reaching into the pocket of her soaking wet shorts, 'then he made me take this.' She took out a fold of white paper and slowly opened it to reveal a five-pound note.

'God 'elp! I've never owned one of those in my life!'

'He hurried off and I went back down to retrieve my book, and my bag fell off my shoulder. I went down to get it and I couldn't find a way back up, there was an overhang stopping me, so I went down to try another route and, well, you know the rest. I thought I could shelter in the cave if the tide came too high but I slipped, and the more I struggled the tighter I was lodged.'

The train was full and the journey seemed endless. Cold, wet and still very shaken, the girls alighted at their stop and hurried home.

Ken sat in the quiet house. The three boys were at school, Eirlys and Morgan were at work and he was supposed to be phoning a few Army and Air Force camps, making arrangements for a concert-party tour. The list was in his hand and he was dressed ready to go out and find a telephone box, but he couldn't rouse the enthusiasm to get up and deal with it. Thoughts of how he had treated Delyth obliterated every other. Delyth and the others he was using so badly.

He was so ashamed of what he had done, frightening the young girl with her sketchbook. It merged with the guilt of him wanting another woman while Eirlys was carrying his child, and was like a volcano inside him threatening to burst and send him to kingdom come. What had happened to him, that he could act like a madman? How had he changed so much? He was never an angry man, yet now he was terrifying young girls and cheating on his pregnant wife. He had married Eirlys for better or for worse and nothing had changed since then except his dissatisfaction. If only he hadn't met Janet. Or had met her before he married Eirlys. Perhaps he was weak and would never have been content. If Janet hadn't happened, would someone else have appeared to destroy his marriage?

The easiest excuse was the war and how it had altered the way people felt about things. He wasn't the only one to be restless. The desperate feeling that 'Today might be all you're going to get' made everyone behave more selfishly, made them greedy for every experience, every chance of happiness in case death or disablement made an end to their dreams for the future. Yet, if that were the case, why wasn't he happy? He was taking risks, threatening the happiness of Eirlys and of Janet, and it wasn't filling every day with joy. Far from it.

He went to the phone box and cancelled his meetings for the next few days, delegating work that he was using simply as an excuse not to stay at home. Better he spent some time with Eirlys and tried to forget Janet. The boys came home for lunch and, because of her father's shift work, it was Eirlys's turn to feed them. She would be surprised to find the table laid, the kettle on and beans on toast, the boys' favourite, ready to serve.

'Ken! This is a lovely surprise. I thought you had to go out?'

'I suddenly tired of dashing about and hardly seeing you, so I made a few phone calls and put everything off for a few days. Can you take a day off tomorrow? I thought we could go out, take a picnic, just you and me.'

'Oh Ken, I'd love to, but I have a meeting I can't cancel. We've decided we're having a beauty contest and as it's something we haven't done before we have a lot of working out to do. I have to get the details as soon as possible so I can display posters and put a piece in the local paper and, well, you know what it's like if anyone does, Ken. You have an idea but however simple it sounds there's always a great deal to do.'

'What if I come along? I might be able to help. I might even be able to arrange for a celebrity to open the proceedings; how would that be?'

Eirlys's eyes were shining as she nodded enthusiastically. 'That would be wonderful, Ken. Thank you.'

The sound of shouting announced the arrival of the three boys. Stanley and Harold burst in, saying they were starving, closely followed by nine-year-old Percival, who was worried in case the meal included one of a long list of things he didn't like.

He came in sniffing, trying to guess what they were being offered. If it was soup he hoped he'd be allowed to mash the vegetables like Eirlys's mother, Annie, used to do. No chance of meat, thank goodness. He didn't like lumps. He peered around his brothers as they threw off their blazers, and sighed with relief. Beans on toast. That was all right, so long as he could leave the crusts.

Eirlys watched him, guessing his thoughts, and shared an amused smile with Ken.

'No lumps to "bover" you today, Percival,' she said kindly.

Ken watched Eirlys as she dealt with the food, talked to the boys, asked about their morning then efficiently cleared away, leaving the kitchen neat and orderly, before starting to prepare the vegetables for the evening meal. She always looked neat, never a hair out of place. Her work area was always swiftly cleared. Even now, nearly five months pregnant, her figure was in control, her skirt and a long cardigan hiding the bulge of the baby. So in control.

He stood admiring her, making himself proud of her, of the way she managed a very complicated job, ran the house and looked after himself, her father and three lively boys, and still looked unruffled and – he repeated the words in his mind – in control. A wave of sadness swept over him. So in control: her clothes sensible and immaculate, her small neat figure, her almost sculpted hair cut to shape and never being allowed to fall into disarray. Janet was careless about such things. She didn't worry about a scarf to keep her hair tidy, but loved to allow the wind to blow through it. She dressed well, but without the anxiety that Eirlys showed. In bed, too, she was less inhibited, not worried about how she looked or behaved. He turned away from his wife and admitted to himself that no matter how he tried to pretend, it was Janet he wanted, Janet he loved. His life here with Eirlys, Morgan, Stanley, Harold and Percival was a prison and, with a baby expected in November, life had thrown away the key.

He walked back with Eirlys, leaving her at the office door.

'I'll try to get out of one of tomorrow's meetings,' she told him. 'Come with me to the first and we can still go out for the rest of the day.'

'Wonderful,' he said. 'I can have you all to myself for a few hours at least.' Leaving her smiling happily, he went to the phone box and began making his calls. With misery overwhelming him he defied common sense; his first call was to the camp where Janet was based. He left a message asking her to phone him at the call box near Conroy Street at ten thirty that evening.

The smile stayed on Eirlys's face until the door closed behind her. Ken was making a real effort but she knew he was unhappy. She had the feeling that he hated coming home and guessed that having the three boys living with them was part of the trouble but there was nothing she could do about it. As for the rest of the trouble, she didn't even know what it was, so how could she deal with it? She only knew that, for her, marriage to Ken was a continuing disappointment and she had to presume it was the same for him. There was no specific cause, they were just misfits who had married in haste and would now repent at their leisure, as the saying went.

If only this baby hadn't happened they might have amicably ended it, but now, like Ken, she felt trapped. She wanted to continue with her job and help at the handicraft shop with Hannah and Beth, not spend hours sitting waiting for Ken to appear and then wishing him gone. If only there was someone to talk to. It wasn't the kind of thing to discuss with her father. It was at times like these she missed her mother so much. If Annie were here, she'd understand and help her decide what to do. She didn't feel able to talk to Hannah or Beth either. They were so much in love with their husbands they would never understand.

Delyth was nervous and tearful; she told her boss she was ill and would be away from work for at least a week. When she ventured outside, the sound of a car approaching was enough to send her diving into the hedge or running in panic to a place where she could hide. He was still out there, whoever he was, watching her, waiting for another opportunity to run her down and this time make sure he killed her.

'Delyth,' Madge said when the weekend was upon them, 'I'm not wasting another day with you acting like a Victorian lady with the vapours. You're coming to St David's Well and we're going up on that cliff for a picnic. You're going to get rid of this fear if I have to drag you there. Right?'

'I can't.'

'Cowards say "can't", sensible young women say "I'll try!"'

'Since when have I been sensible?' Delyth grinned weakly.

'If you don't come with me, I'll go and tell the police what happened, and then you'll have to talk about it, and that stupid Ken Ward will get into trouble and that poor wife of his will know and—'

'All right, I'll come, but if I lose my nerve promise you won't make me go up on to the cliff path?'

'You'll go. And you'll take your sketchbook with you. I want a pictorial record of our youth. Right?' To further her persuasions she added, 'What say we write to Maldwyn and ask him to meet us? Being a Sunday, he'll be free.'

They wrote a letter care of Chapel's Flowers and asked Maldwyn to meet them the following Sunday. He replied and promised to be at the station when they arrived. Madge also wrote to the three young women in the handicraft shop, inviting them to join them on the beach with Hannah's children. She was sure that, with arrangements made involving others, Delyth was less likely to change her mind. 'With five women and a couple of kids, I don't suppose Maldwyn will enjoy it, but he can always escape and pretend he's got something to do in that shop he loves so much,' she said with a laugh.

Delyth began counting the hours, not with happy antici-pation but with dread.

Ken's day out with Eirlys was not a success. They seemed to have very little to say to each other and most of their conversations were about their work, each trying to persuade the other how busy they were, each making subliminal excuses for their disappointing marriage although the words only picked around the edges of the truth.

Ken promised that on the following Sunday he would go with Eirlys to the special meeting she had called and bring with him a few people who had run beauty contests before and might be willing to offer their help.

When they reached home Eirlys excused herself and went to bed. The boys were asleep and Morgan was at work. At ten thirty Ken went out and waited at the call box for Janet to ring.

'I'm free next weekend,' she told him.

'I'm not,' he groaned. 'I'm going to Bedfordshire with a concert party. I have to leave here on Sunday night and drive the loaded lorry up.'

'Perhaps it's for the best, Ken. We shouldn't meet any more. I keep telling myself how cruel it is to treat Eirlys so badly. I've applied for overseas posting and I'll be going for training soon. It's better to end it now.'

Ken wrestled with his conscience. Janet was right. He'd

lost count of the times they had decided to say goodbye. But if she was going abroad then the decision would be made for them; until then . . . 'I'll leave a day early,' he said. 'You can come with me and help set up the stage.'

The arrangement would be perfectly acceptable, as several people were needed by the travelling concert party to set up the stage in the limited time allowed. But it was really only a smokescreen for what would go on when the concert ended.

Maldwyn was a little worried about his original plan to use the cellar for work and holding stock. That someone had come into the premises when he had been in the cellar and taken away the picture frame worried him. Mrs Chapel lived in the flat above and he didn't want people wandering in and out unobserved. He brought a table and a few shelves back up and placed them in the rear of the shop, and it was there the bouquets were made up, where there was a clear view of the shop door when he or Mrs Chapel was alone.

He had been introduced to the traders at the early-morning market and from that day he had been allowed to choose what to buy. Mrs Chapel was thankful for the extra hour in bed and Maldwyn was as excited as a child at Christmas. He selected flowers of varying sizes, from small flowers for posies to large blooms for arrangements large enough to fill a fireplace or a corner of a room. He also went out in the fields and cut branches, which he painted and to which he added a few blossoms. These were a way of filling large areas such as churches relatively cheaply and were in demand at once.

The fruit too began to sell, even though Maldwyn startled his employer by charging higher prices than the shops nearby. He carefully selected each piece and never sold one with a sign of damage. The reputation for quality was quickly earned.

'Wicked waste,' Mrs Chapel told her friends with a certain pride, but the damaged fruit was sold to either Mrs Denver, who cooked for a local café, or to Castle's Café, to be made into pies and other desserts, and the profit made her content.

Maldwyn was pleased with the invitation to join Delyth and Madge the following Sunday, especially as Vera had told him she was working and couldn't meet him for their occasional walk-and-talk hours, as she called them. He hated Sundays when Vera couldn't meet him and usually spent the day cleaning out some corner of the shop.

When she heard of the arrangement, Mrs Denver promised to make a few treats, and he took out his smartest short-sleeved shirt and beige slacks. Madge had hinted in her letter that Delyth had stopped drawing and needed encouragement so he bought a good-quality sketchbook and a selection of pencils, the assistant telling him how lucky he was to have a 2H and a 4B soft lead when most shops could only supply a dubious HB. He thanked her vaguely, not sure what she meant but confident that Delyth would, and packed them with his dippers and towel, spare clothes and the food.

Ken had received a letter from Janet, disguised as a business letter by a brown envelope and a typed address: the weekend had been cancelled because two of the girls were ill and she had to work. That Saturday morning he dealt with several other letters regarding future concerts, went to the phone box and began listing appointments for auditions and confirming previously booked venues.

When Eirlys came home from work at lunchtime, he had gone. There was no message. She presumed he would turn up in time for the meeting with his colleagues, ready to offer advice.

The conversation with Janet and the plan to spend the weekend together had sent all thoughts of Eirlys and her meeting out of his head. Then the letter telling him the arrangement had been cancelled made him set off much earlier: to see Janet for a couple of hours was better than nothing. At nine thirty, while the boys were eating breakfast, he bathed and left the house in Conroy Street without giving the beauty contest a thought.

At the council offices on Sunday morning, Eirlys set out cups and saucers ready for the coffee she had promised to prepare for those attending, and threw anxious glances towards the door. He would come. He wouldn't let her down at such an important time. She'd told everyone of his

97

promises, the expert offering advice, the showbiz celebrity to open the event. He would come.

She delayed starting the meeting for as long as she could. After twenty minutes, when people were becoming restless, and she had been reminded that it was a Sunday morning and people had other things to do, she knew he wasn't coming. With a heavy heart she listened to suggestions and noted in her neat writing the ideas and offers of help that would be useful.

The decision was made to hold the competition sometime in August, when the town was at its busiest, on the sands at St David's Well Bay if the weather allowed or in the large dance hall at a nearby pebble beach if not. There was no famous person booked to open the contest. Ken had let her down badly, made her look inefficient, and it hurt.

She had arranged for her father to take the boys out so she and Ken could go somewhere and have lunch together. Instead she caught the bus to the bay and walked along the promenade, looking down at the families having fun and wondering why she had failed. The families were happy even though incomplete, the children accompanied by mothers, grandmothers and aunts with only a few men: mostly grandfathers, she guessed.

One group climbed down the metal steps from Castle's Café, a young woman with a child and an older man who she presumed was the grandfather, but she was wrong.

'Lilly!' she heard Marged shout from the café door. 'Mrs Denver will look after Phyllis for you so you can come and help your family when they're desperate!'

'I'll think about it our Mam,' the young woman called back. So that was Lilly, Marged and Huw's daughter who had married a man as old as her father. Eirlys wondered sadly whether they were happy. Everyone seemed to be, except herself and Ken.

The sun was strong that day and the men looked uncomfortable in their suits, with knotted handkerchiefs on their heads, some brave enough to roll their trousers half-way up their shins and dabble at the very edge of the waves.

One elderly man was surrounded by excited children who were trying in vain to suppress giggles. They were clearly being reprimanded for splashing the irate man's best – or only – suit.

She pressed her hand against her swelling figure and tried to imagine enjoying such innocent fun with her baby and Ken, and she failed. This baby would be loved, but it wouldn't bring the great happiness she had once imagined.

'What sad thoughts are you harbouring this day, my dear?' The voice came from a strangely dressed woman, wrapped in silky shawls with beads and sparkling jewels adorning her clothes and hair. Two dark, mesmerising eyes stared out from the shawl, preventing Eirlys from turning away and walking on.

'I'm not sad,' she said defensively.

'You can't lie to me, my dear.' The woman shook her head from side to side slowly, earrings clattering musically. She continued to stare. 'Not a death, I think, but a failure. A man, but you think he isn't the man for you.'

Alarmed and not a little frightened, Eirlys tried to pass the gypsy woman, whom she now recognised as the fortune teller from the booth on the far end of the promenade. 'I'm married,' she retorted rather haughtily.

'To the wrong man is what you think, dearie,' the gypsy woman insisted. 'You are seeing a baby who will bring you joy, but believe his father will not be there to see your son grow into a fine young man.' She reached out and held Eirlys's arm in a strong grip. 'Come and see me; cross my palm with silver and I will tell you what you need – maybe not want, but need to know.'

Unnerved, Eirlys watched the woman walk slowly away. How could a stranger know why she was sad? As she passed the colourful tent which advertised 'Sarah the All-seeing, All-knowing Gypsy King's Daughter', she tried not to read the times when the woman would be there, but her mind took in the times against her will and she wondered whether, one lunch break, she might go in and listen to what she had to say.

There wasn't much point. Marriage was for ever and nothing

99

the woman, wise or not, might say could change that. Thoughts of divorce filtered through her mind from time to time but were always discarded; with the baby coming it was not an option either she or Ken could accept.

Ken met Janet in a café not far from the camp where she was working. The lorry, which was loaded with the props for the concert, was parked outside. Ken had been there for an hour when she arrived, in uniform, windblown and rosy from the run from the bus stop. He felt no irritation at having to wait for her, just joy at her arrival.

'Sorry Ken, I was delayed. Some supplies arrived as I was leaving and I had to stay and see them stored properly or the mice will have more than the men.' He had stood up when she opened the café door and opened his arms wide. They kissed affectionately, grinning with the pleasure of seeing each other.

'Another cup of tea then, is it?' the girl behind the counter called.

'I've already drunk three; if I have another I'll explode,' Ken laughed. 'I was afraid she'd tell me to leave if I didn't have something in front of me.'

'Two teas and two doughnuts,' Janet replied and added in a low voice, 'And they'd better be as good as the ones I make, or else.'

They played with the food. Eating was only a pretence, the café being one of the few places they were able to meet. Their talk was casual at first, relating the various activities taking place in their worlds. Then Ken became serious and told her what he had done.

'A young girl, a friend of Beth and Hannah and my wife, saw us together in the park. We were arguing, if you remember. She did a drawing of us together and another of us walking off hand in hand.' He showed her the crumpled pages he had torn from Delyth's book.

'If Eirlys saw it she'd be so distressed,' Janet said, guilt making her look away from Ken.

'She did see it. She told me about the girl with a talent for sketching. Fortunately she didn't recognise the two figures as

100

you and me. Delyth – that's her name – hadn't intended a likeness, just a sketch of two people. But – oh, Janet – I threatened the girl and made her return the drawings.'

'Was that wise? It might have been better to ignore it, pretend it was nothing to do with you.'

'I panicked. I – I followed the two girls, and frightened Delyth, snatched the drawings, then gave her five pounds, pretending it was payment for them. I know I made things worse. She might have suspected the man was me and that I was with a woman who was more than a passing stranger, but now she knows for certain.'

Leaving the café, they walked slowly along the quiet country roads. Janet was on duty in less than an hour and besides the early-evening shift in the canteen she had promised to sing that night in a concert organised by the soldiers at the camp.

'Crowded, it is, lorries, guns, vehicles and all sorts, and hundreds of extra men coming from all over the place ready to embark for foreign parts,' she told him, trying to take his mind away from his worries about Eirlys. 'The barracks are filled to overflowing and there are tents going up all over the fields. So they thought a concert would be a way of passing the evening for those who can't leave camp. As we had to forget our weekend away, I offered to sing.'

Because Janet understood a lot about Ken's work, they had plenty to discuss and the time they had together passed unbelievably fast.

'I want to tell Eirlys about us,' he said as he held her. 'It's the only way. I will tell her, but I want to choose where and when. I don't want someone like this Delyth girl dictating to me.'

'Try to forget it happened, love. You'll probably hear no more about it.'

Walking back to the bus stop holding hands, both wishing the parting could be delayed, they spoke of more personal things, their love and need of each other, the dream of facing the scandal and walking away from Eirlys, but for both the fact that there was a baby involved made the dream more poignant and sad. Both knew their plans were nothing more than pretence. It was too late. It wouldn't happen. Ken would stay with Eirlys, and Janet would be unable to return to St David's Well and the market café.

'Whatever happens, we'll always stay in touch, won't we?' Janet asked.

'Until you find someone else, someone free to love you as you deserve.'

He stood and watched the bus, with her face a vague pale shadow in the back window, until it was no longer in sight, then turned to make his way back to a house he could never call home.

He still hadn't remembered the arrangement to meet his wife. His thoughts were all selfish ones. Anger filled him, not with himself for cheating and for the lies he would have to tell, but with Eirlys for making it necessary. His anger was particular; he felt none for most of the people he knew. It was only Eirlys who brought out that unpleasant emotion and in his saner moments he knew that what he called anger was really only a thinly veiled guilt, which he twisted and distorted to ease his conscience. As anger cooled, he wondered sadly how love, that gentlest of emotions, had turned him into a cowardly bully.

He had delivered the lorryload of props to the venue and, as he was not really needed once his acts had arrived and rehearsals were under way, he left them and travelled by train back to St David's Well. He was shocked when Eirlys berated him for not turning up at her meeting. Shocked that he had forgotten so completely. He promised to do something about it immediately, but she muttered quietly that she wouldn't expect wonders.

The following Sunday, Ken volunteered to take the three boys to the beach and, taking a ball, buckets and spades and the rest of the paraphernalia needed for a day out, he found a place for them on the sand and settled for what he knew would be a boring few hours.

Eirlys had promised to join them later, after spending a few hours helping Hannah and Beth. Leaving her father in charge of the potatoes in a slow oven and the pathetic joint of meat simmering in a pan with vegetables, she walked to

102

the shop. She was very quiet, and Hannah tactfully asked if she were feeling unwell.

'I'm a bit tired: this little baby is wearing me out,' she said.

'Perhaps it's time you stopped working?' Beth suggested, but Eirlys shook her head.

'Ken's money isn't generous, and I need my wage for as long as I can keep working. Dad is good and gives what he can spare, but the boys eat enormous quantities, except Percival, who's still a bit picky with his food. Then there's getting what I need for this baby.' She hesitated a moment and Beth and Hannah waited for her to continue. 'I met that gypsy fortune teller on the prom the other day. She said it will be a boy; d'you think she knows what she's talking about?' She hoped they would speak derisively of the woman's talent and she wasn't thinking of the sex of her unborn child, but the confusing remarks about her being with the wrong man and all the implications of that casually spoken statement.

'I think there are a lot of people who make these things up, but people say she has a way of coming up with the truth,' Hannah said.

'I don't believe in that stuff normally, but from what people say she's able to see things in advance of their happening,' Beth admitted. 'I've made you some romper suits already but I'll make a few dresses as well, in case she's wrong.'

As she thought about the wise woman's words Eirlys realised that what she had actually said was not that she was with the wrong man, she only thought she was. Her spirits lifted. Perhaps things would work out well after all. Hannah and Beth assured her she was right. 'She was telling you not to worry, that everything would be all right,' Beth said.

'And if she's right about the baby being a boy, then she could be right about other things,' Hannah boldly said, acknowledging Eirlys's unhappiness.

'And I'll have to wait until November before I'm sure,' Eirlys laughed, her mood more cheerful than it had been for weeks.

They left the shop early and went to the beach to join Ken and the boys for a last hour or so. The weather had been dull all day and the beach was far from crowded. The cafés were doing good business, and the shops selling the usual seaside gifts were filled with enthusiastic customers. They walked past Castle's Seaside Rock and Sweets, which had reduced its selection since sweets-rationing, announced for the end of July, had made it impossible to continue. Alice Potter was there, selling the last of the novelties made from the sticky confection so loved by children and adults alike. The shop was changing its stock and there were postcards and a few traditional gifts, some made from seashells. Beth popped in to ask whether Alice had heard recently from Eynon. Beth's brother and Alice were engaged and would marry on Eynon's next leave, but as he was in North Africa that day was probably a long way off.

Leaving Beth's Aunt Audrey to cope with the trickle of customers, Alice joined them and they walked towards the sand. Eirlys spotted Ken, and near him three industrious boys digging a moat around a huge castle which had been decorated with everything from flags, shells and rock to what looked like cakes, which had presumably been dropped on to the sand and rendered uneatable. She called and went over, followed by the others. Happiness showed on her face, the words of the gypsy still repeating in her head; Ken was the right man for her, and she glowed with the promise of happiness some day soon.

Ken kissed her lightly and said, 'Shall I go and get a tray of teas? I'm worn out entertaining this lot.' He smiled when he said it, reassuring Eirlys that he was joking.

'I'll go,' Beth offered. 'Mam and Dad give me better rates than you!'

Hannah's children were there with her sister-in-law Evelyn; she had been widowed early in the war, and Bleddyn had determined that she still belonged to the Castle family. A voice called them and they turned to see Beth's brother Ronnie, with his wife Olive and their baby Rhiannon, struggling across the sand carrying the baby's pushchair, Ken jumped up to help them.

Marged, Huw and Bleddyn came down to join them all for a few moments, helping to carry the loaded trays and leaving Hetty and Vera to cope in the café.

'Marvellous, this is,' Huw beamed, admiring his son's baby daughter. 'Practically all my favourite people together on our beach.'

'We only have to think of Johnny and Eynon to know they're thinking of us and feeling happy we're all together,' Bleddyn added.

Then the air-raid siren sounded. There had been few air raids in the town, no more than a couple of dozen, and each time the inhabitants had seen nothing more worrying than enemy planes crossing the sky, very high and clearly intent on other targets. People looked up expectantly, and only slowly began to pack up and leave the beach.

An air-raid warden ran up calling for them to hurry. 'Please, get a move on. Leave your stuff here, you can collect it later,' he shouted between loud blasts on his whistle as people stood casually folding and packing their belongings. 'This is a bomber raid. Hurry up and get to the shelters.'

With a little more haste, but no panic, the exodus began with the impatient warden, joined by two others, continuing to shout and attempting unsuccessfully to impart urgency.

For Delyth, the day had a calming effect. She and Madge had met Maldwyn as arranged and gone up to the place where Ken had scared her. They told Maldwyn what had happened and he agreed that the best thing to do was to go back.

'Here, I've brought you a present,' he said to a surprised Delyth.

When she opened the package and found drawing materials, she smiled and thanked him for his thoughtfulness, but shook her head sadly when he suggested she use them. 'I don't think I can. No, best I forget drawing and just sit here and see nothing.'

Maldwyn took the book and made a few squiggles on it, which he insisted were a boat on the waves in a storm. Laughing, Delyth adjusted his lines and was soon engrossed in depicting the scene around them. She worked fast and with only a few strokes of a pencil could portray a subject that was easily recognised. When Maldwyn, lying on the ground and pretending to be asleep, asked whether she could make a drawing of him if he sat up and smiled, she agreed she would, but later.

As he lay dozing in the warm sun she sat a couple of yards back from his bare feet and filled a page with a cartoon-style drawing of his feet viewed from below, knobbly and exaggeratedly large. Grass grew around them and hanging on one small toe were his heavy horn-rimmed glasses. In one of the lenses, faintly visible, was a likeness of his face.

When he saw it, she jokingly prepared to run from his outrage but he was thrilled and promised it would hang on a wall in the flower shop, if Mrs Chapel agreed.

Daring to go closer to the edge at last, and encouraged by the sound of a small engine, Delyth saw again the small boat with the broken mast. It had a bundle of some sort near the single seat. Her fingers drew the man sitting with his hand on the tiller. Turning to Maldwyn, she said:

'I hope *he* isn't doing something he shouldn't! My nerves won't stand it!'

They were packing their things, ready to leave and meet Vera, when she heard the sound of the boat's engine again. Crawling towards the edge, she looked down and saw the same boat, and the same man, but this time there was no sign of the mysterious bundle. She said nothing to the others but didn't think she wanted to visit this place again.

Like the people on the beach, they took little notice when the wail of the air-raid warning filled the air. Then, as the bombers came over, Maldwyn made them shelter against the rocks until the planes had passed. There were no wardens around to insist they stayed sheltered, so they walked back along the cliff path to Castle's Café to wait for Vera. The sound of the heavy planes was alarming, so different from the usual toy-like aircraft high above them. Fighter planes came and began harassing the bombers, but they seemed indifferent to the attack and continued on their way, ominous, threatening, making people aware of the war in a very different way.

When the first bomb dropped, some distance away, the result was shock. Then the movement of people who had not sheltered changed from a slow stroll into a run as everyone rushed for cover. Several more explosions filled the air and brought fear to the faces of the adults and nervous giggles from the children; when the all-clear sounded everyone looked around, expecting there to be some visible damage, but the bombs had fallen several miles away, no one knew where.

Ken took the hands of two of the boys and they all made their way back to the sands, where the abandoned belongings gave the usually cheerful beach a forlorn look. He looked into the sky and wondered whether the attack was anywhere near Janet. She had told them that the camp had been filling up with soldiers ready for overseas; that would have made a tempting target for the enemy, he thought worriedly.

There were a few half-hearted attempts to revive the mood of the afternoon, with games and castle-building, but many families simply gathered their belongings and left.

Huw went to check that Hetty and Vera were coping in the café then came back down. 'Heard where the raid was?' he asked one of the wardens.

'An Army camp, so we heard. Not sure, like, but that's what we heard.'

Ken asked where the camp was, and at once he picked up his coat and hurried off. 'I have to see if one of my friends is all right,' he explained.

Eirlys ran after him. 'Where are you going?' she demanded.

'I know someone on the camp the warden mentioned and I have to go and make sure she's all right.'

'She? Someone I know?'

'I mean he, Des Cummings, he's my second-in-command.'

'I'm coming with you.'

'There's no need!'

'Ken, wait. I'm coming with you.' She ran back and asked Beth to take the boys home. 'I'll come and fetch them when we get back,' she said.

Later, she had no idea why she had insisted. Perhaps it was the thought that they could share something, if only the news of Ken's colleague's safety.

She couldn't run as fast as normal with the baby slowing her down and Ken ran on ahead as though determined to go alone. She pushed herself and caught up with him at the ticket office. They ran to where a train waited on the platform,

107

filled almost to overflowing with people leaving the beach, and climbed in.

They didn't say much and when the train reached the station where they had to alight Ken left her and told her he would try to phone and get the information from there. He came back smiling. 'It's all right, the camp wasn't the one where Dennis is stationed. I should have thought of the phone earlier.'

Eirlys said nothing, but she wondered why the man was called Des on one occasion and Dennis a short while later. Perhaps she had misheard. But there was also that slip of the tongue when he referred to the friend as 'she'. Her heart began to race as she wondered whether Ken's absences were not always due to his work.

She tried to think herself back into the happiness of a few moments ago but she couldn't. The look on Ken's face told her nothing, except that he certainly wasn't pleased to have her beside him. Even 'All-seeing, All-knowing' gypsy princesses could be wrong.

Beth walked slowly back to Goose Lane, following her father-in-law and with Stanley, Harold and Percival beside her, chatting about the bombing raid. Having lived in London before becoming permanent members of Eirlys's household, they had known the reality of bombs raining down on them far closer than a raid on some distant Army camp, and when she and Mr Gregory spoke of their concern the boys scoffed at their anxiety.

'But men and women could have been killed,' Beth reminded them sternly.

'Yeh, like our mam was, and Eirlys's mam too,' Harold said.

'I wish Auntie Annie was here,' Percival said softly, and she realised he was frightened by the reminder of death that the raid had brought. She picked him up and sat him on one of Mr Gregory's donkeys. Charlie didn't always approve of being ridden once his day on the beach was over, but this time he didn't object.

Beth realised that they couldn't be expected to grieve over strangers, and children's resilience was partly due to the impression that war was a game and people being hurt and killed was a kind of adventure. It was only when it came near enough to destroy someone close that it had any reality.

Mr Gregory cut a stick, which he habitually carried but never used; the donkeys knew the route well enough and the thought of their supper gave them sufficient incentive to keep moving. He lit his pipe and caught up with Beth as they walked slowly on, taking the pace of the string of animals and content to do so.

Six

Vera seemed to be in a bad temper when she met the others after the air raid ended and the café closed. The customers had irritated her with their boring talk, and she was fed up of repeating the same responses to remarks about the weather and the war. She was tired of admiring noisy children and telling proud mothers how remarkable their offspring were. At first, Maldwyn didn't pick up on her sour mood. They leaned over the sea wall and looked down at the continuing exodus from the sands. The sun had gone and clouds were approaching, deepening the shadows, changing the colours to more sombre shades. She was scowling but he was smiling contentedly.

'Don't you love it here?' he whispered. 'Just look at the way everything is changing as the day ends. I don't think I could ask anything more of life than living here, working at the flower shop.'

'Boring people. Small town and small minds!'

'You aren't happy here? I thought you enjoyed living by the sea? I love everything about it. Being a holiday town I feel I'm on holiday too. I find the variety of visitors brings excitement to the town. It isn't the same from one day to the next. Yes, life is good, living here and having you for my—' He hesitated.

'For your friend?' she finished firmly. Every time he thought their friendship might develop into something closer, she made sure he understood that was not her plan. He tried to ignore her tense irritability. Whenever he spoke of his enjoyment of the moment, she snapped some reply; after a while he stopped talking and just drank in the scene spread out before him.

Tables had been formed in the sand, tea towels used as

110

tablecloths held down with seashells, pebbles or pieces of rock, and on them sandy remnants of picnic meals were spread. Mothers searched for toys half hidden in the churned-up sand. Deck-chairs that had been abandoned were being collected by a young man who whistled cheerfully as he stacked them away for the following day. Three young boys were gathering up any empty bottles they could find to take back to the shop and claim the deposit.

'Come on, little un,' one shouted to another, 'you have to help, mind, or we won't give you a share of the chips.'

'Poor dab,' Maldwyn chuckled as he watched the five-year-old struggling to hold two pop bottles pressed against his chest with his small hands.

'Come on, Maldwyn. I want to go home,' Vera sighed. 'I've been working if you haven't.'

Before he could reply a chuckle made him turn to see Delyth laughing at the antics of the boys, who had stuffed bottles up their jumpers and were waddling like ducks, trying to support their load.

'That'll make a good picture if you can capture it,' he said. He watched in fascination as Delyth drew not the children but himself and Vera leaning over the wall, the boys reduced to small matchstick figures far below.

'That's nothing to the picture *I'll* make when I enter the beauty competition,' Vera said, jealous of the way Maldwyn was admiring Delyth's work. She wasn't interested in him, but he was a useful companion until something better came along. He didn't respond to her demand for flattery, and impatiently she pushed herself away from the wall and walked off.

'Wait,' he called, but when she broke into a run he didn't go after her. He was happy, and he wasn't willing for anyone to spoil it. Later he couldn't have explained just what it was about that day, but the hours on the quiet of the cliffs, the frantic rush for shelter when the siren warned of approaching enemy aircraft and the slow, easy end to the evening added up to a day he would always remember.

Delyth smiled at him. 'You've enjoyed today, haven't you? I have too. For the first time since that lorry drove at us I feel relaxed and no longer afraid.'

111

'I'm glad.'

Madge had been talking to Hannah and her children and as she joined them Maldwyn said, 'I'll walk with you to the station, shall I?'

'We're going for a cup of tea first,' Madge said.

'My treat,' he offered.

It was as they were coming out of the café and Madge had to pop back inside for her bag that the man suddenly grabbed them. They were standing not far from the café, near a front-garden hedge. There was an alleyway between the houses and there was no one about when the man jumped out and pushed them both into the hedge, face first. Delyth screamed as twigs cut her cheeks and the man pressed them further into the privet, whispering to Maldwyn, 'Get back home where you belong, or your girlfriend will have worse than a few scratches.'

Frozen momentarily by the suddenness of the attack, Maldwyn swerved out of the man's grasp and turned, but he was pushed so roughly that he staggered. He recovered to see a figure he did not recognise running at great speed and disappearing around a corner.

He started to run after him, but a cry from Delyth stopped him. Holding her close and taking out a handkerchief, he held it for her to lick before wiping some of the trickles of blood from her face. 'Who the hell was that?' he muttered.

'The man who was driving the lorry I suppose,' Delyth sobbed.

'Did you recognise him?'

'No, I didn't really see him. I had the impression he was taller than you by a little, and heavily built. That's all.'

'That's right! Delyth, you're marvellous,' he said. 'It'll help the police a little.'

'I don't want to tell the police. It'll make it worse if the police are involved, make it more real. I can pretend it's a case of mistaken identity or something if we don't report it.'

'Delyth love, it isn't you who'll be talking to the police. I was the one he threatened, and I'm beginning to think that the lorry driver was aiming not at you but me.'

The police noted the story and tried to reassure Delyth

that she had nothing to fear. 'I think you're right, Miss Owen. Mistaken identity, or someone having a bit of fun frightening you.'

'They didn't seem convinced that Maldwyn was the intended victim, then?' Madge asked when they were standing at last on the station platform.

'No, but I am,' Maldwyn said emphatically. 'Delyth was unfortunate being with me each time.'

He watched as the train pulled out and walked sadly back to Mrs Denver's, the happiness of the day destroyed. He wondered whether Delyth would ever be confident enough to visit the town again. Perhaps she would never feel safe there, would find another place for her days' outings. That prospect deepened his misery. He realised now that the joy of the day had been largely due to her company.

Vera was in bed when he got back to Mrs Denver's house in Queen Street. He felt let down, both because she had tried to ruin his happy mood and because she was not there when he needed to talk about the events that had followed.

Alice Potter left the sweet shop on the promenade and went to the bus stop. Twice each week she visited her father. Colin Potter had been a boxer and a blow to the head had caused brain damage which, besides making him totally off balance when he stood up, had increased his temper in an uncontrollable way. She had been going in the evenings but Audrey had given her a hour off once a week so she could see him in the daytime, when he would be sitting out on the balcony in the sun with several others. It was less distressing for Alice than seeing him in the ward, when the gloom of the place seemed to make him even more subdued than he already was by the effects of his medication.

He didn't appear to recognise his daughter. Since he had been in the hospital he had become more and more withdrawn and the only thing he said to her that made her think he actually knew she was there was to warn her there were to be no men in the house, something he repeated several times. Apart from the sharply spoken threat, he said nothing. He didn't look at her but seemed to be concentrating on something far in the distance.

113

She would sit and tell him all that had happened during the days since her last visit, but nothing aroused a response.

Eirlys sat with the sewing basket on her lap, working her way through the boys' clothes, getting them ready for school the following day. Buttons missing, a tear in the corner of a pocket when they had forced some treasure into it. Sleeves that had been taken up and now needed to be let down as their second owner had grown. The pile seemed endless, but she was glad to have something to do. Sitting waiting for Ken to explain would have been worse without something to occupy her.

'If it's another woman I want to know,' she had said quietly, but Ken had only shaken his head. Questioning was only possible when her father was out of the room. Sensing their need to talk, Morgan had excused himself and gone to bed early, armed with a book and two Sunday papers.

'I'm going out,' Ken said, pushing aside the *Radio Times*, which he had been pretending to read.

'Where? It's half-past nine. If you want a drink Dad has a couple of flagons of beer in the pantry.'

'I don't want a drink. I need to get out and do some thinking.'

'So it *is* a woman?'

No reply, only a snatched overcoat and a slammed door.

Morgan came back down in his dressing gown, his face freshly scrubbed and shining. 'Is there anything wrong, love?'

'No, Dad. Go back to bed and I'll bring up some cocoa. Ken's worried about something, that's all.'

'Some problem with this big concert he's booked, is it? Some act let him down?'

Cynically she replied, 'No, Dad. It's more likely he's double-booked.' She laughed harshly at her poor joke and didn't explain.

Ken went to Brook Lane, where Bleddyn Castle lived with Hetty and Hetty's daughter, Shirley. It was Shirley he wanted to see.

When Shirley and Janet had begun to make a name for themselves as singers and dancers, Janet had known that

114

Shirley had the greater talent and would rise higher than she ever would. She had not been envious, just willing to help her friend achieve her goal. But then an accident had ended Shirley's dancing career and for a long time had prevented her appearing on stage; Janet and Ken had spent more and more time together and had fallen in love. The effect of Shirley's accident had spread far wider than she could have imagined. It wasn't only her whose life had been changed because of it.

'Janet and I have been seeing each other and I don't know what to do,' he told Shirley when they were alone.

'Seeing her? Are we talking euphemisms here?'

'All right, we're having an affair.'

'End it, or tell Eirlys and help her face it,' Shirley said sharply. 'If you came here expecting sympathy you've wasted your time!'

'I can't do either of those things. I need Janet, I want her in my life. As for telling Eirlys, how can I? She's having a baby in a few months.'

'Yes, *your* baby! Eirlys is the injured party here and you know what you have to do, don't you? You have to face up to it, Ken; you're committed to Eirlys and to being a father to the child when it arrives. There'll be plenty of children born without a father, thanks to this war. And plenty of women having to face their husbands when they return and explaining a child born while they were away. Can you let your child face something like that? No excuse of war conditions for you, is there? So much misery and there's you thinking about adding to it.' She looked at him, his head bent, shoulders drooped, utterly miserable. 'What does Janet think? She never mentions you in her letters to me.'

'I have to see Janet because she takes part in some of the concerts I arrange.'

'*Have to* see her? That's rubbish and you know it. There are plenty of other singers you could use good as she undoubtedly is. No, you have to make up your mind before Eirlys guesses what's going on and decides for you.'

Ken thought that would be an easy way out. His wife telling him to leave would be a relief. He would make a home for Janet and everything would be perfect.

'I don't even like children,' he said childishly. Then, 'Can you imagine what a start we had, Eirlys and me? Living with her father would have been bad enough, but with those three boys as well, it's impossible.'

Shirley's voice softened and she went on, 'We're all selfish to a degree, Ken. I know I've done things I'm ashamed of.' She thought of the way she had coaxed Freddy Clements away from Beth without a qualm, but she didn't mention that. Instead she said, 'When Janet and I were starting out I put myself first when I shouldn't have. I cheated on her by taking part in concerts without telling her, wanting the applause for myself alone. Yet she's always been such a loyal friend, and she forgave me. I'd be pleased if this worked out for you and her but I can't see it happening.'

'Talking about being selfish, I'm aware that looking after her father and those dratted boys is very hard for Eirlys, and her job is a very complicated one. She does a lot more than me and grumbles far less. I admire her, but admiration isn't enough. I still don't want to be with her.'

'You're seriously thinking of leaving her, with all that and a baby to look after?'

'You make me feel ashamed.'

'Good! That's a start. Now, if you'll set out the cups I'll make us a hot drink and you can go home and start telling yourself how you're going to cope. And cope well enough to persuade Eirlys you're happy.'

'Tall order.'

'Mm.' She heaved herself out of her chair with the aid of a stick and went to the fire where a kettle was beginning to sing. 'I didn't think I would ever learn to accept not being able to dance again, but here I am, standing on stage, singing and pretending every day is a pleasure.' She took some packets out of a cupboard and handed them to Ken. 'You have a choice, Ken: Ovaltine or cocoa,' she said with a grin.

'Tea!'

'If only your other decisions were that easy.'

A letter from his stepmother made Maldwyn decide to go home again. Winifred had fallen while trying to clean windows and

116

was unable to get out. When he told Vera she agreed to go with him if she could get the time off from the café. The hours she worked were long and Marged agreed to her request.

They left straight after the flower shop closed at one o'clock the following Wednesday. He sadly decided that it would be best if they didn't call to see Delyth. If he was the target of the mysterious stranger, then it was safer for her if he stayed well away from her.

He had told Vera about the events of that evening, and the police had called to Mrs Denver's to ask him a few more questions. Their inquiry took an alarming turn when they began asking whether he had any involvement with criminals. Or could there be some activities in which he had become unintentionally involved? After all the questioning no one appeared to know why he and Delyth had been threatened in such a frightening way.

'I wrote to Delyth and Madge to tell them we'd be coming to see them,' Vera said, breaking into his thoughts as they got into the train.

'I wish you hadn't,' he said. 'You know Delyth was badly frightened when I was threatened last Sunday. I don't think she'd want to be within miles of me after that.'

'What are you worrying about, Maldwyn? Proper old woman you are sometimes. It was a mistake, wasn't it? That's what the police think. Unless you've got some terrible secret in your past you aren't telling me about? Are you two up to no good in your spare time?'

'It wasn't funny. She was scared – she thought she was going to be seriously hurt. I thought so too.'

'Aw, poor Maldwyn. How anyone could mistake you two for dangerous criminals I can't imagine. More like Abbot and Costello if you ask me.'

'You go and see her while I see what Mam needs me to do. I'll meet you back at the station at five. We might be back in time for the late picture show.'

'Goodbye, my enigmatic friend. Don't be late or I'll imagine you at the bottom of a mineshaft with a dozen knives in your back and a bomb up your jumper.'

117

He smiled in spite of himself as he went into his step-mother's house.

Winifred was undoubtedly pleased to see him, and he spent the afternoon chatting to her between dealing with a list of jobs she found difficult to manage. He cleaned the windows, and ordered her not to touch them until he came again. Under her guidance he even managed to prepare a casserole of vegetables ready for her to eat the following day.

Neighbours were kind, and he left confident that she would manage until the following week, when he would come again.

Vera was at the station, with Delyth and Madge. Vera and Madge were laughing, Delyth was not. 'Has anything happened?' he asked anxiously.

'My mam is going to marry Uncle Trev,' Delyth wailed.

Maldwyn sighed with relief. For a moment he had imagined another incident like the lorry and the attack near the café.

'Good on 'em,' he said. 'Why the long face? It won't change anything for you, will it? You won't be homeless or anything?'

'As good as. How can I live there now?'

All the time he was with her Maldwyn was anxious, half expecting there to be another incident. He tried not to show his relief when the train came and they waved their goodbyes.

'Did your visit home go all right?' he asked Vera when they had squeezed themselves into a compartment crowded with soldiers, at whom Vera directed saucy smiles.

'Oh yes, except my father told me I have to go back home.'

'I hope you don't. I'd miss you,' he said.

'He's worried that I'll get into trouble – you know – with a boy. Although why he thinks I'm at greater risk in St David's Well than at home I can't explain.'

'It's me,' Maldwyn joked. 'He can see I'm practically irresistible!'

She stared at him and said, 'Well, some girls might think so. Delyth for example.'

'Delyth won't come near me now, so don't worry.'

'What makes you think I'm worrying, Maldwyn Perkins?'

'Because I've got some sweets and a bit of cake from my stepmam and you want some?'

*   *   *

It was after midnight when Ken came in that Wednesday evening. Eirlys was very tired; she knew she would find it hard to continue working until the end of the season and she longed to go to bed. Nevertheless she waited until he came in, the light low, the fire almost out. Trying to make her voice pleasant, she asked:

'Where have you been, Ken?'

'I went to see Shirley Downs.'

Still keeping her voice light, she said, 'I wish you'd said, I would have gone with you. I want her to be one of the judges at the beauty contest and she needs to know the details.'

'Write them down and I'll take them to her tomorrow while you're at work.' He didn't sit but moved towards the stairs. It was clear he had no intention of talking to her. Suddenly her patience was lost.

'No, it's perfectly all right, I don't want to trouble you. Heaven forbid when it's clear that you have plenty to do, coming in at this time of night.'

'I don't mind helping if I can. I wouldn't mind being one of the judges myself,' he said, hoping to make her smile.

'No thank you, I can cope. You are far too busy.'

He threw his jacket down on the armchair and turned to go upstairs. 'Yes. You're right. I'll have to leave first thing in the morning.'

'Good!' she retorted, choking back tears.

They got between the sheets, both chilled by the silence and the widening gap between them in the once cosy bed.

The next morning they rose at the same time. Silently she cooked a breakfast of fried bread, scraping the basin for enough fat to crisp it and serving it with an egg that was half the ration for the week. He ate in silence, watching as she dealt with morning chores, cleaning out the fireplace and setting the paper and sticks with ashes and small lumps of coal on top ready to light that evening. The grate was washed and everything was neat and tidy, an electric fire sending out a small amount of heat before she called the boys.

They tumbled down the stairs, arguing, asking what was to eat. Percival declared that it wasn't something he liked and his

119

brothers increased their rowdy argument as they offered to eat anything he didn't want. While they ate porridge, the frying pan was heated and slices of bread dampened with a small amount of water before going into the last of the hot fat. The result was not crispy bread like Ken had enjoyed, but it was warm and the boys didn't complain.

Sadly Ken watched Eirlys deal with the food and clear away. With a wave at the boys and a nod towards Eirlys, he left.

It was far too early to set off for his first appointment, and that added to his frustration. Having said he was leaving early out of pique, he had no alternative but to leave early.

The beach was not one of his favourite places but it was there he went to kill time before setting off to visit an Army camp and check the stage and the equipment in preparation for a concert he had organised. There were few people about but already the stallholders were opening up in the hope of a good day. The season had only a few weeks to go and they needed every penny they could earn to help support them throughout the winter months.

He saw Bleddyn and Hetty unlocking the swingboats, helter-skelter and various stalls, and walked over to greet them. 'I saw your Shirley yesterday; she's making progress, isn't she? And she's as popular as ever as a singer.'

'Still depressed, mind,' Hetty said sadly. 'Her friends have been supportive and she hears regularly from Freddy Clements, who used to take her dancing. He never sympathises with her, mind. He's very casual about her injuries, treats the fact that she can't walk without a stick with no more concern than a splinter in her foot. She enjoys his letters and I suppose they are a refreshing break from the long faces and sympathetic noises. He makes her laugh, and that does her as much good as anything else. Thanks for persuading her to take part in your concerts. It's good for her to know she still draws the crowds.'

'The accident didn't damage her voice.'

'Hear anything about Janet?' Bleddyn asked.

'Oh, she still sings for me when she can.'

'When you see her tell her we hope she comes back soon. With our Beth running the market café for her we're short on help in our place.' Bleddyn gestured to Castle's Café above the sands. 'Tell her we miss her too.'

'If I see her I will.' He felt uncomfortable talking about Janet, and although Hetty invited him to go with them to the café for a cup of tea he declined.

He walked back along the beach, scuffing his feet childlike through the sand, and when he saw that the hoop-la stall was open for business he impulsively had a try and won a goldfish. 'What on earth can I do with it?' he laughed when the stallholder proudly presented it.

'There must be a child somewhere who'd love you for ever if you gave him that.'

He went back to the house in Conroy Street and left the fish in a large jamjar for Percival, with a note promising to buy 'Glub' a proper tank when he was next home. Before he left, he tried to write an affectionate note to Eirlys but after the first sentence he had nothing to say, so he left the brief scribble beside Percival's, stating just that he would be home on Sunday evening.

Maldwyn came into the shop after buying the daily flowers and fruit from the early-morning market and found Mrs Chapel leaning on the counter, obviously in pain.

'Mrs Chapel, what is it? Shall I call the doctor?'

'He's been, during the night, and I have to have a few days' rest. Sorry, Maldwyn, can you manage on your own?'

'Of course I can. When you feel better, why don't you go to your sister's for a few days and have a break? You enjoy visiting her, don't you? I'll cope. The café will send in a bite to eat at lunchtime and I can spend the hour we're quiet tidying up and making up the orders. Manage fine, I will.'

'I know you will, Maldwyn. You're such a good boy.'

She left the following morning after declaring herself well enough to travel the twenty miles to the village where her widowed sister and her nephew, Gabriel, lived. At once Maldwyn began clearing out the clutter that seemed to gather around the shop whenever Mrs Chapel was there. No matter how often he cleared away, she gathered more until the back room was so full he could barely move. 'So much for the

121

valuable extra space,' he sighed as he reached for the brush and shovel.

He worked until almost ten o'clock that day and went home satisfied that, at least for a few weeks, the workroom and the new extension to the shop looked their best. The following morning his first job after putting the flowers in tall jugs was to bring up some fruit from the cellar and polish it to fill the shallow display boxes in the window. He noticed a softness on one or two and put them aside. He had promised to take some of the rejects to his landlady. Mrs Denver was always cooking and would find a way of using the bruised apples. He was still busy attending to them as customers began to filter in.

When he was closing the door at five thirty, a woman pushed her way in. She was clearly very angry.

'I don't mind paying your high prices for the best, but look at this!' She opened a paper bag and showed him an apple, cut in half and peppered with brown decay. 'I want a replacement and an explanation. I took this to a patient at the hospital and, well, just look at it!'

The following morning there were several other people who had found the fruit far from Chapel's usual standards. Each one showed the same odd brown flecks. They looked as if they had been pierced with something like a small screwdriver or a piece of wire. Near the till he saw a metal needle, pointed at both ends, which Mrs Chapel used for knitting socks. Comparing it with the damage, it seemed likely to have been the cause. But how? There had been no one in the shop to do it and he never left the place unattended. When he had gone to the cellar he locked the door for the few minutes he was away. Besides, why would anyone want to?

The following day the same thing had happened to both the apples and the pears. The doors were all locked and nothing appeared to have been disturbed. So he closed the shop, leaving a note on the door stating he would be back within the hour, and went to the police station.

'Someone stabbing your apples and pears, you say?' The policeman was obviously amused. 'Sounds real serious, that does. Second only to the Great Train Robbery of 1855, I'd say, wouldn't you?'

'What about adding breaking and entering? I locked the shop and Mrs Chapel is away staying with her sister. Someone got in to damage that fruit. Someone must have a key, but there are only two that I know of, and I can account for both of them.'

The policeman took down the details, still smiling. When Maldwyn reminded him about the lorry driven dangerously towards himself and Delyth, and the threats made when he and Delyth were pushed into the hedge near the café, he took the situation more seriously and promised to investigate. 'Someone wants you to leave the town, you think? Can you suggest why? Upset someone, have you? Stolen someone's girl? There's a lot of trouble in that area now, with men away and the women left behind and bored with waiting.'

'I can't think of anyone who'd be interested enough to want me out of the way. I'm only an assistant in a flower shop for heaven's sake!'

They talked around the subject for a while and the policeman made copious notes, but when Maldwyn left the police station he felt no more hopeful of solving the mystery than when he had entered. As he had related the incidents aloud it had all sounded rather silly.

That night he double-checked every lock and bolt and leaned on the shop door after securing it to make sure there was no weakness. He even went back and pushed against it once more, unable to trust his own competence. He had the needle in his pocket. He didn't want to leave anything to chance.

While Mrs Chapel was away, he made a few notes to inform her of what had happened each day. He wrote out a careful report on the damaged fruit and hoped she wouldn't blame him.

When she returned, she walked in to see a few customers being served, the shop neat and orderly and the stock at an acceptable level.

'Thank you, Maldwyn. You're a marvel,' she said, putting down her suitcase and helping to serve.

He waited until she had taken off her coat and was sitting with a cup of steaming tea in front of her before he handed her his notes and mentioned the mysterious damage to the fruit on two occasions.

'You are sure you locked everything?'

'Absolutely sure.'

'I believe you. You could never be accused of carelessness. I wonder how it happened? The fruit couldn't have been damaged before that night?'

'I'd sold most of it the day before and had no complaints.'

'It couldn't have been him next door, could it?' She gestured with a thumb. 'Arnold Elliot and his "Fashion Emporium". He wants to buy me out, doesn't he?'

'He wouldn't! How would he get in? You've never given him a key, have you?'

'No, he wouldn't. And without a key he couldn't. But who?'

Maldwyn was not happy leaving Mrs Chapel that evening. He remembered the occasion when someone had stolen the picture frame and threw it aside a few doors further on. Could they have also stolen a key? If someone had, she was not safe. She refused to sleep somewhere else and Maldwyn made another visit to the police station to let them know that she was alone in a house where there had been a suspected intruder a few nights previously. He casually mentioned the fact that Arnold Elliot wanted to buy the property and extend.

'You're telling me you think he might be behind these threats?'

'No, no. I just mentioned that there might be reasons we haven't thought of, like someone wanting to buy the premises.'

'He's hardly likely to go to those lengths,' the constable said doubtfully.

'No, of course not; I was just thinking aloud.'

Maldwyn went to see Arnold Elliot, but didn't explain fully about the damaged fruit or the other incidents. He didn't want the man to realise he was a suspect. He simply asked him to be vigilant in case Mrs Chapel had an unwelcome visitor.

'What d'you want me to do, sit on the front doorstep all night?' the man asked aggressively.

'No, of course not.' Maldwyn spoke calmly. 'If you do see or hear something unusual will you tell the police or let someone know?'

'Why the sudden concern?'

'She isn't well. I don't like leaving her.'

'She'll be selling up soon, then?'

'I hope not. I like my job and unless it's taken by another florist I'd be out of work, wouldn't I?'

'I'll go and see her, renew my offer on the place. She might be glad enough to retire if she isn't well.'

Maldwyn didn't respond.

There was a telephone in the shop but he didn't phone Mrs Chapel even though he was anxious throughout the evening. Better not to disturb her and make her go down the stairs to the shop. He would probably add to her worry by declaring his own.

Days passed and there was no repeat of the damage to the fruit or anything else to cause concern. Maldwyn began to believe Mrs Chapel's theory, that the fruit had been faulty when he bought it, and thankfully put aside his fear, that he was the target for this as well as the other incidents. He had begun to think no one was safe around him.

The day of the beauty contest was dry but overcast, with a breeze blowing in across the sea and making people add a warm cardigan on top of their summer dresses. The contestants were disappointed: having to parade in a bathing costume would be much less fun in a chilly breeze.

It was the last weekend in August. The town was filled with holidaymakers and hundreds of day trippers making the most of their final fling. As the season came to a close, crocheted hats with floppy brims appeared, many made with matching handbags. Rather than the usual jackets carried over the arms of many trippers, people no longer felt confident to travel away from home without the precautionary addition of a coat or mac. The freedom of summer was already receding. Men put on the sleeveless Fairisle pullovers their wives had knitted, and trilby hats reappeared after their brief summer hibernation. But on that day, the weather made no difference. A beauty contest was drawing the crowds. A walkway was set up near the swingboats, roundabouts and stalls. People began arriving hours before the proposed start, to be sure of a seat with a good view. The sand around the walkway was soon filled with people pressing up closer and closer, mothers keeping a watchful eye on their broods as the concentration of bustling people made it easy to lose sight of the lively, excited children.

The tide was ebbing and the semicircle of people around the walkway became deeper as more sand was exposed. It dried quickly in the breeze and a reluctant sun, and was immediately colonised by the continuous flow of families unpacking buckets and spades, windmills, towels, sunhats and parasols, struggling for room to spread, then good-naturedly squeezing up to accommodate yet more arrivals.

Shirley had taken a taxi to the beach. It would be something to tell Freddy when she wrote. Others probably had the same thought, as it was difficult sometimes to find news to fill the pages.

She thought of Alice then. She would probably tell her father but Shirley doubted whether he would understand. She had visited the hospital once with Alice and was saddened by the emptiness of the man's life, but impressed with Alice's determination to reach him through the vacant expression and the uncanny silence. Alice insisted that while there was a chance he might understand she would continue to tell him about her day-to-day activities. Shirley sent a message to the sweet shop, telling Alice where she was and asking her to join her when she was free.

Eirlys didn't feel well. She had been up since early morning, going over her lists and making sure nothing had been forgotten or left to chance. The boys would go with Hannah and her two girls for the day, and Ken – she wasn't sure what Ken would be doing. They hardly spoke to each other these days, she thought in a moment of melancholy.

She felt strange; her body ached and her legs trembled and seemed unable to hold her. How would she cope for another eight hours? She wondered how long she could continue. There were only one or two more entertainments still

126

to come and she would be disappointed not to see them through.

Her bosses, Mr Gifford and Mr Johnston, called at midday and she went through the plans for the day with them, wishing she could curl up in bed and leave it all to them.

Ken came to the house while they were there and, glancing at Eirlys, could see she was not her usual bright and capable self. When she went into the kitchen to make tea he was alarmed at the slow way she moved. Her eyes were heavy and she looked exhausted. 'Eirlys, is everything all right?' he asked, genuinely concerned.

'I think so, but I do feel rather tired,' she admitted. 'Once today is over most of the summer's entertainments are finished and I can relax. Thank goodness. This summer has been harder than usual.'

'It's time you finished work completely,' he said, 'and I want you to tell Mr Gifford that you will.'

'Let's get today over and we'll talk about it,' she promised.

Ken listened to the final discussion about the day's events and quickly agreed to take on several of the duties to ease the day for her.

At twelve o'clock, when she had taken Stanley, Harold and Percival to join Hannah and her daughters, Eirlys could no longer stand. She collapsed on to a chair, laid her head on the table and sobbed. When Ken returned to the house he took one look at Eirlys, who was bent over the table, head on her hands, crying softly, and ran to call the doctor. He came at once and put her straight to bed.

'I don't think there is anything terribly wrong, Mr Ward, fortunately!' he told an anxious Ken. 'She has been doing too much and should have stopped work several weeks ago, as I firmly told her, not run around organising the entertainments for the town. It's an enormous undertaking at the best of times, and being in an advanced stage of pregnancy is not the best of times. I don't know what you and Mr Gifford have been thinking about to allow it.'

'I didn't really notice how tired she was becoming. She loves her job so much and wouldn't hear of giving up until the season is over. I should have been more aware.'

'Yes, Mr Ward, you should.'

Ken ran around for the rest of the time left before the start of the contest until he felt like crawling into bed with Eirlys. He hadn't realised just how much was involved, even at this late stage, to ensure everything went according to plan. Mr Gifford took over and, with Ken helping and Mr Johnston in tow, they were ready as the town band struck up the tune of 'It's a Hap-Hap-Happy Day' and the crowd settled to enjoy the spectacle.

Ken had suggested a comedian to act as compère and it had been a good decision. Dressed in an evening suit and bow tie, acting the toff, a bottle and a glass at the ready, the talented comic quickly degenerated into performing as a drunk. His humour was aimed mainly at the children and was saucy without giving offence – perfect for the end-of-summer atmosphere. Before the girls had completed their first walk-past he had everyone's full attention. From then on they thought what he told them to think, smiled when he told them to smile and clapped with him as the girls did their brief act.

One by one the girls paraded across the makeshift stage in bathing costumes, their smiles hiding the fact that they were freezing. Vera didn't walk, though: she performed. She didn't just scuttle self-consciously across the stage as many of the others did but paused as she entered, slowly turned and pirouetted and stretched to show her figure at its best. She even returned as though for an encore, and the compère reacted as though frightened by her unexpected reappearance. She made sure she would be remembered.

Next the entrants walked on to the stage smiling. They moved in line along the walkway, first in summery skirts and blouses, then long and elegant dance dresses. A partner appeared for each girl and they danced to the band's rendering of 'Begin the Beguine'. The comedian kept the crowd amused before the girls finally reappeared in bathing costumes, to the accompaniment of cheers and whistles. Judging partly by the volume of applause and partly from their own discussions, Shirley, Ken and the two men from the council offices decided to award the first place to Vera. But to prolong the event, they told everyone that before the announcement they would be entertained by a children's dance troupe.

Janet thought it was safe to visit St David's Well, believing Ken to be in North Wales on a tour of factories with a variety show. She had the weekend off and, having no home to go to, the usual routine was to stay in the room she shared with eight other girls and catch up with some reading, sewing and letter-writing. This time she decided to find a cheap bed-and-breakfast and call on Beth to see how the café was coping with the troublesome shortages of food.

There was a thought in her mind to hint to Beth that the café business might be for sale. The premises were rented and under the jurisdiction of the market management regarding opening times and the limits of what she could sell, but it was a good business. The situation with Ken made it unlikely she would ever be able to return. She would stay in the Naafi at least until the war ended, and perhaps afterwards, to make it a career. If not she would find a place to settle far away from the temptation of seeing Ken, loving him and being unable to show it.

Beth was serving a line of ladies with teas and cakes, taking the orders, delivering the food to the tables and handling the payment steadily and efficiently. After exchanging greetings, Janet took off her jacket, scrubbed hands that were dirty from travelling on sooty trains, set to and helped.

When there was a break in the demand for teas and snacks, Beth laughed, 'This isn't much of a change for you, is it?'

'Only the name. Char and a wad is what we're asked for in the Naafi, which means tea and a cake.'

Clearing tables, washing dishes and the rest of the chores were done in a rush while they were free to do so, then another queue and another busy few minutes. 'Will you take my brother and Olive a tray of tea and a couple of cakes?' Beth asked. 'They'd like to say hello.'

Janet went to the fruit and vegetable stall where Ronnie and his wife were selling the last of some rather weary-looking cabbages and carrots.

'Life saver,' Ronnie said as he took the tray. There was no

129

time to chat because the queue at the café was growing, so after exchanging a few words Janet went back.

It was almost four o'clock, and Beth and Janet were able to think about clearing up and closing. Beth told Janet about the beauty contest and about Delyth and Madge, who had come on a day trip to watch their friend Vera Matthews taking part. 'Perhaps we could see the end of it if we hurry.'

They joined the crowds, who were still being entertained by the young dancers, and stood with the rest to see Vera being presented with the prize – a large bouquet, a book on flower-arranging and a £5 note – by Shirley Downs. Vera accepted the applause like a professional and as soon as she was off stage gave the book to Maldwyn, who had just arrived. Janet tried to get through the crush of people to talk to Shirley, but she failed and turned the other way. Perhaps she would go to the house later. Soon afterwards, she came face to face with Ken.

'Where's Eirlys?' she asked, looking around, trying to avoid his eyes.

'She was tired and had to stay home,' Ken told her. 'Pity, after all the work she put in.'

The crowd was impatient to move away now the show was finished and in the pushing and struggling Ken and Janet found themselves together, with no sign of the others.

Delyth spotted them and, worried that Ken might look up and see her, she pulled Madge away. She still wondered if he was the one trying to frighten her with repeated threats.

Janet saw Shirley watching her, disapproval on her face, and tried to move away from Ken. 'I have to go,' she said, but his hand on her arm gripped her firmly; he led her to a café, where he found a space and sat down facing her.

'This can't go on,' he said.

'I wouldn't have come, but I wanted to see Beth and I thought you were away from home.'

'I'm glad I wasn't.'

'I'm not! I don't want to see you again, Ken. Eirlys was my friend and now I'm her worst enemy.'

'Stay with me, please; we have to talk about this,' he said as she stood up to leave.

130

She sank back into the bentwood café chair, her arms defensively folded, and stared at him. 'What can we do? You will be a father in a matter of weeks. How can we let this continue?'

'Where are you staying?'

She gave him the name of the bed-and-breakfast; Ken told the waitress they had changed their minds, gave her a shilling tip and they left. Without telling her what he planned, he went to the house calling itself Mon Repos and asked for the bill. Instructing Janet to pack, he paid for the two nights she intended to stay and took her to a small hotel.

They stayed together until long past midnight and when he went home and crept up to bed, hoping not to disturb Eirlys, their bed was empty. He ran back downstairs where he saw a note propped up on the teapot. It told him that Eirlys was in hospital and he sat for several minutes staring into space, his eyes moist, his heart heavy with remorse. What sort of a person had he become that he could have abandoned his wife at such a time, abandoned her without even remembering she was ill?

Seven

The note shook in Ken's hand. He threw it down and, without stopping to change, he ran to the hospital, too anxious even to find out if Morgan was awake. He entered the rather gloomy reception area and all but collapsed on the desk, where a young girl was staring at him fearfully. He was unaware how wild he looked, or how loudly he spoke when he made his demand.

'I want to see my wife,' he panted. 'Mrs Eirlys Ward. She's having a baby.'

'Sorry Mr Ward, but visiting isn't until two o'clock tomorrow,' the girl stammered, wondering if she were about to be attacked.

A doctor and a nurse came then and calmed him, assuring him Eirlys was not in danger.

'Mrs Ward is resting. We don't want your baby born before we're ready for him,' the doctor said, encouraging Ken to sit. He felt guilty and ashamed, and in spite of that wanted to see Janet, to have her tell him everything would be all right.

'I want to see her!'

'And you will, but not in the middle of the night, Mr Ward. Go home and come back tomorrow.'

He dashed home at the same speed with which he had reached the hospital; guilt and worry made it impossible to slow down. Morgan was asleep, the boys too, but he didn't think there was any chance of joining them. He made a cup of tea and sat in a chair, wondering how he could make up to Eirlys for his disgraceful behaviour.

The day following the beauty contest was a Sunday, and Vera woke up to the knowledge that after all the excitement and admiration of the contest she had to go to Castle's Café and wash dishes. It made her resentful. Why wasn't she on the stage, or posing for fashionable pictures for magazines? How did people with as lowly a start as she manage to break out of the conventions that choked them? She washed in the chilly bathroom, which wasn't a bathroom at all, just a room Mrs Denver had set aside for them to wash in. It was on the north side and always cold. The wash-stand had a dark grey marble top and seemed to create an extra chill in the room. The towels hung on the side of it; there was a bowl in which to wash herself; a jug, which Mrs Denver never failed to fill with warm water for her; and the soap dish with its slab of green washing soap which the old lady supplied for them. She hated everything about the room that morning.

The soldier who had talked to her after the competition and asked her to meet him was nice, but she didn't think he held the key to an exciting future. Soldiers moved on, and there were too many girls already who had succumbed, in the belief that their handsome soldier would return with love and a wedding ring. She heard Maldwyn whistling as he got out of bed; with a towel around his neck, he came to where she was, applying make-up in front of the mirror on the windowsill.

'Finished?' he asked. 'I'll go down and get some warm water if you are.'

'I'm beginning to hate it here,' she whispered. 'I want something better. Don't you?'

'I've never been away from home before, and I can't compare this with anything else, except the place we were thrown out from! I think we're very lucky. Mrs Denver looks after us as though we're her own. Spoils us in fact. I don't think we'd do much better if we paid twice as much as we pay her.'

'I hated living at home and I'm beginning to think this isn't much better. If only I could get work in the fashion world. D'you think I'm attractive enough to work as a photographer's model?'

'Of course you are . . . but I think it takes more than beauty.'

'You think I'm beautiful?' she asked, lowering her head

133

and glancing up at him sideways in what she hoped was a provocative manner.

He grinned. 'Fishing for compliments, is it? Isn't winning that beauty contest enough for you?'

She looked thoughtful for a moment, then replied soberly, 'No, I don't think it is.'

She was vague all morning. Marged had to repeat orders for her and she forgot several things she was supposed to do.

'She's in love, I think,' Huw chuckled as he picked up a used cup she had left on a freshly set table.

'In love with herself if you ask me!' Marged snapped. She went into the kitchen, where Vera stood looking out of the window towards the cliff path, ignoring the sink filled with unwashed dishes.

'Vera!' she shouted, making the girl jump with shock. 'We'll be running out of clean plates if you don't get a move on!'

'Can't I do something else, Mrs Castle? This hot water is ruining my hands. Look at them, all red and ugly.'

'Dishes! And please hurry.'

Disconsolately, Vera washed and dried and stacked, and dreamed about a different sort of life, where she left all the menial jobs for someone else to do.

As the day went on, Vera was more and more reluctant to do her work. She was off-hand with customers, impatient when they hesitated while choosing their order. The children she told to be quiet, and brushed up any mess with huge sighs of irritation. Marged warned her that 'Winning a competition is meant to be fun. You shouldn't allow it to ruin your life by dreaming of something that will never happen.'

'How d'you know it won't happen? Look at Shirley Downs. She dreamed of being a singer and she achieved it.'

'Shirley has a wonderful talent and she's worked very hard to develop it. A pretty face isn't enough, not on its own. Life isn't froth and bubbles for most of us, just hard work. Getting as bad as our Lilly you are, Vera Matthews!'

Huw chuckled and said she'd soon come down to earth. 'Let her have her few days of fantasy. She'll soon accept that froth and bubbles are only to be found in a washing-up bowl.'

*   *   *

134

Janet waited in the hotel where she and Ken had spent several happy hours the evening before. He had promised to come but it was getting late; maybe he couldn't get away. Being a mistress, she berated herself, had its drawbacks. Unreliability was just one of them. She asked at the small reception desk if any messages had come for her and at midday she went for a walk.

She ate a lonely lunch in a small restaurant that promised an 'Old Fashioned Roast Dinner', swallowing the dry potatoes and unidentifiable meat with difficulty. At three she decided he wasn't coming, paid her bill and went to the railway station.

The blissful hours with Ken had left her low in spirits and ashamed of being so happy. She had to get away from him, move to a place where he would never find her.

As usual, the platform was crowded with people waiting for the mid-morning train: soldiers, sailors and airmen returning from leave with their loved ones standing near, seeing them off, not knowing what to say. As the time for the train drew near, the groups huddled closer, as though needing protection as the time to part approached with each loud tick of the platform clock.

But Janet was not in the midst of a crush of people; she was isolated within the throng, and she knew that was what the future offered her. Isolation even in the middle of a crowd of people. She had no place here, or anywhere, no roots, no one to care whether she were dead or alive. Staring into the future, she couldn't imagine a situation where life could be any different.

Ken dozed for a few hours, then he washed and changed his clothes and set off back to the hospital. He didn't want to telephone, he wanted to be there, to see her, hear her tell him she was all right.

The doctors had reassured them both about the baby, but before Ken returned Eirlys was warned that she had to rest more and it would be advisable for her to give up work completely.

'Advisable, not necessary?' she asked.

'I would strongly recommend that you stay at home for the remainder of your pregnancy, Mrs Ward.'

135

She smiled her thanks but said nothing of this to Ken when he arrived. She couldn't give up work, not at this stage. She had to oversee her summer-entertainments plans to the end. There were only a few arrangements to follow through. Most of the work was done and she hated the thought of leaving it to someone else. It was her project and she wanted to hang on to it greedily. It was only a couple more weeks. Surely the baby wouldn't object to that?

Ken was told he was not really allowed to enter the ward until visiting hours but he persuaded the matron to let him go and sit beside Eirlys for a few moments. She didn't seem very pleased to see him.

He sat beside her bed and tried to talk to her about the success of the contest, repeating some of the flattering comments about her management of it that he had overheard, but she hardly seemed to hear him.

'Are you tired?' he asked after an uneasy few moments.

'Yes, Ken. I think I want to sleep. Visiting time isn't until this afternoon and the nurses have lots to do. Why don't you go?'

He kissed her unresponsive lips and went out, turning at the door to see her pick up a magazine and begin to read. She couldn't possibly know about Janet, so why was she so withdrawn from him? Perhaps their marriage was a failure for her too, he thought with some surprise.

He didn't go back to Conroy Street. Instead he went to the hotel where he had taken Janet, running as he drew near, afraid she would have left early. He was told that she had left fifteen minutes before and, thanking the porter, he ran to the station just as the train pulled Janet, with a fuss of steam and smoke and noisy chuntering, out of his reach.

When Vera left the café she went back to Mrs Denver's feeling very deflated. Yesterday she had been admired, told she was beautiful, and today she was washing dirty dishes, clearing up after families of boring people who didn't even notice how lucky they were to be served by a beauty queen.

'What is it, love?' Mrs Denver asked as she handed her a cup of tea. 'Anything I can do?'

'Not unless you can tell me how I get out of this rut I'm in.'

'Leaving home was an adventure, then finding a place to sleep in that railway carriage, and getting a job in Castle's Café. That doesn't sound like a rut to me. Be patient, dear; you'll find something better, more suited to your talents.'

'D'you think so? Really?'

'Really. Daring, you are, bold and brave. One day soon you'll know what you want and you'll go out there and make it happen.' She leaned over and patted Vera's hand. 'Until then, make the best of what you've got. Maldwyn is a good friend when you need company and doesn't bother you much when you don't. You have a job that pays well enough. Specially if you started being nice to the customers and earned a few more tips,' she said pointedly.

'I have been a pig today, Mrs Denver,' she grinned.

'I thought you might have been. Now, what about a nice wash and a change of clothes? Put that nice blue skirt and blouse on, the ones you bought last week, and make yourself feel less like a skivvy and more like a beauty queen, eh?'

Eirlys came out of hospital on Monday afternoon and went straight up to bed. Morgan fussed over her, glaring at Ken whenever he had the opportunity, making certain his son-in-law knew he considered him partly to blame for Eirlys's problems. On the landing outside their bedroom, he asked, 'You're going to stay around for a few days, aren't you? See that Eirlys is all right before you swan off somewhere to entertain the masses?'

'I can't. I have to go to North Wales and London. There are things I have to do, and I have to arrange for someone else to do them if I'm to have time off. I can't just drop everything.'

'Your wife's more important at the moment, I'd say.'

'Unfortunately the war doesn't stop for illnesses, even for someone as important as Eirlys.'

'This war is about people!' Morgan pointed towards the three boys huddled together near the fireplace. 'They are terrified. Afraid that if anything should happen to Eirlys they'd lose their home. I've tried to reassure them but seeing you so indifferent, not looking after Eirlys as you should, is making it worse for them.'

'Father-in-law,' Ken said sharply. 'Those boys are your responsibility. Not mine and not really Eirlys's. We'll be moving out of your house one day and they will stay with you. You allowed their mother to live here with you and that implied they were staying for ever. Now you have to deal with them. Not me, not Eirlys, *you*!'

In the bedroom. Eirlys covered her ears with the pillows. Downstairs, the three boys looked subdued and frightened as the men argued, their voices raised in anger.

'What will happen to us if Eirlys dies, like Mam did?' Percival asked in his low, slow voice. 'Will we have to go back to London and stay in a room like before, sleeping three in a bed?'

'Course not,' Stanley assured him, with more confidence than he felt. 'Eirlys ain't going to die, she's 'avin' a baby, that's all.' He looked towards the stairs and added in a whisper, 'Anyway, if she does, Uncle Morgan'll see us all right, won't he?'

'Why does she have to go to bed and sleep just because there's a baby coming to live with us?' Harold asked.

'Oh, Harold,' Stanley groaned in worldly-wise tone. 'Do you 'ave to ask all these questions?'

Morgan came down the stairs, followed by Ken. 'Go on,' he grinned, pointing a thumb up the stairs, 'you can all go and see her now.' With a whoop of delight they scuttled up the stairs and into her room and sat gently on the bed.

'When's this baby coming then?' Percival asked with a sigh. 'It's taking ages. Uncle Morgan says that's why you're ill. How come it's troubling you before the postman brings it?'

It was two days before Ken felt able to leave. He went straight to the camp where Janet had worked, to be told she had moved on.

'Can you give me an address where I can reach her?' he asked, taking out a notebook and fountain pen. 'She's promised to sing at two of the concerts I've arranged and I need to let her know about rehearsals.'

The guards at the entrance to the camp eyed him suspiciously. 'There's no message here for you, and if I were you, mate, I'd clear off and stop asking questions.'

'You could be risking arrest and possible interrogation if you hang about trying to get information, even about the Naafi girls,' the other added. 'And you could get the lady in question suspected of spying too.'

He walked away. From behind a counter, Janet stood up, thanked them and returned to the Nissen hut where she slept.

With a heavy heart Ken moved on, wondering how he could find Janet, whether he should, and how he could face the rest of his life without her if he didn't. He realised that, if she had moved on without telling him where, his only hope of contact was through Shirley, who used to partner her on stage, or Beth, who ran the market café which was still in her name. Surely she would come back to it one day? Like thousands of others, he cursed the war and the upheaval it created and wondered whether anything would ever return to how it was.

He changed some money into penny pieces, found a phone box and began booking halls and arranging meetings, and all the time he wondered where Janet had gone and if she would get in touch. It took a long time and today he was impatient. Few people had telephones and he would sometimes have to wait while the owner of the phone, often in a corner shop, ran to find the person he wanted.

With the holiday season at an end, the children back in school and fewer day trippers and visitors arriving in the small town, it might be expected that everything would slow to a more sedate pace, with the average age of the crowd being greater than during high summer, and no silly hats or bursts of laughter at things that were not really funny. The mood did change, but the people who did come were still determined to have fun, and were making the most of every sunny day, crowding into the town through the first weeks of September, by train, bus, bicycle and on foot. Restrictions on using petrol for pleasure reduced the number of cars, but there were a suspiciously high number of vans and lorries crowded with children arriving with the rest, the owners hoping that if the police saw the illegal use of their firms' vehicles they would sympathetically turn away.

Delyth and Madge still came whenever they could, usually on Sundays and often on Wednesdays as well. Cutting down the cost of the day out by bringing food and a bottle of pop from home, they were beginning to feel like locals, and were treated so by many of the traders and shopkeepers.

Vera had been the one to introduce them, firstly to the Castle family and then to others. They always met her and gave her news of her family and friends. Together with Maldwyn, her friendship gave them a greater sense of belonging. They knew that their life would be sadder once the season ended, and the stalls and entertainments on the sands were dismantled and stored away until the spring.

The only continuing disappointment for Delyth was not seeing Maldwyn. He seemed uneasy and anxious to be gone when they did meet. It seemed to Delyth that he was not interested in even a friendship with her, and it made her sad.

They went to the rock-and-sweet shop, which was no longer filled with joke pieces of seaside rock in the shape of giant dummies, enormous teeth, eggs and bacon, funny faces and a dozen other gimmicks. These had once been bought in enthusiastic quantities for people to take back home to tease some member of their families. Now, with sweets on ration, the stock was depleted and for future seasons there would only be local views, saucy postcards and inexpensive ornaments. Even the traditional views of the area had restrictions, some being withdrawn if the council considered them capable of helping the enemy.

Alice Potter, who was engaged to marry Marged and Huw's youngest son, Eynon, was not there. Audrey explained that she was visiting her father. They hung around outside, looking at the funny postcards, until she appeared. She smiled when she saw the friends, and pointing to the clock mimed that she would be free for lunch in an hour. Arranging to call back, Delyth and Madge moved on.

Delyth had a camera with her, intending to take photographs of the beach to look at during the winter when they would not

140

be able to visit so often. When Alice stood outside the shop, adding more cards to the display, she snapped her without being seen. It would be a nice gift for her to send to Eynon if it was a success.

Maldwyn was on the sands, the Sunday a break from the shop.

'Where's Vera?' Madge asked when she saw him talking to Huw Castle.

Maldwyn shook his shoulders dismissively. 'She met some chap she danced with after the contest. I've hardly seen her. She's been out with him every spare moment since.'

Madge and Delyth looked at him for a sign of dismay but he showed none. 'Fancy a cup of tea?' he asked.

'We're meeting Alice in a while.'

'Great. The more the merrier. Envied I'll be, escorting three pretty girls.'

Delyth held back and allowed Madge to walk with Maldwyn. She didn't want to make him feel pressured, but she hoped this was a softening of his unexplained indifference to her.

When Alice caught up with them she was worried. She hadn't heard from Eynon for several weeks. 'That's not un-usual,' she explained. 'When I do get post I often get several at once.'

'So why are you worried?' Delyth asked.

'I don't know. His parents haven't heard either and he writes to us all so regularly. This time it's much longer than usual and, I don't know, it's different,' she told them as they sat in Castle's Café and tucked into Marged's chips and Spam fritters.

They tried to comfort her during the rest of her lunch break, but she still looked sad and afraid as they walked with her back to the sweet shop. Outside the shop stood a soldier, a kit bag beside him. He was chatting to Aunt Audrey but scanning the crowd as though waiting for someone. For a moment Alice didn't take any notice. Then the soldier opened his arms and shouted, 'Alice!'

'It's Eynon!' she said in a disbelieving whisper. Then she ran.

The two girls watched as they hugged each other, then turned

141

away to see Maldwyn grinning as though he had engineered the surprise himself.

'Nice to know there are some good moments in this damned war,' he said.

After spending some time alone locked in the sweet shop's store-room, declaring their love, Eynon and Alice went arm in arm to see Marged and Huw and begin to spread the joyful news.

This was cause for celebration. Neighbours spared some of their hoarded tins to make sure Eynon had a good welcome-home party, the neighbours in Sidney Street joining in. Huw and Bleddyn went out for a few flagons of ale and, happiness being the special ingredient, it was a success. No one asked when he was going back, not even Alice. She didn't want to think about saying goodbye; she had to make sure Eynon enjoyed this first day without a thought for the tomorrow which would come all too soon.

When the family had gathered and the talking and laughter was threatening to buckle the walls, Eynon asked for quiet and handed Alice a folded piece of paper. It was a special licence. They were to marry in ten days' time. 'A couple of days after that I have to go back,' he said, trying to sound cheerful. 'Just for a while, till me and Montgomery have got this Rommel bloke on the run, and Hitler's been put in his place.'

'Back to Africa?' Huw asked.

'Of course, our dad. They can't manage without me just yet.'

Alice asked Eynon to go with him to tell her father, but sadly there was no response to add to their joy.

When Delyth and Madge heard about Eirlys's plans for moonlight dancing as a finale to the summer entertainments, they were determined to take part. Accommodation was still difficult to find in the overcrowded seaside town, but a word with Marged and they were offered a night and a breakfast in a house in Sidney Street, a few doors away from her home.

'Nothing special, mind,' she warned, 'but you'll be comfortable, and if the breakfast isn't enough come to us and we'll fill you up with toast, right?'

'Now all we have to do is tell our parents,' Delyth sighed. 'Although I don't suppose Uncle Trev will be anything but pleased at the news of me being out *all night*,' she emphasised meaningfully.

'You mean – they don't, do they?' Madge gasped.

'Course they do. So if I get him on my side Mam's bound to say yes. Then you can tell your mam and it's all sorted.'

Eirlys was still resting for much of the day. One morning, as Ken was leaving, she asked for his help.

'Can you go and see Mr Gifford, please, Ken? He and Mr Johnston will need to know that the arrangements for the rest of the summer entertainments are more or less in place.' She held up her notebook, in which she had written everything needed for the main events and several smaller ones. 'Most of it is typed out and on his desk but the last-minute details are here. Phone numbers and so on.'

'I thought the beauty contest was supposed to have been the last big event?'

'No, we hope the Dancing by Moonlight will be as big a draw as the beauty contest, if the weather holds. And there's the final parade, of course.' He looked doubtful and she added, 'It helps the town; bringing more visitors helps everyone. And with the weather holding out we'd be crazy not to make what we can.'

'We don't want to be crazy, do we?' he muttered.

'Please, Ken.'

'I suppose I'll have to take it,' he said, picking up her notebook. 'It'll mean catching a later train.'

'Thank you.' She watched him put the book in his pocket and said, 'Don't lose it, and can you bring it back today so I can check what's happening? I'll be back working normal hours next week and I don't want to forget something.'

'Full-time? I thought the doctor said—'

'The doctor said I have to rest, not spend the next six weeks in bed!' She laughed to hide her irritation. He really hated her to be so involved with the summer entertainments. It was a very important job and took so much of her time and energy, time she knew he felt should be spent looking after him, as a

143

proper wife should. She knew he was as unhappy as she, but wasn't convinced that he would be any happier if she were at home, being a full-time wife. And as he was away for so much of the time, she couldn't imagine that that would ever be enough for her.

Ken went to the office, where he found Mr Gifford and Mr Johnston looking thoroughly harassed. There were members of staff standing patiently in a queue holding papers on which they needed a decision, a group of women asking them to help them decide where they should send money they had collected. The phone was ringing; Mr Johnston picked it up and dropped it back on its rest.

'Talk to the WVS, they're the ones to help,' Mr Gifford was saying as he tried to coax the women out of his office. 'Oh, Ken, come in. I hope you've come to tell me Eirlys is coming back? I'm getting desperate managing without her. It's amazing how much she does. All the men are being called up as soon as they're useful. The women too. Mr Johnston and I didn't leave until nine o'clock last night, the third time in ten days.'

Ken was about to tell him that Eirlys would be back on Monday, but during the man's diatribe on the troubles brought upon him by the war he changed his mind. This wasn't the place for her to be, he thought in a moment of genuine concern for her. She was expecting a child and she shouldn't have to deal with chaos like this. 'No, I'm sorry, Mr Gifford, but Eirlys asked me to pass on the details of the remaining events. She won't be returning to work, on doctor's advice,' he added firmly.

He handed over the notebook and walked away from the man's crestfallen face without a qualm.

He went back to the house and told Eirlys what he had done. 'It's for the best, Eirlys,' he said, avoiding looking at her. 'I've spoken to the doctor and he agrees: this job of yours is something two men would normally do, and with extra help too. And there's you risking our baby and managing on your own.'

'That isn't true. I have several assistants, and besides Mr Gifford and Mr Johnston are really in charge of it all. The

144

responsibility is with them. All I wanted to do was put the office in order for them after a busy few months.'

'Well they'll have to sort it out between them; you are staying home.'

'The doctor said that, did he?'

Ken didn't reply. He turned away, collected his suitcase, which was packed ready for his departure, and after a brief nod he left.

Eirlys lay there for a while then got up and went out to telephone the doctor. He called later that day and declared her fit and well. When she suggested returning to work he looked a bit doubtful, but guessed that with the season almost over she was disappointed not to see it through. He made her promise to take things easy but assured her that a few hours only for no more than another week would do no harm. 'Young Stanley and Harold will help you, I'm sure, and even little Percival can do something.'

'And Dadda. He's very good and does all the heavy chores.'

'I gather that the entertainments are almost over, so things should coast along gently for a few more weeks, but you really will have to think of retiring. I don't usually recommend ladies working so late in their pregnancies, although in your case I think you'd be more stressed if you gave up with the job unfinished. A few hours only and for one more week. All right?'

'Yes,' she promised sadly. 'I'll have to stop and become a housewife and mother, won't I?'

'You are happy about this baby, Eirlys? Most women can't wait to give up on work and enjoy motherhood.'

'I want this baby very much, doctor, but that doesn't mean I'll be glad to finish working. I love my job, particularly now when I've been given so much responsibility. I just wish I didn't have to leave.'

'You've worked hard for the summer's activities, haven't you?'

She nodded. 'I'd like to have seen it through. It isn't that I don't want this baby, but if it could wait just a few more weeks before taking all my attention I'd welcome it even more. Does that sound dreadful, doctor? Wanting to keep my job?'

'Not at all, my dear.' He could see how disappointed she was to have to give it up. 'I shouldn't say this, I suppose, but do you have to? If you can manage – and you tell me you get plenty of help from the boys and your father – you might be able to carry on. It's only a few weeks to finish the season. As long as you're sensible I think it would be a pity for you to have to hand over to someone else. For them to take the credit,' he added with a smile. 'Shall I leave it to you? You're a sensible young lady and as long as you promise to visit me regularly and not do anything to put yourself or the baby at risk.'

'Some women manage to work *and* bring up a baby, don't they?' she said, sensing an ally.

'Perhaps I shouldn't say this either, but if you make good provision for the care of your child during the hours you work I see no reason for you to be a stay-at-home mother. My wife works and she's managed three children successfully.'

Eirlys's eyes were bright as she said, 'You're a very modern thinker, aren't you?'

'For a boring old doctor, you mean?'

She laughed. 'Thank you. Thank you very much.'

The boys came home for lunch and she prepared an omelette with dried egg powder, served with Percival's favourite baked beans and tomato sauce, then after Stanley had helped her wash up she went to the office to see her boss. It was after one o'clock and as she had guessed he was still there, intending to work through his lunch hour.

He was clearly relieved to hear that Ken had been wrong and Eirlys would be back in her office the following Monday.

'Your notes were thorough, but any event will be more successful with you at the helm,' he smiled.

'You won't be able to keep my job for me while I take leave and have the baby,' she said sorrowfully. 'It will probably mean being away from work for a couple of months. So shall I prepare an advertisement for my replacement?'

'A couple of months, you say?' Mr Gifford said thoughtfully. 'Give me time to think about it, will you? The winter is less hectic and if you could be back before, say, March, not full-time, perhaps four days, we might manage until then with a temporary person.'

146

Eirlys was so excited as she left the office, she felt slightly sick. She patted her swollen stomach and told the baby, 'You'd better be a good baby, or we'll have a problem, you and I.'

She went to the gift shop where she knew Hannah was working and asked if she knew anyone who would be prepared to look after a baby for four days a week.

'Your baby, d'you mean?' Hannah asked.

'My baby. Hannah, I have a feeling I will be bringing this baby up alone and that means I'll have to work. I don't suppose you'd consider it, would you?'

She felt she had to explain to Hannah what she'd said and told her she suspected her husband of indifference if not more. 'There might even be another woman,' she admitted sadly. 'I don't know what went wrong but we've been drifting further and further apart. When Ken realised that we didn't have any privacy, sharing the house with Dadda and the three boys, he became so irritable. Most of the time he hasn't any patience with Stanley, Harold and Percival, and the fact we never have a moment alone doesn't help. They even knocked the bedroom door and walked straight in until I explained. It's all gone wrong. As soon as he gets home he can't wait to get away again.'

'And you?' Hannah asked softly.

'If I'm honest, I can't wait for him to go.'

'I'll look after the baby, for a while at least. But I don't want you to think I'm taking sides. I think you should continue to work, not with the intention of driving Ken away, but to give you a chance to see which is the most important, the baby and Ken, or work.'

'Thank you,' Eirlys said tearfully, unaware of Hannah's gentle criticism.

When Ken came home a few days later Eirlys was out, at work.

'Where have you been?' he demanded when she came through the door.

In her first words, closely following 'Hello,' she asked him to move out.

'No,' he said calmly. 'I won't give up on our marriage even if you will.'

'Then I'll go.'

147

'What, and leave your father to cope? Remember last time, when he got into such debt it took you months to clear it? And the boys, can you leave them? Haven't they had enough to cope with in their young lives?'

'Since when did you care?'

'I care. I care for my child too and I want to be here to look after him.'

'The point is you never *are* here.'

'But you knew about my job when you married me.'

'It isn't your job keeping you away, not all the time. There's someone more important than me or your child, isn't there?' She stood in the hallway, never having moved more than two steps into the house. She was still wearing her coat and she looked up at him, unblinking, accusing him.

Ken was about to agree and tell Eirlys the truth, but her swollen stomach reminded him of what was at stake. 'No, Eirlys. I love you.'

'Love? How can you even use the word? Love is trust, and loyalty.'

'And support!' he added. 'And understanding. When did you give me any of that?'

'So it's all my fault, is that what you're saying, that I ruined our marriage?'

'What marriage? If we go to the pictures we have to take the boys, if I suggest a walk, some time on our own, you invite them along. We sit here in the evenings and hope for some time to talk, but your father is always the last to go to bed. And we speak in whispers, afraid of waking the boys.'

All the resentment poured out of him, but Eirlys didn't hear what he was saying; she heard only the explosion of excuses, justification for destroying what they'd had. Anger and fear blocked her ears to the truth.

'I work hard.' She was outraged by his words. 'I do my best.'

'Not for me you don't!'

She turned and left the house, slamming the door behind her. She didn't care about the boys needing their meal, or whether or not they had heard the argument. She had to get away.

*   *   *

148

The following day Janet left with a small group of girls who, like her, had volunteered for overseas posting and were going to start their initial Army training to join the Naafi Expeditionary Forces Institute. She hoped the training would be as harsh as she'd been told to expect: she needed to obliterate all feeling. She also hoped she would be sent to the furthest possible point from South Wales.

Eight

The wedding of Eynon Castle and Alice Potter was better than some wartime weddings, but not by much. The fact that the Castles owned the seaside café and a fish-and-chip restaurant meant they had a place to hold the reception and a licence to cater for the guests. The venue was automatically the café above the sands, where Marged and Huw, helped by other members of the family, were able to seat thirty people or provide a buffet for more. To seat them seemed more proper, both from convention and because with food so scarce most would appreciate a good meal. For the evening party the more spacious church hall had been booked.

Bernard provided chickens and most of the vegetables. The wedding cake was a three-tier sham made from cardboard, decorated with paint and topped with a bride-and-groom relic from someone's attic. A late rose from Marged and Huw's garden was laid across it and the result was pleasing, if not edible.

Alice looked lovely in borrowed finery, a white dress altered by Hannah to fit her slim figure and a veil already used by several neighbours.

The wedding was at two, and the plan was for the couple to leave for two days' honeymoon at a small hotel further down the coast, and for family and friends to gather again in the evening to continue the celebrations without them.

Ken asked Hannah and Beth where Janet had gone. 'I need her to take part in a concert and I've lost her address,' he told them, taking out a small notebook.

They shook their heads in unison. Beth stared at him with a strange expression on her face, and alarm bells rang. She knew! She knew about Janet and himself being in love. He glanced around. How many other people knew? He thanked the girls and moved away. He tried to analyse how he felt about Eirlys finding out. Would it be a relief, a chance to be able to leave her and find Janet? Something tarnished the vision. Something he couldn't define. He was fond of Eirlys and with the baby coming he had a responsibility, but was that all? Was that enough?

He longed to see Janet, to be reassured they were both still dreaming of being together for always. She had sometimes phoned him at a phone box at a certain time on a certain day, but no arrangement had been made and he had no way of getting in touch. He had written to the place where she had last worked. Perhaps someone would forward it to her, but he didn't feel hopeful. Things were very confused, with secrecy at Army and Air Force camps more important than a letter to a Naafi girl.

Delyth had ignored Maldwyn's plea for her to stay away from St David's Well, and with Madge had been among the congregation at the church. Marged saw them and invited them to join the party later. Delyth took a few photographs and smiled as the beach photographer fussily told them to move away from his groupings and generally ordered everyone about. 'Prima donna,' she heard Bleddyn whisper to Huw.

While the guests were enjoying the wedding breakfast, to which they hadn't been invited, Delyth and Madge sat on the beach below the café, from where they could hear the occasional burst of laughter as speeches were made and toasts proposed and drunk.

The day was warm, the breeze scented with past summers and echoing that special buzz of families crowding amiably together, enjoying the traditional pleasures. Fewer people colonised the sand and the atmosphere was calmer as the visitors had changed and consisted mainly of older people without the ties of children.

Maldwyn saw them as he went to join the wedding party after closing the flower shop. 'I thought you were staying away,' he said with a frown.

'I couldn't miss seeing the Castle wedding, could I?'

'And I couldn't come alone,' Madge added. 'We've been invited to the party later. Are you going?'

'Yes. I haven't been to a wedding before.' He patted his pocket. 'I bought them a little gift. A picture frame for one of their wedding photographs.' He didn't suggest going to the party together. He wasn't happy about being close to Delyth, in case whoever was causing trouble was near. It gave him a sensation of unease to imagine someone watching him, and he was glad when the girls told him they were off to find something to eat before going to the evening celebration.

Delyth hid her disappointment. He was probably meeting Vera, she thought sadly.

Wedding guests were spilling out of the café both on to the cliff path and clambering down the metal steps on to the sand, with much laughter, evidence of the wine they had consumed. Delyth picked up her camera. 'I didn't bring my sketchbook,' she explained. 'I'm beginning to feel a bit conspicuous using it. So I brought a camera instead. It belongs to "Uncle" Trev.' She emphasised the epithet as usual, to indicate her disapproval. 'I took a few photographs at the church and as they went into the reception. There are a few shots left so I think I'll finish them as this lot make their way down the steps, that should be a laugh. I'll give them to Marged and Huw when they're printed – if they're good enough.' Then she frowned as she examined the camera. 'That's funny, there's only two left. I thought there were more.' She shrugged, and hurried to where a stream of guests were still making their way down the steps, the women exaggerating the difficulties in their finery, which included high heels and tight skirts, and enjoying the ensuing laughter.

It was one of those days when it seems summer will never end. People strolled along, in no hurry to be home, stopping to lean on the strong sea wall and look back at the emptying sands, at the stalls now disappearing into their winter stores. A man was gathering litter, another collecting the deck-chairs and putting them into a lorry to be taken away until the spring. Two men were sweeping the promenade, whistling cheerfully as they worked, and as always there were groups of children with their arms filled with empty bottles and other

152

finds: handkerchiefs, sunhats, coins, forgotten toys, buckets and spades and the flags with which children and adults decorated their ephemeral buildings. There was a forlorn look about the abandoned castles and channels as the tide crept up to wipe them smoothly away, cleaning the sand ready for another day.

Before leaving for their brief honeymoon, Alice and Eynon went to see her father. He sat with several others on a row of chairs against a wall in the day room. The room was sparsely furnished, just chairs, a couple of tables and a wireless playing softly in the background. The walls were pale cream, the woodwork a sombre dark green, and heavy curtains kept out much of the day's sunshine. The smell was a cocktail of disinfectant and boiling cabbage, and as always Alice was upset from the moment she entered.

Colin Potter was leaning to one side and they could see that attempts had been made to prop him more comfortably with pillows. He saw them coming, his sharp eyes brightening, but he didn't speak. They sat one each side of him and offered him a piece of sponge cake as a substitute for the wedding cake they hadn't had. Quietly they told him about the celebration.

As always, he looked at his daughter and said, 'No men in the house, mind.'

Alice looked at Eynon tearfully and he held her comfortingly in his arms. 'Perhaps that's the only way he can tell you he recognises you. He's doing all he can to show you he knows you're there and that he loves you.'

The thought cheered her. It meant a great deal to her to think she might be recognised by this shell of a man who had once been a strong, loving father.

They stayed awhile until, running out of subjects for their one-sided conversations, Alice kissed him and they left.

Arms around each other, they went to pick up their cases and walked to the train to start their journey to Tenby and a few days of rare and wonderful privacy. Then they would have just two nights in the home Alice had made, in two rooms of a house in Holby Street, before saying goodbye.

Maldwyn went back to Mrs Denver's after the reception, and

soon afterwards Vera arrived to change out of her waitress uniform, specially worn for the wedding, and put on a dress ready to go to the party. Vera wondered why Marged and Huw had invited so many people who were neither family nor close friends.

'You and me, well, we've worked there, but Delyth and Madge, who are only day trippers? You'd think they'd want only their family there, wouldn't you?'

'With so many men and women in the forces it would be a bleak celebration,' Maldwyn said. 'This way the gaps will be less noticeable. People support each other with more than words. Besides, a party is always welcome.'

'Of course. Bleddyn's son was killed, wasn't he, and his other son, Johnny, is far away and hasn't been home in ages.'

'It isn't only the men. Women are being called up now, remember. Girls of seventeen are leaving home these days. That's something that didn't happen before the war, except for maids going into service. Eynon will be going back overseas as soon as the week is over. The thought in everyone's mind – especially Alice's – is that he might not come back. Being able to look back on an evening filled with dancing and laughter and friends having fun will be a help in the days to come.'

'No one knows how long they'll survive, do they? I don't think I'd like to get attached to anyone until the war's over. To find someone then lose them would be terrible.'

'I don't think everyone looks at it that way. Some are determined to enjoy what they can. Certainly those involved in the fighting.'

'Still feeling guilty not being in uniform, Maldwyn?' When he nodded, she went on, 'Well *I'm* glad you didn't go away.'

'Are you?'

'Of course.' But she didn't look at him; her eyes stared dreamily into space; she was already looking ahead to the party and the possibility of some fun.

Ken was going to Alice and Eynon's wedding party and, although she had been invited, Eirlys had declined. Trying to look happy was exhausting and served no purpose. It was probably her imagination but everyone seemed to look at her as though guessing the sadness within her. She and Ken were hardly speaking and he was away from home even more than usual. He didn't even bother to tell her where he was going or when he would be back. She dragged herself around the house, doing the usual cleaning and cooking, but she had no heart for any of it. Once there had been pleasure in making everything shine and filling the house with the smells of meals cooking, knowing her efforts were appreciated. Ken was indifferent to it all and made it clear he would rather eat before he came home and avoid sitting around the crowded table listening to the boys talking about their day – often with overloaded mouths.

She had left the church before the photographs were taken, walking home with the boys and urging them to get out of their tidy clothes before they were ruined with boisterous games. Ken returned an hour later. He didn't come straight inside but hovered as though expecting someone. He was putting his key in the lock when he suddenly turned away and ran to the telephone box on the corner. Opening the door for him, she heard it ringing. Curious, she went to see why he had moved so hastily to answer it. Did he think it was for him? Ken didn't notice her there and she stepped back in disbelief when she realised that he was speaking words of love. She stood, frozen to the spot, not wanting to know, yet unable to move away. Although his words came to her clearly, she didn't learn who was at the other end of the conversation. She was trembling as she turned away.

Saddened, but in one way relieved to have confirmation of the real cause of his indifference, she went back to the house while the conversation went on, and didn't respond when he came in and called cheerfully to let her know he was home.

She didn't know what to do. There was an impulse to run away, to hide from the cruel truth of his betrayal, but another part of her wanted to shout, tell everyone how he had behaved: she wanted to hurt him, hit out at him for his disloyalty. She did nothing. She couldn't tell her father and there was no one else with whom she wanted to share the shame that was partly hers.

*　　*　　*

The wedding party and dancing couldn't have been accommodated in a small café, so a hall was booked, which had been decorated by Chapel's Flowers. As usual, much of the display was made up from what could be gathered free, from the hedgerows. With autumn giving its beautiful swansong as the leaves changed colour before covering the ground with a rich carpet of red and gold, it was easily done. Maldwyn had even managed to cut branches of bramble, with attractive leaves and berries becoming part of the table decorations. Many commented and Marged told them all proudly that it was the work of one of her guests. On the table where Marged, Huw, Bleddyn and Hetty sat, he had placed a bowl of chrysanthemums, but Bleddyn had moved them away, their pungent scent too strong a reminder of funerals. His thoughts were with Johnny, his only surviving son, and the reminder of Taff's death was distressing.

There was the usual shortage of men and Maldwyn was much in demand. Delyth and Madge spent most of the evening dancing with each other. Vera hated to sit out a dance and made sure she had his attention. When she did find another partner, Maldwyn would take the opportunity to dance with each of them before being taken away again by Vera or another of the unattached females. Although they enjoyed the social occasion, and the rare excitement of staying away from home for the night, both girls were disappointed not to see some of Eynon's Army friends there, offering the opportunity to flirt a little or even make a date with a boy who was handsome and free.

'Even having someone to write to would be better than nothing,' Delyth sighed.

'Given up on Maldwyn then, have you?'

'It seems unlikely he'll give up on Vera.' Delyth sighed again, looking towards the corner where Vera danced with both hands clasped behind Maldwyn's head, hands ruffling the hair on the nape of his neck.

'I don't know what he sees in that tart,' Madge said to comfort her.

'D'you think she is a tart?' Delyth asked, the implications of the word filling her heart with dismay. Until then she hadn't thought of what Maldwyn and Vera might do in the lodgings they shared, and it shocked her. Madge's description brought visions of Maldwyn and Vera writhing about on a bed, as she had seen her mother and Uncle Trev do one night when they thought she was asleep. She turned away to blot out the vision.

There was a break in the dancing and they were pleased to see Shirley being helped up on to the stage. She still had difficulty walking but her voice was as strong and melodious as ever and she sang three songs to great applause. They went up afterwards and congratulated her, then Vera pushed her way between them and began asking Shirley about where to go for singing lessons so she could perform too. Over Vera's head, Shirley gave the slightest of winks, as though to share with them the amusement at the confidence Vera displayed.

Sammy Richards the carpenter was playing the accordion, people were beginning to hum the well-known melodies and the crowd was quietly happy when Ken walked in. At once Delyth was nervous. He had been at the church but she had hoped he wouldn't be at the dance. With Eirlys unlikely to enjoy the party, she had expected him to stay home with her. She looked around the faces, trying to recognise the girl he had been quarrelling with that day in the park.

'What a heel,' Madge whispered. 'There's his poor wife expecting and he's out enjoying himself. And I bet he's still meeting that other woman.'

'He frightens me,' Delyth admitted. 'I still think he might be the one trying to drive Maldwyn away.'

'Why would he do that?'

'As a warning for me to keep quiet about his other woman.'

'Sorry,' Madge laughed. 'That's far too complicated for me.' A young soldier approached and asked her to dance, and Delyth watched Ken, and wondered.

When Maldwyn suggested they went to the table and filled a plate with food, she took his arm, glad to be away from the occasional hostile glances from Ken Ward.

Vera left the hall with a soldier, and it was an unhappy Maldwyn who walked Delyth and Madge back to their accommodation. He had imagined Vera would be with them, but he

157

had seen her red coat disappearing as she left without even a wave. He was disappointed, but couldn't really blame her. She had never promised more than friendship, in spite of her sometimes passionate kisses.

All the time they were on the street he was on edge, listening for some suspicious sound that threatened Delyth or himself. He sighed with relief when the door closed behind the girls, thankful that the walk had ended without incident.

With the end of summer, Mrs Chapel and Maldwyn were busily sorting out their autumn and winter plans. They had ordered spring bulbs, and bulbs for forcing into early flowering to add to the Christmas displays. Some were already planted to sell in pots, part-grown. These were in a dark shed or under the stairs, and others were buried in the garden, ready to bring out when the time was right. When he was tidying up, Maldwyn had found a few hyacinth vases and half filled them with water and set the bulbs on top. These were popular with children, who were fascinated to watch the growth that was usually hidden from their sight.

Maldwyn went to jumble sales and bought anything that he could use as a container: jugs, old kettles, teapots, shallow dishes. The damaged vases and pot he had found in the cellar had given him the idea: even the broken ones would have an air of beauty when the flowers bloomed. The shallow dishes were filled with pebbles from the beach, he added water until the pebbles were half covered, then stood bulbs on them. They made unusual gifts when the buds were beginning to show and the roots were slowly working their way around the pebbles. He hoped to have them at their best in time for Christmas. These things took up a lot of space, but Mrs Chapel cheerfully moved into a smaller room and gave up her bedroom to the shelves that Maldwyn knocked up and rapidly filled with carefully nurtured stock.

Dried grasses and branches were popular, mainly because of their cheapness. Quaking grass sold for threepence a bunch and lasted throughout the winter months, displayed dry in a vase. Mrs Chapel continued to paint twigs, which, with a few artificial leaves and flowers added, offered inexpensive

158

displays to passers-by. They were in such demand that most evenings were spent preparing them for the following day. They both worked hard, but enjoying each other's company made the time pass pleasantly, and on one of these occasions Mrs Chapel spoke about her nephew, Gabriel.

'He was always a resentful boy, never pleased with anything he was given, always looking for more. He failed at school, failed at every job he tried and blamed others every time.'

'Why isn't he in the forces?' Maldwyn asked.

'He failed at that too,' she said with a cynical laugh. 'They said he was unsuitable, but no one told him why.'

'He's not strong?'

'Oh, he's strong all right, but not all that right in the head, between you and me. Gets on well enough though, cheating and wheedling his way through life. I feel sorry for my sister, but I can't help the boy.' She looked at Maldwyn, who was intent on painting some tall willow branches with a pale green dye, to form a frame for a corner display in the window. He waited for her to continue, concentrating on his brush strokes, saying nothing, afraid of adding to her criticism of a member of her family, thinking she might one day regret telling him.

'I did think at one time that he could come here, work with me and one day take over the shop, but it wasn't any good. He won't work and, although I can't prove it, I think he stole cash from me,' she said sadly. 'I didn't tell my sister but I think she guessed.'

Maldwyn hadn't been home for a while, although he kept in touch with Winifred by letter. When he finally arranged to go home the following Saturday, he was tempted to cancel his visit. He was not happy about leaving Mrs Chapel in the flat alone. He still had no idea who had driven that lorry, or frightened Delyth, or ruined that fruit. All he knew was that it was in some way connected to him and his moving to St David's Well. He also knew that, like Delyth, Mrs Chapel might be in danger – at least of threats – because of her connection with him.

As a precaution, and making light of the idea, he arranged for Sammy Richards to change the locks on both doors and add a bolt on each. He made sure this was done before he left, and again asked the miserable Arnold Elliot to be aware that Mrs Chapel was on her own.

The Castle family were looking for winter work. Once the stalls, helter-skelter and swingboats had been stored for the winter and the café had been cleaned and closed, Huw and Alice had to find jobs to help them over the following months. Bleddyn was responsible for the fish-and-chip restaurant, which he ran all the year, as did Beth the market café. Vera and the one or two casual workers were also hunting for work they could leave when summer returned. But many of the jobs in the town were seasonal, so there were plenty of people in the same situation as themselves.

Alice was tempted by the higher wages of the factories. It would mean more money saved for when Eynon came home. And the shift work would give her more time to spend on her garden when spring came. Many local women had been sent to work in a large munitions factory in a town about twelve miles away, travelling to and from the place by train. Alice didn't want that. She needed to be here, close to Eynon's home, where he could imagine her whenever he thought of her.

Vera still had visions of glamorous work. She believed that, as a winner of a beauty contest, she owed it to herself not to accept menial jobs like serving in a vegetable shop, as Beth had done a few winters ago. With a display of confidence she didn't really feel, she went to Brook Lane to see Shirley. Shirley invited her in and Vera tried to explain how she felt.

'Can you sing?' Shirley asked. 'Or dance?'

'Well—' Vera was about to admit she couldn't, but changed her mind and instead said, 'I haven't really tried.'

'Try now,' Shirley coaxed. She limped over to the piano which Bleddyn had bought for her and picked out the beginning of a well-known melody. Vera lost her nerve completely.

'I don't think I can, not here, not like this, I need a proper stage and accompaniment.'

Shirley smiled and said, 'Perhaps you just aren't ready yet.'

'I'd feel more confident if I had a few singing lessons.'

'Why don't you find work in a shop where you can use your

talents to advise customers about what clothes to buy and how to wear them? That way you could earn the money to pay for lessons.'

'Fashion, you mean?'

'Well, with twenty-six clothing coupons to last a year, fashion is hardly a consideration these days. But yes, a clothes shop like the one next to Mrs Chapel's flower shop. You'd be very good at it, I'm sure.'

'D'you think so?' Vera stood up and swirled around the room. 'Yes, I think you're right.'

'Leave the singing until you're ready.'

Shirley saw her out and knew that the following summer Vera would be back in Castle's Café, still dreaming of a wonderful career on the stage. She knew that for some dreaming was as far as they got, and sadly Vera was one of them. Unless she concentrated on earning a living, placing her feet firmly on the ground, her life could be ruined by being the winner of that one local beauty competition.

Pushing the chairs aside, she stood up and began her exercises. She had to work at getting strong, or she would be nothing more than a dreamer herself.

Vera called to see Arnold Elliot later that day and asked for a job.

'Nothing at present,' he told her. 'Me and my son manage all right, until we expand, then I might have need of an extra assistant.'

Vera looked around the shop with a frown. 'It seems to me, Mr Elliot, that you could do with some help now, not some time in the distant future. Look at the way those dresses are displayed. I know clothes are rationed, but you want people to spend their coupons here, not somewhere else, don't you? Boring, they look, but by giving them a touch of an iron and pinning them properly in your window display, I bet you'd sell more than you do now. Give me a try, I'll definitely increase your sales.' Her heart was thumping like an out-of-control engine, her legs were shaking, but she kept the confident smile on her face, and the spark of devilment shone in her eyes.

'I'll think about it. Give me your address,' he said gruffly. Perhaps the girl did have a point. So many came in and left

161

without buying. He needed something to boost sales if he were to have the confidence to buy old Mrs Chapel's shop when the time came. Marking time while he waited was dangerous. A business went down faster than it went up.

Delyth took her film to be developed and waited excitedly for the snaps. She collected them on Saturday at lunchtime, and shared the first viewing with Madge. The pictures taken at the church were good: clear, with subject and background well balanced. Moving through the twelve shots, she was surprised to see two of herself, taken from behind as she sat on the beach. The shadow of the photographer was spread over her, contrasting with the brightness beyond. 'Did you take these?' she asked. Madge shook her head.

'Then who did? Someone picked up my camera and snapped me, and –' her hands shook as she pointed to something on the sand beside her – 'oh, Madge! What's this?' On the ground behind her chair was a long-bladed knife. 'Madge!' she gasped. 'Look at this! What does it mean? Who did this?'

Madge was frightened, but determined not to show it. 'They've got your snaps mixed up with someone else's; that's always happening. A customer told me the other day she had a view of a caravan she had never seen.'

'It's him again, isn't it?' Delyth whispered. 'He's telling me to persuade Maldwyn to leave St David's Well. But why?'

'I think it's a mistake,' Madge insisted.

'But it's me on the photograph. How can it be a mistake? He was standing behind me while I was unaware of him. Madge, I'm frightened.'

'Check the negatives before you panic.'

With shaking hands, Delyth examined the negatives and there it was: just before she had gone to snap the wedding guests coming down on to the beach, all laughing, having fun. As she had sat there, unaware of the danger, someone was threatening her, placing a knife beside her and making sure she understood his intent.

'We have to go to the police,' Madge said, looking through the negatives to confirm the truth.

'No. I want to speak to Maldwyn. He *must* know what

162

this is about. There has to be a reason and he'll have to work it out.'

'We can't go to St David's Well again. It's too dangerous.'

'I have to talk to Maldwyn. Whether he realises it or not, he knows why this is happening.'

She wrote to Maldwyn that evening, unaware that he was staying with his stepmother not far from her home, and told him what had happened. She arranged to go to St David's Well the following Wednesday.

Maldwyn was at the station to meet them. The weather had changed; the warm summer days had gone as though for ever, and a cold wind blew across the platform as they stepped from the train. They went first to a café, where they ordered toast and tea, and showed the photographs to Maldwyn.

'Police?' Madge suggested.

'Yes, but not yet. I want to think about this, and try to work out why I am the target.'

The bread was stale, and the toast was cold before they took a first bite; the minimal amount of margarine didn't alleviate the tastelessness.

'Even the seagulls wouldn't be thrilled with this,' Madge muttered, scraping the toast into a handkerchief.

'Don't dare give it to the birds, or you could be fined for wasting food. It will go into the bins to feed the pigs.'

'Poor things too,' Madge said sympathetically. 'Who'd be a pig in wartime, eh?' She was trying to lighten the mood but nothing took the anxiety from her friend's eyes.

Delyth wanted to go to the bay. 'I want to defy him, show him he isn't worrying us. We've brought a few sandwiches and some more life-threatening food – a slice or two of fatless sponge cake. So why don't we go up on the cliff path and find a sheltered spot to sit for an hour?'

'Don't you think that's dangerous?' Maldwyn warned. 'Until we find out who's doing this, we ought to stay away from dangerous places, and from each other.'

'More toast?' the waitress asked and they all laughed when Delyth said, 'No fear!' and added in a whisper, 'I reckon her toast is more dangerous to life than the cliff path!'

The wind made them hurry, bending forward against the

163

chill, but they were all suitably dressed in overcoats and scarves, and the girls wore head-hugging knitted hats. Delyth went to the top of the precarious path and down through the rocks a little way until she could see the entrance to the cave. The tide was high, and moving up and down at the entrance was a long shape that could have been a roll of carpet but just as easily could be a body. Giving a scream, she ran back to the others. This time they did call the police.

It was more than an hour before the mysterious package was recovered and examined. Firstly they had to wait for a police launch to make its way around the coast, with the Army standing by in case it was an explosive. While they waited, a police constable talked to Delyth, trying to get information but at the same time taking her mind off her fear that the object was a body.

She told him about seeing the boat with the broken mast and her hobby of sketching what she saw. As he coaxed her to talk, she also told him about Ken. 'He warned me not to tell his wife about the drawing I did of him with another woman, one day in the park back home. I knew it wasn't his wife, see, because I met her and she's not as tall as the woman he was with.'

'Very observant of you, Miss Owen. I don't suppose you did any drawings of the boat you mentioned?'

'I did, but they were lost.' She didn't want to add to Ken's troubles by telling the police it was he who had destroyed them, but Madge did.

'That was Ken Ward again,' she said. 'He took all Delyth's drawings.'

'Could you draw what you remember?' the constable asked.

On a scrap of paper Delyth sketched the boat as she remembered seeing it, with the bundle athwart the vessel, half hidden below the seat.

Maldwyn muttered, 'Well done. You're amazing, Delyth. Quite amazing. Isn't she, Madge?' He took her hand and held it in both of his, looking at her from time to time with pride – and was there something else in his gentle eyes, something like affection? Whatever it was glowing there, it warmed her and made her feel safe.

Still trying to take her mind off what was happening below,

the constable admired her simple drawing and said, 'You're very observant. We could do with people like you in the force. What about the man in the boat? What can you tell me about him?'

'The mast was snapped, so I don't have a very good guide, but I'd say he was about as tall as Madge's dad.'

'It wasn't him!' Madge gasped, and they all laughed.

'Tall, but although he looked heavily built, he had so many clothes on I could be wrong. Dark trousers tucked into wellingtons and a coat that looked like the stuff tents are made of, sort of stiff and pale beige, brown, nondescript. Oh, and the wellingtons had been cut down and spread, you know, so he could slip them on and off easily.'

The policeman made copious notes and again congratulated her on her sharp observation. Maldwyn continued to hold her hand and told her how well she was doing. 'You've been given more help than the police usually get, eh, constable? I imagine most witnesses remember very little and what they do recall is only partly accurate. Marvellous, isn't she?'

'She is that, sir. A quite remarkable witness.'

Maldwyn held her closer, as though sharing in the man's praise.

They could hear from the voices below that the object had been discovered, and Maldwyn put an arm around each girl to comfort them in case the discovery was an unpleasant one. It could be a sailor thrown from a wrecked ship, or an airman from a ditched plane, or even a careless walker fallen and dragged into the cave by the tide. When the object was taken aboard the police vessel, one of the men shouted up to tell them that it was nothing frightening. It was food: tins of powdered egg and milk, as well as carefully wrapped joints of bacon and several packages of meat.

Excited now and unwilling to leave, they waited while the cave was explored and learned that it contained more food, as well as clothes and equipment that appeared to have been taken from Army supply stores.

The constable, whose name they learned was Charlie Groves, walked them back to the police station, where they were asked to make a statement. The police phoned through to Bryn Teg

165

and an officer informed their families that they would be late and would be taken home by police car. The afternoon that began with such fear was turning into an exciting adventure.

There was a sense of anticlimax when the questioning was over and Charlie Groves told them he was ready to take them home. Before they left they were told that an examination of the photographs suggested that the knife was not a real one but a children's toy.

When they reached their gates, Charlie Grove told Madge that if she came to St David's Well again to be sure to call and see him. She smiled and said she might, but thought she wouldn't. She was still grieving for John and it would be a long time before she was ready to date someone else. 'Pity, though, he was very nice,' she told Delyth as they went their separate ways to report to their families on their eventful day.

The next morning, when the unsigned letter arrived, Maldwyn hid his panic, said nothing to Mrs Chapel, and opened the shop. He didn't look at it again until he had finished arranging the displays in the window and doorway, and had the shop looking as Mrs Chapel liked it. When she called down to tell him she was making coffee, he took the letter out and read it again.

Liked the pictures of your girlfriend, did you? Go back home or you know what will happen to her. Not all knives are toys.

He took it to the police at lunchtime, but they seemed to think that finding the cache of food and supplies was the connection and that now it was discovered he had nothing more to fear.

'It seems to us that someone didn't like you and your friends spending so much time up on the cliff, where you might see what was happening. Now we know about their hiding place, they won't be going there again. Forget it, Mr Perkins, I'm sure the men will soon be caught.'

He wasn't convinced, but decided to write to Delyth and tell her what the police said, to reassure her, without divulging the contents of the threatening letter he had received.

He had enjoyed the time they had spent on the cliff that day. He and Delyth had been brought closer by the anxiety of wondering what the men would find in the bundle that looked suspiciously like a body. Life with Delyth would be good. She was pretty, talented and certainly interesting company, and one day, when he had a shop of his own, he could imagine her sharing it with him, helping him to make a success of it, either here in St David's Well or some other small, friendly Welsh town.

That evening he sat for a long time with Vera on the periphery of his mind, her image slowly fading while thoughts of Delyth grew. He knew he had no chance with Vera. She had ambitions and hopes far beyond owning a flower shop. Though perhaps one day she might settle for less, like most people did. The vision of her standing beside him in a flower-filled premises grew for a while then faded away, and Delyth's was the face he saw smiling up at him.

He went back to his letter and ended it by saying he hoped to see her very soon but would come to see her rather than wait until she visited the seaside again. 'I can't wait until next season before seeing you,' he added rather boldly, and signed it *Your loving friend.*

Vera burst in then in great excitement, to tell him she had persuaded the owner of the clothes shop that she was just what he needed. 'I went back to ask if he'd thought about it and I've got a job, Maldwyn! I don't have to go home for the winter. Isn't that wonderful? We can spend the winter here, you and me, having fun. There's bound to be plenty of dances and you aren't too bad on the dance floor.' She kissed him fiercely, then again more tenderly, and ran upstairs – to take all the hot water as usual, he sighed with a wry smile.

When she came down, she asked plaintively whether he had any more clothing coupons to spare. 'I've got to have clothes, Maldwyn. D'you think Mr Elliot will let me buy some without coupons?' Without giving him a chance to comment she went on: 'Stockings! They take coupons too and I won't be able to paint my legs now winter's coming. I'll get chilblains and they won't look very glamorous for a beauty queen, will they? Trousers are all right for Land Girls, but not for a fashion salesgirl.' Maldwyn was laughing as she continued, 'Mr Elliot will want me looking my best. I'll go and see Hannah Castle. She might be able to help. Oh, Maldwyn, isn't it exciting?'

He wondered, now the romance of the summer season was over and there would be fewer chances of finding someone more to her taste, whether she might look at him as more than someone to use when she had need of company. She was beautiful and such fun. If only she would stop thinking of him as a friend and see him as something more. A minute of hope with Vera and all thoughts of Delyth were wiped from his mind.

He picked up the letter he had written to Delyth and read it through. He frowned, and looked up the stairs to where Vera could be heard singing. The song was a Cole Porter number, 'You Do Something to Me', and he wondered, with more optimism than was justified, if she meant the words for him. 'Come to the pictures?' he called up.

'Love to, Mal. We might even find a couple of seats in the back row, eh?'

He read the letter again. He had intended to persuade Delyth to go out with him on her own, without Madge, but with the promise in Vera's voice and those excitable kisses his thoughts had somersaulted him back to where he usually was, half in love with Vera. He folded the letter and walked towards the glowing fire. What he had written was too affectionate. He tore it up and watched it burn before going up to wash – in cold water.

Nine

When she heard someone banging rather loudly on her front door, Eirlys was ironing. It was a Monday morning and she had been given the day off by her grateful bosses because of the work she had done on the previous Saturday. She frowned as she put the iron down on the hearth and patted her hair to make sure it was tidy, wondering who it could be. So few people would know she was at home. Two policemen stood there, not local bobbies, but strangers.

'Mrs Ward? Mrs Ken Ward?'

'Yes?' She frowned, waiting for an explanation, then horror made her clutch her unborn baby as the thought of an accident came to her. 'Ken? Is he all right? Has something happened?'

'So far as we know he's fine, Mrs Ward. May we come in?'

She stood back and allowed them to enter, and stood staring at them, waiting for them to tell her the reason for their call. In 1942, the third year of the war, news was more likely to be bad than pleasant.

'It's Mr Ward we'd like to interview,' one of them said.

Interview? This sounded alarmingly serious. Gesturing for them to sit, she asked, 'Will you please tell me what this is about?'

'Can you tell us where he is? We'd like to see him as soon as possible.'

'I don't know where he is. London, I think. I know it sounds vague but he travels around the country arranging fund-raising concerts, and entertainments for the forces, factory workers and other organisations.'

'We know what he does, Mrs Ward. If you could give us

an idea of how we can contact him and when he's likely to be at home, we won't disturb you any further.'

'But what's wrong? Why do you want to see him?'

'An address? Or a phone number? A friend, maybe, who would know where he is?'

They weren't answering her questions. 'Tell me what this is about,' she demanded, 'then I might be able to help you.'

One policeman sat with a pencil poised; the other just looked at her.

Unnerved, she stood up and took an address book from the sideboard. 'You could try his parents.' She gave them the address and, to her further alarm, she was told they had already tried the house in London. Fumbling now, her brain leaping around between unanswered questions and a need to ask more, she thumbed through the book. She gave them a few phone numbers of people Ken regularly worked with and they thanked her and stood to leave.

'It isn't anything for you to worry about, Mrs Ward. It's just a case we are investigating that we think his movements might have some bearing on.'

Hastily finishing the ironing, Eirlys grabbed a coat and went to find Beth. She had to talk to someone. She found her in the market café, serving a couple of shoppers with tea and scones, and waited impatiently until they were settled.

'They used phrases like "interview", "investigation", "his movements might have a bearing on a case". They want to talk to him as soon as possible. What on earth can it be? He's hardly a criminal.'

'There are lots of reasons for them wanting to talk to him,' Beth soothed, handing her a cup of steaming tea. 'He might have been somewhere near at the time of an accident and they'll want to know if he saw something. Or perhaps someone he knows has been in trouble or hurt. Don't worry until there's something to worry about,' she teased.

'But they were so cold. They sat there and asked for his whereabouts and just ignored my questions.'

'Well,' Beth said, still trying to make light of it, 'if he's a master criminal, they don't want you, as a gangster's moll, to warn him, do they?'

'All right, I'm panicking,' Eirlys admitted. 'But it was so frightening.'

'Can you get in touch with him?' Beth went on serving the straggle of customers as they arrived and in between came to sit with her friend.

'No, not unless he phones the office, and today I'm not there. Oh! D'you think I should go in? He might be trying to get in touch.'

'Go home and rest. You and that baby of yours need an hour lying on the bed thinking of nothing more than what to feed the boys on.'

'Heavens, I have to get back. They'll be home in twenty minutes!'

'Get some chips to go with these.' She wrapped four pasties and handed them to Eirlys. 'Cut some bread and jam to fill them up and they won't complain – although Percival might,' she laughed.

Ken was in a boarding house near Brecon. The landlady had a strange expression on her face when she came to tell him he had uniformed visitors and, like Eirlys, his first thought was of an accident.

'What's happened? Is my wife all right? My parents?'

'So far as we know they are fine. It's you we want to talk about, Mr Ward.'

When they began to question him about Delyth and the cliff path beyond Castle's Café, he bluffed for a while and insisted he knew nothing about the girl. When they calmly made it clear that they knew about the meeting with a woman in the park, and the threat to Delyth Owen, during which he had taken her drawings, he admitted it.

'And the photographs of her taken on the beach on the day of Eynon Castle's wedding?'

'Photographs? I don't even have a camera!' Then he remembered the baby Brownie his mother had bought him a couple of years before, which lay at the back of the wardrobe at home. 'Well, I do have a camera, but—'

'Forgive me, but are you saying you do have a camera or you do not have a camera, Mr Ward?' The pencil of the note taker was poised and they both looked at him. This was ridiculous. They made everything sound like a confession of guilt.

'I do own one but it isn't something I use. My mother bought it; it cost a pound and I thought it was a waste of money as photography wasn't something that interested me. It still doesn't! And I certainly didn't take photographs of Delyth Owen on the day of Eynon Castle's wedding. Now, when are you going to tell me what is this all about?'

The questions went on and he answered as fully as he could, in the hope that would hasten their departure. He had a concert that evening which included new acts, and he needed to be there for the rehearsal as everything had yet to be timed and the running order decided.

As the subject changed and he was asked about lorries being driven at Delyth, and illegal food and supplies, he began to panic. Then, just as he was expecting to be arrested, they stood up and left, promising him he would be contacted again a day later when he was back home.

'You won't have to mention the – er – woman in the park to my wife, will you?' he asked as they stepped outside.

'There's enough of the world at war without us adding to it, sir.'

He went to the rehearsal and saw the concert through without being aware of whether it was good or bad, and instead of going back to the guesthouse and sleeping he caught the milk train. Unless there was an air raid to cause delays, he would be home before Eirlys, or Morgan, was awake.

Eirlys waited anxiously for Ken to come home. She knew he wouldn't be there until the following day but still jumped up every time she thought she heard the gate, and insisted on the wireless being played low so she would hear his key in the lock. Then it occurred to her that he might have been arrested, and she listened for the door, expecting not Ken but the police. Her father was working the night shift and when the children were in bed she went too, wanting the day to be over, to lose anxious hours in sleep. But sleep wouldn't come.

She went downstairs several times, even opened the door

and looked out as though that would make him come more quickly, like impatient people looking around the corner to hurry the arrival of a bus, she thought foolishly. She made cocoa, and tried to read, then filled a hot-water bottle to hug, and settled with the light low to try again to find peace in sleep.

Before the alarm clock gave its strident demand for her to rise she heard the sound of a key in the door and for a brief moment thought it was her father. Then memory flooded back and she went down to see Ken dropping his case and throwing off his coat.

'I've had the police here looking for you, Ken. What's happened?'

He put an arm around her and murmured reassuringly, 'It's all right. They thought I could help with a case, that's all.' He switched on the electric fire while Eirlys filled the kettle. 'I'd been in the area where some illegal foodstuffs had been hidden. I wasn't involved and neither would I be. I think it's disgraceful. Food isn't something to make money from when everyone is so tightly rationed,' he said. 'You know me better than that. The black market is something I disapprove of, the same as you do.'

'Why didn't you tell me?'

'I didn't want to alarm you. I knew the police would soon find out the truth and then it would be over, so why upset you for nothing?'

He was so convincing, and told the story with such brevity, that she relaxed and believed him. He sighed with relief and hoped the rest of the inquiry, regarding Delyth's sketchbook and his shameful, bullying behaviour on the cliffs, would never reach her ears.

They sat on the couch, close together, Ken's arm protectively around her, and she felt more secure in his love than she had for a long time. They had talked, shared a worry, and it made her feel more hopeful about their future. When Morgan came in at seven he found them there in each other's arms, fast asleep.

Although the night had been restless and disturbed, she felt restored when she went to the office to deal with the last of the summer events. The final game in the giant chess tournament was easy. All she had to do was arrange for a team of young people from the local school to be there in fancy dress to set out the three-foot-high pieces and move them around to the players' instructions. The mood was a carefully balanced one: the more the helpers fooled around, the more irate the participants would be, but the more the audience would enjoy it. Most onlookers would know little about the finer points of the game and were ready for more relaxed entertainment. The commentator would try to add a little sobriety to counteract the children's actions.

The Dancing by Moonlight was hardly difficult either and for the most part was just left to chance. She had no idea how many would turn up, and knew that if the weather didn't co-operate there could easily be no one at all. It had been advertised, the charities which hoped to benefit had a number of people ready to run around the crowd with their collecting tins, and a small committee had been set up to count and distribute the money.

Vera was furious. She had been promised a job in Mr Elliot's clothing shop, then a letter had arrived telling her she had to report for war duties. She went to the employment offices and was told that she had to do something and they had arranged for her to go to the local factory that made engine parts. She protested, insisted she wasn't strong enough, and even tried to tell them she was considering ENSA, the forces entertainment organisation, but when she could produce no evidence of an audition they handed her the card and told her to present it the following Monday morning at eight.

She had to get out of it somehow, but as she was now in the age group when the government had the final say, she had no idea how. She thought she would call on Ken. He might be able to arrange an audition to give some validity to her claim to being considered by ENSA.

She called to see Ken and was fortunate enough to find him at home. She explained her predicament truthfully and asked if he could help.

'I won that beauty contest, so I know I have the looks. I

174

just want a chance to prove myself and I know I could be successful.'

'Successful at what?' he asked.

'Well, singing, dancing. I'm sure I can learn.'

Ken tried to be sympathetic, but with no proof of her talents nor evidence of experience, he could do nothing. 'You'll have to do this on your own,' he told her. 'Everyone is too busy to train people; they have to prove themselves before they'll be offered an audition.' She looked surprised, then disappointed, and, letting her down lightly, he suggested she took singing lessons and went from there. 'Your teacher will advise you on the best way of getting started.'

'Shirley Downs and Janet Copp did it without teachers,' she protested.

'Shirley and Janet were naturals. They had a terrific talent.' The mention of Janet saddened him; he ended the conversation abruptly and closed the door.

Vera turned huffily and went back to talk to Mrs Denver about how difficult it was for someone like herself, who wanted to rise above waitressing. 'And I refuse to work in a dirty factory ruining my hands,' she added with a shudder.

The weather was not kind to the chess competitors. A misty drizzle kept many people away, but the entrants seemed not to notice. This left Bernard Gregory, puffing amiably at his pipe, which defied the rain and continued to burn, facing a headmaster who had come out of retirement when most of the teachers had been called to fight.

The children, dressed as clowns, moved the pieces, ducking in and out of the shelter of the tents where the competitors stood cogitating on their moves. Bernard lost, but it was a satisfying event and he looked forward to writing to tell his son of his success in the tournament. Peter would be proud of him.

Once the result was announced and the prize given, the children began leap-frogging the pieces, and the small audience joined in. So in spite of the uncooperative weather the day ended happily. Eirlys was once again congratulated on her success.

Although it was a Saturday, Mrs Chapel had insisted Maldwyn went to watch, and he had invited Vera, thinking it would be fun even though neither of them understood the game. Just to be in a crowd, taking part, supporting the town's efforts, seemed to Maldwyn to be sufficient reason for going, but at the last moment Vera declined.

'All right, we can go somewhere else if you like, as I have the afternoon off,' he offered. They had been seeing a lot more of each other recently and he was beginning to hope for more than an occasional hug. She kissed him from time to time, but only when she chose. She still pushed him away when he wanted to kiss her with any depth of feeling, telling him not to be so daft. 'Pictures?' he offered, although he didn't really want to spend the money. He was going home on Sunday to see his stepmother and wanted to take her a gift. And there was the Dancing by Moonlight on the following Saturday. He had high hopes of the dancing.

Vera screwed up her nose. 'I don't think so. I promised one of the girls from the shop that we'd go dancing, so I'll want the afternoon to get ready.'

'All right. I don't mind dancing, it'll be a bit of practice for next Saturday.'

'I mean just her and me. A girls' evening.'

'Oh, I see. Well, all right, but don't forget the dance next Saturday. You're definitely coming to that one with me.'

'I'll be there,' she said gaily.

He watched the chess then went home. Vera had washed her hair and wore a new outfit, a very short skirt and a blouse with a low neck. Jealousy was hidden as he smiled and hoped she would have a good time. He sat with Mrs Denver and listened to the wireless, but he couldn't settle and at half-past eight went for a walk, his feet taking him to the school hall where the dance was being held. There were records being played and he heard the sound of Henry Hall's signature tune, 'It's Just the Time For Dancing', and wondered whether he could risk going in and claiming just one dance. He paid and went in.

As the music faded he saw Vera dancing with a soldier. He smiled and was about to go over and say hello when

176

there was a drum-roll and the compère announced the singer. Shirley Downs stepped on to the stage. With the aid of her stick she walked over to the piano and began to sing.

Her voice was powerful and utterly enchanting. No one moved as she sang, 'Embrace me, my sweet embraceable you.' Slowly, as the words wove themselves around his heart, Maldwyn turned his head to look at Vera. Surely she must be thinking of him. But she was moving her head too, and with a sinewy movement her body was wrapping itself closely around the soldier sitting next to her.

Tapping her feet, Shirley sang 'Mountain Greenery', and the mood changed. She softened it again with a rendering of 'I Get Along Without You Very Well', which filled Maldwyn with melancholy emotion. He left, to walk the streets, berating himself for being a fool. He had to accept that Vera thought nothing more of him than someone who was available when there was no one better. He passed the hall again as the crowd inside were singing the national anthem and he hurried home, unable to bear seeing Vera come out on the arm of her soldier.

But Vera didn't walk home with her soldier. She left the hall just before the last waltz was played.

Eirlys was light-hearted. The police had not returned and Ken was more affectionate, even loving. They had talked about the baby they were expecting in a few weeks and he had assured her he was as excited as she. He came home twice that week, told her exactly where he would be between visits and even gave her telephone numbers in case she had to call him. 'I know it's too early, but I want to know if you're worried, even if it's only a slight twinge of anxiety.' He even promised to delegate his Saturday plans and come with her to the moonlight dancing, even though she would only be a spectator.

The weather had turned chilly, and girls who had been excitedly looking forward to showing off their summer dresses for probably the last time were disappointed. Hand-knitted angora-wool boleros were popular and had been in use for several years. Many searched for them in drawers or borrowed

177

from friends, adding them to a dress and hoping the dancing would keep them warm.

No one wore stockings. With clothing coupons being far from generous they couldn't afford to buy them. Instead they bought packets of 'liquid stockings', a powder which was mixed to a paste and spread with a sponge over the legs. Some were lucky enough to have a friend who would draw a seam for them and a block on the heel to make them look more realistic.

Maldwyn looked at Vera sadly. She had dressed in the outfit she had worn to the previous Saturday dance, which revealed too many of her charms.

'Won't you be cold?' he asked stupidly. 'It's being held out of doors, remember.'

'If you think I'm covering this with a cardigan you're mistaken. Honestly, Maldwyn, you sound like my grandmother sometimes.' She straightened up to show him the blouse she had so carefully remodelled to show the titillating glimpses of her shapely figure. 'Don't you think I look nice?'

He didn't reply.

Fortunately the night was clear and the moon shone across the water like a golden path. Musicians who played by ear, without the need for music, had gathered and formed a small band. Everyone who came was determined that this final occasion would be fun, and at once the mood was set.

Half the town seemed to be there, the dancers spreading along the prom and even on to the sand below. Even Mrs Chapel came for a while, before the cold persuaded her back to her flat and the warm fire. Bernard Gregory came on his horse and cart, bringing Beth and promising to come back for her later. He sat beside Mrs Chapel and they watched as the lively couples danced. 'Pity we aren't a few years younger, eh?' he said, tilting his hat with its notebook tucked into the lining band, something he always carried. 'I've got some nice holly in the field; want to place an order for Christmas, Mrs Chapel?'

'A bit ahead of yourself, aren't you?' As he took out his notebook and a stubby pencil, she laughed. 'Go on then, put me down for what you've got, although I bet young Maldwyn will be walking along the lanes getting some for free. A bit of holly and ivy will be the only things we'll be able to rely on for tradition this Christmas, and that's for sure.'

'There'll be a few chickens and a rabbit or two. We'll celebrate with over-eating as usual, you see if we don't, even if it means there's nothing left in store.'

'D'you know, even now, with the shortage of so many foodstuffs, there's many a pantry where a few special tins are still hidden. Salmon, a bit of tinned fruit, a tin of cream, hiding there for when the boys come back. Never tempted to use it – birthdays, Christmases and even weddings, there it stays, waiting for the biggest celebration of them all, when this awful war ends and the boys come home.'

'What a party that'll be, eh? We might even join in the dancing ourselves that day, Mrs Chapel.'

Eirlys was too weary to enjoy dancing, but she found a place to sit, with a blanket around her knees and Ken's jacket around her shoulders for warmth, and watched the participants having a happy time. The musicians responded to requests; once or twice one started in a different key from the rest, but no one cared, or even noticed.

Madge was encouraged on to the floor by Constable Charlie Groves, who, after shuffling around the crowded area for three dances and sitting one out, shyly asked if he might walk her back to her hotel.

'Hotel?' she laughed, 'Nothing so grand. We're staying with a neighbour of Mr and Mrs Castle in Sidney Street.'

'Then I'll see you safely back there.'

She was about to refuse, but thought that with Delyth and Maldwyn, and probably Vera, it would do no harm. 'Thanks,' she said. 'I'd like that.'

When Ken left Eirlys and asked Delyth to dance she almost ran away. But he took her arm gently and waltzed her around the very edge of the dancers, smiling as he passed his wife before saying, 'Delyth, I want to apologise. I'm ashamed of the stupid way I behaved. I love my wife and the brief – friendship with another woman was a terrible mistake. I'm not a violent person and it was only fear of Eirlys being upset,

179

her expecting our child, that caused me to panic. I really am ashamed and very sorry.'

Doubtful at first and still nervous of him, Delyth allowed herself to be reassured. She smiled as they passed Eirlys for the second time and when the music stopped she found herself standing next to her.

'Everyone's talking about you, Eirlys,' she said, leaning to make herself heard over the conversations and the laughter as the band began another number. 'Everyone's saying how marvellous you are to have arranged all these events. You must work very hard.'

'Not any more,' Eirlys said. 'I've retired, at least for the time being.'

'You must be very proud of her,' she said to Ken, and Ken took his wife's hand, kissed it and said he was.

Maldwyn watched Vera, in the hope of managing at least one dance. She seemed determined to avoid him, taking a partner from the willing group surrounding her before he could reach her. He heard complaints about her uttered, the tarty way she was dressed, the way she pushed herself forward when she chose a partner. There was the usual shortage of men and she seemed to be taking more than her fair share.

As Delyth moved away from Ken and Eirlys, she touched his arm. 'Will I do instead, Maldwyn?'

'Oh, what do I say to that? You make it sound as though I'd consider you second-best.'

'Just dance,' she laughed, sliding with ease into his arms.

'Eirlys, you look happy,' Hannah said as she sat beside her. 'Is it because you've finished work at last?'

'Partly. I was getting very tired. But Ken has told me everything. It's all out in the open, and we're closer than we've been for a long time.'

'Really? I'm glad, and I think it's very brave and sensible of you to forget and start again. Life's too short to hold on to anger.'

'Hardly anger,' Eirys laughed.

'You aren't angry? Then you're a saint. If I heard that Johnny had been with someone like Janet Copp I'd break my heart.'

180

'Someone like—? What d'you mean?'

Hannah stared at her, begging for the words to come that would take away those she had just spoken. Obviously Ken hadn't told her everything. 'Sorry, Eirlys, I wasn't listening properly. Weren't you talking about the man from the shoe mender's who's been keeping his affair a secret for three years?'

'No,' Eirlys said slowly, 'I was talking about me and Ken, as you well know. You might as well tell me everything. I'll find out anyway, and it's better that you tell me. Come on,' she said as Hannah hesitated, the shock of her thoughtless remark clear on her gentle face. 'I need to know.'

'I know nothing about it. I just heard that he was suspected of being involved with some black-market food then was found to be innocent. He tried to keep it from you in case you worried. What else is there to know?' She pointed out the three boys, Stanley, Harold and little Percival, running through the dancers and being chased by Eirlys's father, in the hope of distracting her. Eirlys said no more but Hannah knew the damage had been done.

When the last waltz was being played, Maldwyn looked in vain for Vera. It was implicit in his invitation and her acceptance that they would walk home together. She seemed to have disappeared. Instead, he invited Delyth to dance at the same moment as Charlie Groves came for Madge.

The musicians packed away their instruments and a few people began to disperse, but suddenly someone began to sing and dance the 'Lambeth Walk', and at once the exodus stopped. Afterwards someone began to sing 'I'll See You in My Dreams', and almost immediately couples and groups of friends found places to sit, leaning on the sea wall or the shops or against each other, and the crowd settled for a sing-song that went on for another hour.

Charlie Groves told Madge where he lived and asked whether he could write to her. She shook her head. 'Perhaps in a while, when I've sorted things out in my head,' she said apologetically.

Eirlys didn't wait to find Ken. As soon as the strains of the last waltz faded away she joined her father and the three boys

181

and hurried home. When her father asked about Ken, she told him he had other things to do, and refused to explain.

Hand in hand, Madge, Delyth, Charlie and Maldwyn walked along the road, laughing as they remembered some of the events of the evening. Maldwyn forced gaiety into his voice and they sang their favourites, silenced to spluttering laughter when a bedroom window opened and a voice called for them to respect the Sabbath and shut their row. 'Half an hour to go yet,' Charlie shouted and they ran like foolish children, making their way through the dark and empty streets.

Maldwyn tried to put Vera from his mind and was relieved when Mrs Denver, who had waited up to make him a hot drink, told him she was already in bed. 'I tried to find her and bring her home but she was nowhere to be seen,' he protested when Mrs Denver accused him of not looking after her.

'Well, she's safe enough and fast asleep by now. No harm done.'

He knocked softly on her door as he went to bed but there was no reply. In her room the bed was neatly made up, and empty. The window was partly open and outside it a tree gave precarious access to the ground.

The soldier with whom she had danced so many times that evening had walked her home. He hoped for a few minutes of kisses but was disappointed. As soon as they had arrived at Mrs Denver's house she had thanked him, said good-night and gone inside. A few minutes of Mrs Denver's fussing and being persuaded to drink some hot cocoa and she made her excuses and went to bed. Turning the key in her bedroom door, she had made her escape and hurried to where another young man was waiting. His kisses were passionate and she responded with joy, the secrecy of their intimate association an added piquancy to the time they spent together.

Whether it was the excitement of the dance, or anticipation of the meeting, or the tension of climbing out of her bedroom window so late at night, which was something she hadn't done before, or whether her feelings for the man had changed from a bit of fun to the moment when another stage of their relationship had been reached, she later couldn't be sure. But she found herself wanting him desperately, her body

182

crying out for him. Their kisses became urgent and impatient. He pressed her against him, the sensation bringing an abandonment of common sense, blotting out the oft-repeated warnings. Thinking only of the moment, desire growing to an almost painful degree, she allowed herself to be led to a place where they could lie down and succumb to their need of each other.

It was a couple of hours later, as she was climbing back up the convenient tree and slipping in through the window, absolutely exhausted, that fear returned. What had she done? This was one of her father's worst fears, that one of his daughters would 'give in' to a man; yet the sensations left her in a haze of contentment. Worries were for another day. Now she could relax and relive the blissful joy of love. Fear of her father's anger drifted quickly away. In that magical moment, her body crying out for relief, the need for loving had been stronger than her fear of his heavy hands and the thrashing he had constantly threatened.

She lay, not sleeping, her body still trembling with the aftermath of love, floating in a soft, gentle world where there was no harshness, no decisions needing to be made, and wondered how much longer he wanted them to keep their love a secret.

Soon, he promised they would tell the world. He was exempt from conscription, although he didn't explain why and she was thankful he wouldn't be leaving her. But he *was* going to London, where a job awaited him. It was her dream come true, leaving Bryn Teg and St David's Well and going to live in London. It was the place to be if she wanted to start a career as a singer. Until then they would write, and she could join the band of women waiting for their man.

After searching unsuccessfully for Eirlys, Ken walked home. She was in bed, her face turned away from him, her body rigid and unwelcoming to his touch.

'Eirlys, tell me what's wrong and we can put it right. I don't know what to say to you. How can I, until you tell me what's wrong?'

'I want you to leave. Move out. Now. I want you out of here before Dadda and the boys are awake.'

'No!' he said simply. 'My home is here, with you, and here I'll stay. If you won't talk to me now, then we'll talk this through in the morning. I won't leave the house until we do.' He slid in beside her but they didn't touch, both almost leaning over opposite edges of the lonely bed.

The air of tension was something of which even the boys were aware. As it was Sunday there was no rush to get to school and they asked Morgan if he would take them through the fields to Mr Gregory's smallholding. They loved visiting the animals, especially walking on up to Sally Gough's field, where the donkeys were settling into their winter quarters.

Morgan took one look at his daughter's face and read the anger there. 'Hurry up then, lads. We'll go as soon as we've helped Eirlys with the dishes,' he said. 'We might be in time to see the chickens fed.' As well as his laying hens, Bernard Gregory had several dozen young cockerels, four months old and being fattened for the Christmas market. The boys had watched them from day-old chicks settled around broody hens and heated substitutes, and were fascinated by the way they were changing. 'Whether they'll still eat their Christmas dinner after treating them almost like pets is something I don't like to think about,' Morgan had whispered to Eirlys once or twice.

When the house was quiet, Ken asked, 'What is it, Eirlys? What's bothering you now?' His tone suggested she was being unreasonable, and even that it was part of a tedious pattern.

'Wrong? Don't you know?'

'Tell me, then we can sort it out.'

'Does the name Janet mean anything to you? You and Janet, having an affair like some sordid film story?'

'Who told you that?' he protested, glaring at her, about to deny it, but then his shoulders drooped and he nodded his head.

'Don't tell me it isn't true. It explains so much.'

'It isn't true. It was true but now it's over. It was a brief mistake and it's finished.'

184

'That it happened at all is enough. I want you to leave, Ken, and the sooner the better.'

'Why? I admit it, I made a stupid mistake, but I love you and only you, and I want us to stay together. I want to be here when our child is born and stay, watching him grow.' She waited, watching him and wondering if she could ever trust him again. 'It was because we were thrown together so much with the work we do – did. Janet isn't involved with my concerts any more. She's working for Naafi and has applied for an overseas posting.'

'So that's why you want to come back to me? Because she's no longer available?'

'No, Eirlys. I – we – finished it a while ago. Someone saw us as we were ending it, quarrelling and trying to sort out the mess we'd got ourselves into. Someone saw us, and that was when I realised how stupid I'd been; I knew in that moment where I belonged and who I really loved.'

'Fear of being caught out in your sordid affair made you run out on Janet and come back to me? That's supposed to make me feel better?'

'No. You're twisting everything I say. It was that day tripper who's become friendly with you and Beth and Hannah. Remember the drawing she showed you of two people quarrelling?'

'That was you and Janet? Then she knows!' She turned away from him, stood up and began banging saucepans about on the cooker, throwing vegetables into the bowl for peeling and generally acting the outraged woman. 'Who else has been talking about me, calling me a poor stupid woman who doesn't know what her husband is up to? Hannah knows. It was she who inadvertently told me. So how many others have guessed?'

'I'm so sorry, but no one else can actually know, and if we behave as though there's nothing wrong they'll all believe the story was nothing more than rumour. Let's face it, rumours usually are wrong.'

'I think I hate you.'

'I love you. I always have, in spite of all this. I love you and I want our marriage to be a success.'

185

She cried then and he held her in his arms until the outburst had subsided.

'One chance, darling Eirlys. We owe it to the baby to try again. I promise you'll never regret it.'

It was so easy to give in; there was so much at stake, not the least their child. How would she manage? Did she have the right to deprive a child of his father?

She went to talk to Hannah, who was distressed at her dreadful mistake and, somewhat hesitantly at first, Hannah talked about her first marriage.

'It wasn't just other women,' she said in her quiet voice. 'I ended up in hospital on several occasions and I feared for my life once or twice. And all the time my mother was insisting I stay with him, that a marriage was for ever and I had to obey the vows I had made in church. I had to defy my parents to leave him, and they still haven't forgiven me for the embarrassment I caused them. It's different with you and Ken. Love can get a bit battered around the edges in a stressful time like this, but I believe he loves you. I also believe that, however you feel at the moment, you still love him.'

Eirlys was sobbing as she walked home, but she wouldn't have been able to explain whether it was for the sad marriage of Hannah or for the difficulties she and Ken had built around themselves.

Mrs Chapel was not feeling well. 'Nothing serious,' she assured Maldwyn, 'but I think I'd like a few days away from the shop, so I can sleep late and be utterly lazy for a while. I get so tired these days.'

'You know I'll look after things here, so stay with your sister as long as you like. I'll write to tell you how things are; and I'll keep a journal for you to look at when you get back; and of course I'll bank the money every single evening, even if it's only a few shillings.'

'Thanks, Maldwyn. I'll go on Saturday, after we close the shop. Then when I get back we can start planning for the winter and you can take a few days off yourself. You haven't had a holiday since you started.'

'I don't need holidays. I love my job. It's great working

with you, learning from you. You've been really kind to me and I appreciate it.' He smiled as Mrs Chapel waved a hand energetically to push away his compliments. 'Now,' he said in a businesslike tone, 'is there anything you want me to do while you're away?'

On Saturday he walked with her to the station and carried her small case. 'I'm glad we had new locks on the doors,' he said. 'Otherwise I wouldn't be too happy about leaving the premises empty. I'd have asked if I could sleep there myself.'

'You and that Vera?' she asked wickedly.

'Mrs Chapel!' he laughed. 'Be'ave, will you? No, not Vera, she has other fish to fry. Fish in uniform, I believe,' he added sadly. Not being in uniform still made him feel ashamed.

'Don't forget there's a spare key with Mr Elliot,' she reminded him. 'And my sister has another if I lose mine.'

While Mrs Chapel was away he took the opportunity to do some tidying. He tried to strike a happy balance between his fastidiousness and Mrs Chapel's messiness, not wanting to irritate her by being over-zealous. The walls were given a fresh coat of whitewash and a few broken items discarded. The pots and containers he had collected ready for flower arrangements were stacked neatly on shelves and he knew that when she returned she would be pleased with his efforts.

Her intention had been to stay with her sister for three days, but a letter came on Tuesday to tell him she was still very tired and had seen a doctor.

Dear Maldwyn,
    The doctor thinks I might have a bit of a heart problem – nothing to worry about, but a little rest wouldn't do any harm. Gabriel is being very kind, spoiling me a bit, and my sister is enjoying my company. So, if you are sure you are managing all right, I'll stay another week.

He wrote straight back and told her to stay until she felt well, assuring her that the shop was doing fine and he was happy to manage alone. He enclosed the week's accounts and copied out the bank statements so she knew exactly what was happening, and also described the flowers he had bought and the new ideas he had for the winter displays, when flowers were so scarce and expensive.

She returned a week later, looking relaxed after her ten days away, and was glad to be home. She praised his efforts and coaxed him to take a few days off.

'Later perhaps, but there's no use you coming back rested then taking on the shop on your own and getting tired again. I don't think you ought to be up early to go to the market just yet. My stepmother has a few jobs she wants me to do, so I might go late on Saturday and come back Sunday. But no longer, not until you're back to normal.'

He called on Delyth while he was at his stepmother's house. She was pleased to see him and invited him in to listen to a couple of new records she had bought. She wanted to know all the news from St David's Well.

'It's very quiet now the season's finished,' he said. 'There's only the pictures or the dances, and I'm not much of a dancer.'

'You are, you dance well! At least I think so,' she added shyly.

'If you could stay at the house in Sidney Street again, you and Madge, we could go one Saturday night. If you'd like to that is.'

'Love to! And I think Madge would enjoy it. She's written to that policeman and I think he's rather smitten.' She grinned. The thought led her to ask, 'How's Vera?'

'She's hating working in a factory, where she has to cover up her hair and wear overalls, but she's making friends and seems happy enough. I suspect she's got a boyfriend but for some reason she won't let on who he is.'

Delyth smiled, and hoped her relief didn't show.

Maldwyn left her, happily thinking of taking her in his arms and dancing a slow waltz. It was a far from unpleasant prospect. When Winifred asked him why he was smiling later that evening, his smile only grew wider.

He caught the evening train back to St David's Well on Sunday, and arrived in the town at eight o'clock. Although

188

it was rather late for social calls, he went to see Mrs Chapel. He had been unhappy about leaving her alone.

As he walked along the street, he could see shards of glass on the pavement ahead. Quickening his pace, he found that the shop had been broken into and most of the stock destroyed.

Ten

The police investigating the break-in at Mrs Chapel's flower shop made it clear that they suspected Maldwyn. Leaving Mrs Chapel in the shop with nothing to sell and a huge mess to clear, they took him into the store-room, where every dried flower and leaf had been broken, every vase smashed, every bucket buckled, and questioned him.

'The incidents both here and involving Delyth Owen have all been when you were around, Mr Perkins, and you are the only one apart from Mrs Chapel with a key to this shop. I find it very difficult to consider a third person being involved. There's you, Mrs Chapel, and this mysterious person no one ever sees and who has managed to get himself a key. You do see my problem, don't you?'

'What about the key left with a neighbour in case of fire? The regulations insist on that, don't they, in case of incendiary bombs?' Maldwyn suggested, helpfully.

'That would be Mr Elliot next door. We've checked and it's still there.' He waited patiently for Maldwyn to offer more suggestions.

'Delyth thought the "incidents", as you call them, were due to her habit of drawing people and perhaps catching someone where they ought not to be. I've tried to make her believe they were connected with me and not her, so she'd be less afraid.'

'If you are responsible she has every reason to be afraid, Mr Perkins.'

'But I'm not!'

The detailed examination of the premises, particularly of the doors and their locks, went on, and when he told them where he had been over the weekend, they told him his alibi would be thoroughly checked as well.

'Alibi? What do I want with an alibi? You can't really believe I'd do all this? It's made a lot of extra work for Mrs Chapel and me to replace all that's been lost, and the containers we've collected over the past months ready for Christmas sales can't *be* replaced,' he said angrily. 'Why waste time investigating my movements instead of trying to find the person responsible?'

'Calm down, sir. We're doing everything we can but we have to eliminate the most – er – those closest to the crime.'

Maldwyn knew the officer had been about to say 'the most likely', and the fear shrank his insides in an unpleasant way. He could protest all he might but he was the main suspect. 'Go and see my stepmother and Delyth; they'll tell you where I was, and the porter on the station saw me coming home on Sunday.'

'We already have, sir. But St David's Well is only an hour or so away from your home. And the night is long.'

'It couldn't have been at night. The damage caused couldn't have been done without noise. Mrs Chapel would have heard.'

When they had gone, he went into the shop and persuaded Mrs Chapel to go upstairs and leave the clearing-up to him.

'I only went to church for the morning service. I wasn't out for more than an hour and when I came back—'

So why did they make me think it had happened during the night, when I could have conceivably been responsible? he wondered angrily. Trying to trip me up. That's why!

'You make us a cup of tea, Mrs Chapel, and I'll clear this lot, and first thing tomorrow morning I'll see what I can find at the market.'

'There'll be nothing much there on a Monday,' she said sadly.

'Mrs C, there'll be something in your windows tomorrow, even if it's a row of Mr Gregory's cabbages. Right?' Coaxing her to go back up to her flat, he began the task of clearing away the mess.

He worked until long past midnight and when he left Mrs Chapel was safely in bed, the doors were firmly locked and the shop was empty but ready for business. He had no idea who could have caused the damage, but had a suspicion that Mrs Chapel had forgotten to lock the door. Seeing the premises open, some opportunist idiot had walked in, had some 'fun' and managed not to be seen or heard.

This couldn't be connected with Delyth or with him. Surely there was no one who disliked him that much? To his knowledge he had never offended or hurt anyone badly enough for them to seek revenge in such a cowardly way. He was frowning as he walked through the dark and silent streets back to Mrs Denver's and slid the key into the lock. But he didn't turn it. Instead he withdrew it and returned to the shop. Leaving Mrs Chapel alone was something he couldn't do. Letting himself back into the silent shop, he curled up on the floor and slept restlessly till morning. At five he got up, afraid to go back to sleep in case he woke too late for market.

When Mrs Chapel woke, the shop was full of flowers and Maldwyn was whistling cheerfully as he filled the tall, battered containers with his purchases.

'Maldwyn, you're such a good friend,' she said emotionally. 'I'd never manage without you. It's all getting too much for me.'

Her words chilled him. If she were to give up and sell the business, he'd be out of a job, and he doubted whether he would ever find one he liked more. 'Come and sit here and serve while I go and make us a nice cuppa,' he said. While the kettle boiled on the small ring in the back room, he began to think about what the future held, and it made him sad.

He couldn't go back home. Winifred didn't want him there, even though no man had appeared so far to take his father's place. Vera had made it clear she was not interested in him. There was Delyth, of course. Her face appeared in the shadows of his mind and he began to weave his dreams around her. A shop of his own with Delyth as his partner. The future began to look more rosy and he was smiling as he handed Mrs Chapel her steaming cup and offered to go to the baker's to get them a cake.

*   *   *

192

Ken and Eirlys no longer slept in the same room. Eirlys made the excuse that being so ungainly, and having to get up several times each night to go to the lavatory, Ken wasn't getting his rest.

Morgan guessed that all was not well with his daughter's marriage, although he said nothing. He took the boys out whenever he could, giving Eirlys and Ken the chance to talk, but on several occasions Eirlys elected to go with them, preferring not to listen to the tedious repetitions of Ken's promises.

October was almost ended and the mornings were dark and rather cold. Her first task of each day was to light the fire but she came downstairs one morning to see it lit, and a kettle on the hob beginning to sing. She went into the kitchen, expecting to see her father there, but it was Ken.

'Oh, it's you,' she said ungraciously.

'Yes, it's me. Is that all you can say? Even the milklady gets a polite good-morning from you, but you're too self-righteous to give me anything more than a snarl. Well, you've won. As soon as the baby is born and arrangements have been made, I'll do what you ask and go. But remember this, Eirlys: you'll be on your own, and it might be for the rest of your life. You left me once before, convinced that Johnny Castle was your love. Then that ended. Now you're back with me and telling me to leave. Are you incapable of love?'

She set the table for breakfast, made some toast against the glowing fire and planned what she would give the family for the day's meals, but his words refused to leave her brain. They repeated themselves time and again. Could she love someone enough to forgive their mistakes? Was she even capable of inspiring a love that would allow them to forgive hers? Being efficient was one thing, but being convinced of her own perfection was another thing entirely.

When the boys went to school and her father left to put in a couple of hours on his allotment, she sat wondering whether she was too sure of herself. So sure that she had invented the illusion that she didn't need anyone else?

Looking into the future that dull, late-October afternoon, she could see a life of looking after her father as he grew older and less able, and caring for the boys and her own child until they found their own homes and produced their own families. She saw herself with a slowly fading role in their lives, leaving her with nothing but memories.

Even the job she loved might possibly end once the war had been won and the men came home. They had been promised jobs to come back to, and that meant her returning to her previous, less interesting role of supporting others while they did the work of which she was capable. It was time to think about love and life, and stop being locked in her own selfishness. But what could she do? She could hardly tell Ken she had changed her mind and expect everything to fall into place. They needed some catalyst, some event to make them both see whether their love was worth fighting for. But what?

'How did you know you loved Mam?' she asked her father when he came back from the allotment with a few early sprouts and a root of Welsh onions. 'How could you be sure?'

'I didn't want to be with anyone else. I was only really happy when she was happy, and, if I'm honest, I needed her to look after me, do all the things I couldn't do, and in return I did the things she needed help to do. I failed her though. My father had a good business which he left to me and I let it run down and down, so we lost the beautiful home we had, and she had to work, and I'm always ashamed of that.'

'She forgave you.'

'I don't think she ever really forgot what I had lost for us. If I'd been a better businessman we'd have been comfortably off, and she wouldn't have had to work in the bakery. She never stopped loving me though. I know that.' He was staring at her as they talked, wanting to say something useful, helpful, guessing the reason for the questions. 'Has Ken done something that makes you think he's stopped loving you?'

'He *has* stopped loving me. There was someone else, for a while. He tells me it's over, but I can't forget it.'

'Your mam managed to forgive me, remember, and we returned to the happiness I'd all but thrown away.'

She blushed at the reminder of her father's involvement

with Bleddyn Castle's first wife, who had committed suicide in the cold waters of the docks in a distant town. She shivered at the memory of that terrible time.

'Ken is here, isn't he?' Morgan went on. 'He might have been tempted but it's you he wants to stay with. This war has agitated and thrown aside so much we could once depend on, people dragged away from their homes instead of staying close to their families and all the security that gives.'

'The war's an excuse that's worn a bit thin if you ask me.' She sounded bitter.

'He must be tired and lonely at times, and there are girls who would deliberately set out to – you know.'

'This wasn't like that, Dadda. Not a momentary madness, sudden temptation. It's someone I know, and like.'

'You have to decide whether Ken's worth forgiving, and if so you have to accept what's happened and make up your mind not to throw it up at him every time you have a row. That will be the hardest thing, not to use it whenever you have a row.'

She hugged him and silently admired his common sense. But was she capable of being sensible at a time like this? The baby kicked, rubbing its foot across her belly as though trying to get out and join in the argument. He had to be considered in all this. She couldn't condemn him to a life without a father, and with an absentee mother who worked for most of her waking hours. So many children were already facing that deprivation.

In the gift shop, Hannah and Beth discussed the letters they had received. Hannah told Beth that Shirley had received several on one day from Freddy Clements.

'I had one as well.' Beth smiled. 'Oh, it's all right, Peter doesn't mind. He understands the need of men so far away to have news from home. Father-in-law writes to Freddy too.'

'I think Freddy's letters have cheered Shirley and helped her cope with her injuries,' Hannah said. 'He doesn't offer sympathy. Rather the reverse. According to Shirley, the closest he gets to sympathy is to tell her she needs to get strong again because when he gets home he's going to get seriously legless and will need her to carry him home!'

They were silent for a while, each thinking about their own men and the importance of their letters. Then Hannah told Beth about her unfortunate misunderstanding when she more or less told Eirlys about Ken and Janet's affair.

'When she said Ken had told her everything I took her at her word and presumed she knew about Janet. How could I have been so stupid?'

'Perhaps you weren't. Perhaps it's better to be honest and know what you're dealing with than have something simmering under the surface and Eirlys not knowing what it is.'

'Ken's a fool!'

'I agree with you there,' Beth smiled. 'It's strange; I have never once thought about Peter finding someone else.'

'Nor I with Johnny.'

'We're the lucky ones.'

Maldwyn came into the shop to buy a tea-cosy for Winifred. 'I burnt hers by standing it too close to the fire to keep warm,' he admitted.

'How's Vera? We don't see her these days,' Beth asked.

'Oh, off with some boyfriend when she can. I hardly see her either, and I live in the same house!'

Vera refused to tell anyone about the boyfriend she occasionally met. Maldwyn and Delyth presumed it was the soldier she had met at the dance, but she received no letters and no one saw her writing any.

Maldwyn saw much less of her now she was working in the engine-parts factory. She had to contend with shift work, although she didn't have to work nights: young girls were exempt from that. There were plenty of older women, and the few men who remained who were glad to earn the extra money it entailed.

The money was more than she had earned in Castle's Café, and she occasionally treated herself to some new clothes when she had the coupons, and sometimes when she did not. Several of her new workmates were willing to sell their clothing coupons for ten shillings and although this was illegal she took advantage of their need for money and spent happy hours wandering around the shops before deciding on how to spend her wages.

When she met her boyfriend she dressed smartly, whatever the weather dictated. But they didn't dance and they didn't often go to the pictures. Instead they walked around the parks – now devoid of their gates and railings, which had been collected for scrap metal – and sat close, whispering about how much they loved each other and how, once the war was over, they would marry and build a home.

He didn't want their love to be known until he was in London and settled in the job he said was waiting for him. 'Dad isn't too keen on my getting involved with anyone, says it isn't fair, so best he doesn't know. You can write to me, and we can tell everyone then,' he promised. 'I just want to wait until I've got a place for you.'

'I don't care what my father says. He's a bully, always thinking the worst of me and my sisters,' she said, and explained about his fears that she would end up 'doing something silly'.

'Like this?' he said, slowly lowering her to the ground and wrapping them both in his overcoat.

'Just like this,' she murmured against his lips.

Maldwyn persuaded Mrs Chapel to stay upstairs most of that Monday, and when she came down on Tuesday morning she looked refreshed and much brighter. While he went back to Mrs Denver's at lunchtime, she closed the shop and went up to the flat and made herself some tomatoes on toast, wishing she had asked him to stay. He really was very kind and she was well aware how fortunate she had been the day she had offered him a job. When the phone rang downstairs in the shop she sighed and hurried to answer it. Lunchtime or not, she didn't want to miss a sale.

She missed her footing on the bottom step and almost fell. By the time she had reached it, the phone had stopped ringing. She swore mildly and went back upstairs.

When it rang again an hour later, Maldwyn answered it.

197

'It's your sister, Mrs Chapel,' he called. 'She won't be long,' he said into the phone. 'She's out the back getting some foliage for a bouquet.'

'In the garden you mean? But it's raining. Why aren't you doing that?' the voice said angrily. 'Sending her out in this weather! I thought you were paid to save her from that sort of thing?'

'Mrs Chapel makes up her own mind, she won't listen to me,' he replied cheerfully, but he was puzzled by the sharpness of the woman's tone. He handed the phone to Mrs Chapel with a shrug.

'In the rain? What do you mean? There's a shelter out there, and anyway, I can't sit and watch Maldwyn do all the work when there's a lot to do. We work together, and thank goodness I've got him.' She looked at Maldwyn and mirrored his shrug. 'What's upset her?' she said as she replaced the receiver. 'She's never criticised you before.'

'I seem to be suspected by everyone lately,' he sighed. Then he asked something that had puzzled him from time to time. 'When your father died and you took over the business, was there any jealousy on your sister's part? I mean, why you and not her?'

'What business?' She smiled ruefully. 'He'd let it run down to almost nothing, and even the premises weren't his. They were rented and the rent was in arrears. There was absolutely nothing for us to to inherit except memories of a once-successful flower shop. My sister wasn't interested, so we shared the pieces of furniture, china, ornaments and things between us and that was about it. I applied for the tenancy, got it and started rebuilding the business. Dad had taught me a lot and I was a willing pupil. The rest I gradually picked up for myself, talking to other florists, listening to people in the wholesale market and reading books. You know, if you're interested you learn by enjoyment. Better than school, believe me!' she added with a smile.

'So it's all yours and there's no reason for your sister to resent it?'

'I bought the property. The mortgage was paid off a few years ago. Don't worry about it, young Maldwyn. She isn't

198

afraid of you stealing the family funds, if that's what you're thinking. I once said I would leave the whole lot to her Gabriel, and offered to train him, but he hasn't shown any interest. She'd probably had a bad day and was looking for someone to have a go at. She gets a lot of pain from her knees and can be a bit grumpy at times. But she's not really unpleasant. You'd like her.'

'I'm sure I would, Mrs Chapel.' But he still wondered whether her sister had entered the shop while Mrs Chapel was at church and shown her resentment in destructive rage. Anger didn't always need to be justified. She could get in – she had a spare key. But no, Mrs Chapel must have forgotten to lock the door, there was no other explanation.

The police returned a few days later but had nothing to report.

'What's puzzling us, Mr Perkins, is that no one heard anything. The work of throwing things around, and of pots and things being broken, couldn't have been done in silence, so why didn't anyone report a noise?'

'Have you asked Arnold Elliot next door? He lives on the premises and was probably at home.'

'We have interviewed Mr Elliot, and he told us there was so often noise from this place he wouldn't have taken much notice. Banging and shifting things around late at night and once on a Sunday, he said.'

As they were leaving, Maldwyn's mind returned to Arnold Elliot. He made no secret of the fact that he wanted the shop in order to extend his own. He was a person who would benefit by Maldwyn's leaving the town. Without him to help her, Mrs Chapel might not be able to run the business for much longer. He saw the policemen out but said nothing of his suspicions. Best he bear them in mind and keep an extra eye on the man.

Young newly-wed Alice Castle enjoyed looking after the two rooms in which she and Eynon would start their married life. She didn't feel lonely; she was saving and planning for when Eynon came home. He had gone back to his unit a few days after their wedding and was now in North Africa. She read the newspapers avidly and tried to follow the to-ing and fro-ing of Montgomery's determined battle for El Alamein.

When she read of casualties in the desert war, she had a way of dealing with it. She forced herself to visualise her husband running, fully equipped, approaching the victims, stopping to look down at them, then running on, unharmed. It was one of the many ways she had of coping with the dread of the telegram boy knocking at her door with the news of Eynon's death.

She had been sent to work in Vera's factory, and although the wages were better than she had earned in the sweets-and-seaside-rock shop on the promenade she still spent very little, putting money aside for when Eynon came home.

Putting aside the money she saved when she refused an invitation to the pictures, or managed without a fire for an hour or so longer, was another way of dealing with the minute-by-minute fears for his safety. She was one of the girls willing to sell her clothing coupons, buying second-hand garments and asking the patient Hannah to help her adjust them to fit. Everything was building towards Eynon's return and she told him so in her letters.

It was five o'clock in the morning and almost time to leave for the six-till-two shift. She put the empty milkbottle on the doorstep. No milk today. With the ration cut to two and a half pints per week, the half-pint bottle arrived on five mornings only. She had used some of her precious food points to buy some condensed milk and although it was over-sweet she drank a cup of tea sweetened and whitened with that.

She hated the early-morning shift. There was always the chance of a letter from Eynon and she would have to wait until she finished at two o'clock to know whether he'd written. Like Hannah, she always took the letter to the family and read passages that would interest or amuse them. That way they all enjoyed them and it seemed to make their loved ones closer, more in touch, by having more than the occasional letter themselves.

She walked into the factory with Vera Matthews that morning, Vera running up and getting in just in time to

200

clock on without losing a quarter of an hour's pay by being there even seconds after six o'clock.

'We're going to see a fortune teller on Wednesday, want to come?' she asked as they took off their coats and walked to the workbench.

'Who's "we"?' Alice asked. She was reluctant to make a friend of Vera, who seemed so bold.

'Me and Delyth and Madge. We're going to see that Sarah – the gypsy who has the tent on the beach in the summer.'

'I don't know . . .' Alice was thinking of the half-crown the woman was likely to charge them. 'No, but thanks for asking.'

'Please yourself.' Vera flounced off, shaking back long hair that would soon be pushed up into a snood for safety; there was also a hat, something she hated and considered unnecessary.

Alice collected her first box of engine parts, took the seat of someone who had just finished the night shift and started work without delay. It was piecework, paid by the number of items she completed, and she needed every penny for when Eynon came home.

The postman was popular in the Castle family that day. Hannah heard from Johnny; Marged and Alice both heard from Eynon. Much of his news had been obliterated by the heavy blue pencil so loved by the censor. But they were assured that all was well. That evening, letters were read out in Marged and Huw's living room and the contents, or those parts that were revealed, were discussed over cups of cocoa, made with condensed milk mixed with a spoonful of cocoa powder to which was added boiling water. For a while a sense of euphoria kept them happy. Their men had been well and safe when the letters were written; surely they must still be so? Illogical, but such a relief that for a few nights they were able to sleep.

Maldwyn was lucky too. He had a letter from Winifred telling him she hoped to see him home at Christmas. There was also one from Delyth, saying she and Madge were coming to St David's Well the following Wednesday and asking would he like to meet them. He wrote straight back telling them he would be at the station.

He put aside Winifred's letter. Christmas was a long way off, and who knew what would happen in two months? He half hoped to be invited to stay with Mrs Denver. He knew she hoped so too. She had been saving what special food she could buy, queuing for hours when a tin of salmon or fruit was on offer. Even with the points system these things were in short supply.

Perhaps Winifred could come to Mrs Denver's? It would mean moving a lot of furniture around again, to make room for her, but he thought his amiable landlady wouldn't mind – as long as his stepmother brought some rations!

Delyth hadn't mentioned their intention to see the fortune teller to Maldwyn. She thought he would think them silly. Having no concerns at all about what Maldwyn thought of her, Vera did. 'You coming with us then?' she asked, and explained about going to visit the wise gypsy who could see into the future.

'I think I'll give that a miss,' he said, and smiled as she teased him and accused him of being afraid.

Dressed in their smartest clothes, Delyth, Madge and Vera went to the dark, over-furnished house where Sarah lived. Maldwyn went with them but elected to stay outside. Life was full of mysteries and suspicions, and he didn't think she would solve any; it was more likely she would add a few more. 'Better to let tomorrow be a surprise,' he insisted. 'I don't think I want to know what's ahead. Knowing could make it harder to deal with.'

Calling him every kind of coward, laughing to conceal their own trepidation, the girls went in.

The woman, whose age they couldn't guess, was dressed in dark clothes and swathed in scarves. Jewels twinkled in the light of the candles that surrounded her, and her dark eyes watched them with amusement as they stepped into her consulting room.

'Together? Or separately?' she asked and they chorused, 'Together,' without the need to discuss it. There was such a weird atmosphere, the shadows dancing on the walls from the flickering candles so unnerving, that they sat as close together as the chairs allowed and leaned towards the table, glancing occasionally towards the door as though preparing for flight. Their hearts were beating faster than normal and in the semi-darkness even the faces of their friends looked strange and unrecognisable. Sarah knew how to set the scene and make a visit memorable.

Madge reached for Delyth's hand. Vera, who had joined them after her shift ended at two, seemed the least affected by the atmosphere built up by the clever woman.

Sarah talked to them about their lives, saying nothing to alarm them, flattering them, promising them all they desired. Then, as she stood to dismiss them, she said to Vera, 'Beauty isn't enough.' To Delyth she said, 'Talent in your hands will grow.' To a trembling Madge, she said softly, 'And you, my gentle lady, you have to learn to let go. Don't hold him, let him go free.'

Madge was sobbing when they were once more in the fresh air. Maldwyn came at once to comfort her, but she wasn't sad, just emotional and, she insisted, very glad she had decided to visit the 'All-seeing, All-knowing Sarah, the Gypsy King's Daughter'.

Inside, the heavily clothed woman looked troubled. She made it a habit never to worry people by what she saw, unless it was something that could be prevented. Sometimes she saw a problem in isolation, and revealing it could worry customers unnecessarily when another piece of the puzzle, unknown to her, was ready to drop into place and solve it.

Around Delyth, the talented one, she had sensed danger, but it was too nebulous to be of any use. Occasionally, another visit helped, but at other times you had to let the fates do what they will. She went out on to the pavement and beckoned to Delyth. 'Come and see me again – no fee – I might be able to help you further.' She went back inside and stood for a long time looking thoughtfully at the uncooperative crystal ball. 'If only my talents were greater,' she sighed.

It was only two thirty and Vera was hungry, having had no food since a break at ten thirty, when *Music While You Work* came on the wireless and got them all singing. They wandered through the town, buying some pasties with mysterious contents and stopping in a café for a piece of flat, fatless sponge optimistically called chocolate cake, and a pot of weak tea.

Eirlys was passing when they came out; she looked flushed and feverish.

'Are you all right?' Delyth asked. 'Can we do something for you?'

'I heard there were some broken biscuits for sale without needing to use food points and I wanted to get them for the boys,' Eirlys said.

'Go home and we'll get some,' Madge said. 'Tell us where to find you and we'll bring them, right?'

Eirlys thanked them and turned for home. She was feeling most odd and the pains that she'd felt for the last few days were becoming severe and beginning to worry her. It was too soon for it to be the baby and she was afraid something was wrong. She felt so weak she wondered whether she would get home without help. At a phone box she rang for a taxi and at the same time phoned her doctor. She would be all right, there was nothing wrong with the baby, she told herself, it was only reassurance she needed. How she wished her mother had lived. She wanted her so much it hurt. But greater than the need for her dead mother was a longing for Ken to appear, to tell her she would be all right, that he loved her and would always be there.

In the taxi she sat back and closed her eyes. She wanted Ken by her side, but was that love, or a need for the moment? She still doubted her ability to love, and Ken's words during that row worried her more and more. All she knew for certain was that at this moment she didn't want him to leave her. In a less emotional part of her mind she also knew that the way he dealt with the birth of their child, whether he was genuinely pleased and proud, or politely so, would decide their future. She didn't want him to stay out of a sense of duty and all the time wish he were somewhere else. He deserved better than that, she thought sadly: as much, if not more, than she did.

The taxi took her home and she sank gratefully on to the couch. Where was Ken? If only she'd had his itinerary on her, she could have left a message for him too. She felt the emptiness of the house closing around her, isolating her from everyone, enclosing her with this pain and the accompanying fear.

Half an hour later Vera, Delyth and Madge arrived, proudly carrying three bags of broken biscuits, the shopkeeper allowing one per customer. Smiling with an effort, Eirlys thanked them, then asked Vera to go to the phone box and leave a message with his parents to tell Ken he was needed.

Vera did so, and also spoke to the doctor's wife. She knew very little about babies and their birth, but she could see that this one was anxious to arrive and she didn't want to be involved in all that!

When she returned to the others, Eirlys was curling up with pain. They gave her sips of water, held her hand until they thought their fingers would be crushed and, in silent prayers, urged the doctor to hurry.

Ken was at a meeting at the ENSA headquarters in Drury Lane. He had contacts with up-and-coming singers and comedy acts and was arranging for them to be auditioned to join a concert party. Although he was a small-time organiser, he always encouraged those performers with talent to aim for better things, and whenever possible he helped them further their careers, even when it meant his losing a valuable act.

Today he had come to discuss Shirley Downs, and Janet. Talking about Janet wasn't easy for him. He knew that if he wanted to save his marriage and hold his child in his arms, he had to forget her. Before he did, he wanted to give her career as a singer a boost. Once the war ended she stood a chance of making a good living in the world of entertainment. She and Shirley had once been partners, so it was natural for him to discuss them both.

His father phoned the theatre and told him he was needed at home; he had no further information, just that Eirlys was unwell. He made his excuses, left details of how both girls could be contacted through Shirley, and hurried to the station.

An air-raid siren began to wail its warning and he tried to ignore it and run through the streets, pushing past those already making their way to the underground shelters. A warden stopped him and insisted he went with the rest. Impatiently he waited, pressed in with the others, and as the minutes passed he felt tempted to make for the doorway and run. Nothing was happening and he wanted to be with Eirlys.

The explosion briefly deafened him and as it cut out the lights he was blinded too. There was only his sense of smell, and even that suffered as his nostrils filled with dust and cement. He was choking in a silent darkness. As he began to recover, blinking rapidly to clear his eyes, there was a second explosion, followed by several more. A final blast rocked the shelter. A part of the roof caved in and there was a scramble as people were pulled away from the fallen masonry. No one had been seriously hurt and he heard murmurings as they were comforted. He covered his mouth and nose with a scarf and waited for what at that moment seemed to be certain death.

Torches flashed and lanterns were lit, and at once everything improved, hope revived. People wiped the dust from their eyes, smiled their relief at having survived and waited for freedom, trying not to think about what was happening at street level.

The rumbling and roaring of fires and more distant explosions went on for a while, then the thin, single note of the all-clear was heard and they trooped back out to see what damage had been done, many running towards their homes, afraid of what they would find there.

Ken hurried through the rubble-strewn street, but the scene that awaited him at the station was one of the devastation. A bomb had exploded, leaving a huge crater, and the trains that weren't damaged would not be able to leave. Ambulances were taking away the dead and injured and he was directed to a bus that would take passengers to the nearest station that had been undamaged by the raid.

At Paddington he was able to board a train, and, although it was crowded and he had to stand, he was taken without many delays to Bristol, where he had to change to the local train. It was there he was told that the trains were all delayed because of trouble further up the line. Impatient now to reach home, he went outside and thumbed a lift from a delivery van advertising utility furniture for newly-weds. The driver stopped and agreed to take him as far as he was able towards St David's Well.

After two miles the van lurched, and an examination showed that a tyre was flat. A lack of tools meant the puncture would take hours to fix. Ken thanked the man, apologised for not stopping to help and stood at the corner in the hope of another lift. Although the fear of invasion was past, there were still many unwilling to pick up a hitch-hiker in case they were helping a spy. After several vehicles passed him without stopping, he began to walk.

The doctor examined Eirlys and declared that she should be in hospital. The baby had turned and was lying breach, so it was likely to be a difficult birth. Maldwyn waited for Morgan and the boys, to tell them what had happened, and the three girls took a bus to the hospital and prepared to wait.

'I'm going to phone the corner shop and ask them to tell our parents we might not be home,' Delyth said. 'I don't want to leave until this is over, do you?'

'I've got work in the morning,' Vera said.

'So have we!' the other two chorused. 'But if Ken doesn't get back in time, Eirlys will need friends around her.'

Eirlys's father arrived, having left Maldwyn looking after the boys, and they all sat there with nothing to say, being frowned at by the staff, who hinted that they should go home and leave people to get on with their jobs, hints that were smilingly ignored.

'Where's Ken? Why hasn't he come?' Eirlys sobbed.

'He's not likely to be in here, is he?' the nurse said briskly, looking around the operating room with a disapproving frown. 'He'll be in the waiting room. I'll send someone to look for him when we have you settled ready for the surgeon.'

'Surgeon?'

'I'm afraid you have to have a Caesarean section, Mrs Ward. Don't worry, we'll just need to empty your stomach first. Now, try to swallow this tube for me.'

Ken was hurrying along the dark country road, stopping

hopefully every time he heard a car approaching. None of them stopped. He should have stayed at the corner, where he could be seen, or even stayed to help the van driver change the wheel. Perhaps he would catch him up. He stared back along the empty road, briefly encouraged, then his shoulders drooped; he would be ages yet. No one else would stop for him out here. They would be past before they saw him.

The drone of a large engine was heard; it sounded as though it was going slowly. It had to be his best chance. He stood in the road and waved his arms frantically. The driver stopped and leaned out of his window to ask what was wrong.

'My wife's having a baby and I want to get to the hospital,' Ken said.

The driver grinned, his teeth showing brightly in the darkness. 'I'll get you there, lad, but first I have to go behind a hedge. I drank too much tea at my last stop.' He jumped down and went across the road to where a break in the hedge offered a chance of privacy.

Ken stood in the road a few yards away, impatient to be off. As the driver walked back he stopped to light a cigarette. Unaware of anything except the man's irritating delay, Ken called him and, when he didn't move, started pulling him towards the truck. Until it was almost upon them, they didn't see the car that came speeding towards them. The lorry driver threw himself back towards the hedge. Too late, Ken tried to follow him and he was spun into the air, falling close to where the shocked driver lay. The car slowed, then picked up speed and quickly disappeared.

When the operation was over and Eirlys was recovering, Delyth, Madge and Vera hugged themselves, considering themselves a part of the happy occasion.

'If only she could wake up to find Ken here,' Delyth sighed.

'He'll be on his way,' Morgan said, more to convince himself than them. 'She wasn't even sure where he was. It might have been Scotland! He'll come as soon as he can.'

208

As Eirlys opened her eyes and looked at her baby being proudly held by the nurse before being placed in her arms, she had no idea that Ken was lying unconscious in the same hospital.

Eleven

Maldwyn settled the boys, providing toast and cocoa and a bag of biscuits that Percival had found in the pantry, supervised teeth-cleaning and sent them to bed. Percival insisted he would never sleep unless he was read to. 'I'm bovered by nightmares, blood and daggers and—'

'All right.' Maldwyn capitulated before he was given a more detailed précis of Percival's imagination, and read a couple of chapters of *Three Men in a Boat*, which Percival didn't quite approve of but which sent his brothers into paroxysms of laughter. 'I'm going to ask Uncle Morgan for a dog and I'm calling it Montmorency,' he announced before falling asleep.

Maldwyn sat in the chair and tried to stay awake, expecting any moment for either Ken or Morgan Price to walk in. But eventually he dozed, and woke confused at six a.m., wondering where he was and why he was there. He hadn't realised that it was a knock on the door that had woken him and when a second knock came he went to answer it, expecting to see one of the men, complaining about a mislaid key. It was the police.

'Not again? Are you following me around?' Maldwyn gasped. 'What am I suspected of now!'

'You? What are you doing here?' Constable Charlie Grove asked. He checked his notebook and asked, 'Does a Mr Ken Ward, or a Mr Morgan Price live here?'

'They both do, but Morgan is in the hospital with his daughter, who's having a baby. I don't know where Ken is.'

'We do. He's in hospital, and I'm looking for his father-in-law to tell him what's happened. What are you doing here? I thought you lived with Mrs Denver in Queen Street.'

Maldwyn explained the events of the previous day and ended by saying, 'The last I heard, Morgan Price is at the hospital.

Delyth and Madge were there too. Perhaps you should see if they're still there? I'm sure Madge will be pleased to see you, eh?'

Charlie smiled and nodded. 'Good idea. I can always tell my sergeant I was acting on information.'

When Ken came round he tried to ask what had happened to his wife, but his thoughts wouldn't gel, his mouth was unable to form the words. He was soothed and reassured and he slept normally without rousing sufficiently to understand what was happening.

Charlie found three sleepy people still in the waiting room. Vera had gone to work, unwilling to miss a shift unnecessarily, leaving the two girls and Morgan waiting for news. A nurse had come several times to tell them to leave, but each time they were propped against each other sleeping peacefully and she hadn't disturbed them. Charlie shook Morgan awake. 'Looking everywhere for you, I've been. Congratulations on your grandson, Mr Price.'

'All we have to do now is find Ken Ward and everything will be fine,' Delyth said sleepily.

'He's found. Unfortunately he's in another ward. Had a bad accident, he did, knocked over by a car, and the doctors are trying to decide which of them to tell first – Ken about his baby, or Eirlys about her husband.'

It was Morgan who broke the news to his daughter, and only a few minutes later Ken woke, fully *compos mentis*, and asked about Eirlys. After the doctors had examined him again, and dealt with a broken arm and a badly bruised head and body, he was wheeled in to see his wife and their son.

He leaned over, looked at the sleeping child and burst into tears.

'He's beautiful. You're beautiful. Oh, Eirlys, you're wonderful. I'm so lucky. I love you, my darling girl, I love you both, so much.' He reached out awkwardly and hugged her and together they stared down at their son, Ken trying to stifle his sobs and Eirlys wondering when she had ever been so happy.

Delyth and Madge were escorted to the railway station by Charlie. They got on the train and fell asleep at once, almost missing their stop. When they went to the shop – nothing further had happened about the threat to send them to more important work – and began to explain the reason they were so late, their boss took one look at their tired faces and told them to go home.

During the next few days, Eirlys had several visitors. Two at a time was the strict rule, but the boys found a window near her and stood there smiling and blowing kisses to the baby they had yet to meet, until they were chased away.

Her father came, and Maldwyn, who shyly handed her a beautifully arranged bouquet of chrysanthemums from himself and Mrs Chapel then hurried away, embarrassed at the sight of all the young women in bed with babies at their sides. Several members of the Castle family called with gifts, including Beth and Hannah.

When Matron relented and allowed the three boys in to see the baby, Stanley and Harold marched in and leaned over the cot in delight, making coochy-coo noises like veterans. Percival held back, standing beyond the next bed, afraid to look at the tiny child.

'Percival? Don't you want to see him?' Eirlys asked gently.

'He might not like me,' he muttered.

'Of course he will. You'll be like a big brother to him, someone to look after him and love him, just as I love you. Come here.' She held out her arms and he ran to her, hiding his face, ashamed of wanting to cry. 'I'll look after him for you,' he whispered. 'But I'll be glad when he ain't so small.'

Vera walked through the town soon after two o'clock and saw Maldwyn busily washing the windows of the florist's, whistling cheerfully. 'How d'you do it, Mal? Why aren't you dragging yourself about like me? Perhaps you had more sleep than me!'

'I probably did. I was woken first thing by the police and I thought they'd come to arrest me, thinking I was in hiding or something,' he laughed. 'Fancy the pictures tonight?'

212

'Not likely. I have to be up at five and the way I feel now I could sleep straight through until then.'

At the corner of Queen Street her boyfriend was waiting, and instead of sleeping she checked that Mrs Denver was out on one of her endless shopping trips then led him inside through the back lane. She wasn't sure what time he left, as she was deeply asleep.

Many letters from St David's Well during those weeks included the story about the dramatic birth of Anthony Kenneth Ward. The news that Ken had recovered from his accident was another episode to the story and news of the infant's progress filled many paragraphs. Good news was welcomed, no matter whom it concerned.

Ken was overwhelmed with love for his son, and his feelings for Eirlys were stronger than they had ever been. The baby's helplessness was appealing and brought out a strong desire to protect him from any harm. He was proud that, although helpless and utterly dependent, the child managed to get what he wanted. He would screw up his little face and protest loudly when things were not to his liking and Ken would hold him and talk to him, utterly enchanted.

There was other good news too. In November 1942 church bells rang for the first time since 1940. No longer a warning of invasion, they were a celebration of the success of Mongomery and the Allies in the final battle for El Alamein, a battle that had raged for several months. For those in the know, there was still a very long way to go. But for many the sound of the church bells gave hope.

Christmas came and went, and 1943 offered little change to the tedious routines of most women. Many were dashing about practically every hour of the day, trying to fit in everything they had to do. More and more women found work; they would look after a friend's children so that friend could work, then hand over their own children to the same friend so they could do their own hours of work, in factories or stores or sometimes in an office. Washing, cooking, cleaning and shopping had to be fitted in when there was a moment to spare. Everyone was exhausted. Their only consolation was their escape from the air raids suffered by the larger towns and the south-east of England.

Beth looked up one Tuesday afternoon to see Janet standing there, smiling and asking for a cup of tea. 'And I hope it's as good as I used to make,' she said, laughing at Beth's surprised face.

'I doubt that,' Beth replied. 'I have to get so many more cups out of every packet, it doesn't have much colour or taste by the time I close.'

'Don't bother to explain. I work for the Naafi and you wouldn't believe how many cups we have to get from two ounces of tealeaves!'

'What are you doing home? How long have you got?' Beth asked a stream of questions as she served a queue of patient customers, many of whom recognised the previous owner and stopped for a brief chat.

'I'm only here for two days, and there's something I want to discuss with you,' Janet said.

When the market closed the two young women went back to Mr Gregory's smallholding, and after eating Janet and Beth stood outside in the cold darkness while Mr Gregory fed the dogs and cats, and Janet put forward a proposition. 'I want to sell the café. At least the business – the property isn't mine to sell, as you know. What d'you think?'

'I'll be sorry if I have to leave,' Beth said, quickly wondering where she could find a job until May, when she could return to the work she had always done, in Castle's Café on St David's Well Bay.

'Why leave?' Janet asked. 'Why not buy it yourself? You've run it successfully all this time; it wouldn't be much of a change except you'd keep all the profit.'

'I don't think I'd be able to raise the money,' Beth replied, but her face shone with excitement.

'Are you sure?'

'Perhaps I could borrow from the bank. Maybe Mam and Dad might help.'

'Or me,' her father-in-law said as he joined them, taking his ever-present notebook from the inside band of his old trilby.

He led them back indoors and with his stubby pencil made notes and eventually agreed on a price.

Ken didn't stay away from home so frequently since the arrival of baby Anthony. He delegated whenever he could and found people in various places to act on his behalf. If only they could have a phone installed he would cope much better, but that seemed to be an impossibility, although he wondered sometimes whether the phone company enjoyed making people wait.

He continued to be thrilled with his baby son and wrote long letters to his parents describing his progress. He and Eirlys were happy too, sharing the joy of their child. There were moments when he thought of Janet, but even the best memories couldn't compete with what he now felt for Eirlys and his son. 'It's like I've been reborn,' he told Eirlys affectionately.

He hadn't contacted Janet since she had been posted to the training camp and presumed she was already overseas, so he was stunned to bump into her as she was leaving the gift shop on Wednesday afternoon. The shop was closed for business but he could see Hannah and Beth inside, busily sewing, and they had been joined by Delyth and Madge, refusing to abandon their day trips in spite of the cold, dark weather.

'Janet!' he gasped. 'I thought you were far away. What are you doing home?' He looked uneasily at the four women watching from inside the shop.

'Selling the café business and saying my goodbyes to St D,' she said sadly. 'There's no place for me here, not any more.'

'I'm sorry. I feel guilty, letting you down after all the dreams we had.'

'Don't be sorry, Ken, your decision was the right one. Is the baby all right?'

'He's wonderful. Already trying to lift his head, and I'm sure he smiles at me.'

She laughed then. 'You're just like all the other proud dads. Only one perfect baby, and every father has him.'

They moved away from the shop; Ken was trying to work out what to say to Eirlys. Perhaps nothing. It was obvious they

215

had met by chance and not by arrangement, and surely the four women wouldn't say otherwise?

At the corner of the street, Eirlys stopped pushing the pram and stood watching them. She turned, went home and sat waiting for him to come in, then waiting some more, for him to tell her about meeting Janet, but he did not.

The local Red Cross had arranged a concert in aid of parcels for prisoners of war and Janet and Shirley Downs were singing. She and Ken had been invited and her father had promised to look after the baby for the hour and a half she would be out. Unable to face meeting Janet, and unwilling to tell Ken he had been seen talking to her, Eirlys left the concert early; Ken left with her.

'What is it, love? Are you feeling all right?'

'I'm fine,' she said sharply. 'And what about you?'

'You're in a funny mood. Was it seeing Janet?'

'Not this evening, no,' she replied enigmatically. Ken shrugged and tried to put her arm through his but she resisted and they walked the rest of the way in silence.

The next morning she made an appointment to see her ex-boss and before she kept it she called on Alice Castle.

That evening she was so angry and upset that there was no need for Percival's urging for her to make sure all the lumps were out of the mashed potatoes; she almost beat them to a pulp. After they had eaten, she told Ken she was going back to work part-time as soon as the baby was changed to bottle-feeding, leaving him part of the time with Alice and part of the time with Hannah.

Ken was furious, and demanded to know why. She didn't explain, except to say she wanted to. How could she tell him she was alarmingly insecure? How could she put into words her conviction that one day, sooner or later, he would leave them, and she needed to be sure she could earn the money to look after herself and Anthony?

With no explanations or even accusations, they began slowly to drift apart once again. Someone told Ken that women sometimes became unreasonable after they'd had a child, and he wondered if that were Eirlys's problem and how long it was likely to last. There was also the dread that she would take Anthony away from him; he loved him so much. If they separated, the baby would have to stay with his mother, and Ken wasn't sure how he would cope with such a loss.

The flower shop was quiet during the early part of the year. What flowers were available were expensive, and things wouldn't change until the arrival of spring. Flowers for graves were almost a thing of the past, as most people were too anxious about the living. The recently bereaved had no graves to attend. Post was a daily hope, telegrams a daily dread.

Maldwyn did extra work for Mrs Chapel, painting walls and repairing shelves and the outside work area. He was worried about her. She became tired more easily and was leaving more and more of the decisions to him. When he opened the shop after a lunch break one day and found several displays of flowers cut into pieces, she did no more than sigh and reach for a brush to clear the mess.

Maldwyn said he would talk to the police again, but she shook her head. 'Whoever's doing this will get bored eventually.'

Mr Elliot called as the broken flowers were being cleared away, asked for an explanation and offered sympathy. Maldwyn was suspicious. Was the man there to gloat? He knew he had a key. He imparted his suspicions to Charlie Groves, but with little hope of an outcome.

Unable to accept her mother's new husband, Delyth was dreading the marriage, feeling uneasy about Trevor Gronow moving in and sharing her mother's bedroom. It was embarrassing and didn't seem right, although she knew she was being selfish by begrudging her mother a happy life.

Like all wartime weddings it would be a meagre occasion with no great spread, no beautiful dress and no honeymoon. Instead, the neighbours had all promised to contribute something and join the couple for a knees-up in the Owens' house. In an attempt to please her, Mrs Owen told Delyth she could invite as many friends as she wanted, and at once she wrote to Maldwyn and Mrs Chapel. She also invited Hannah and the children, Beth and Peter if he were home, and as many of the Castle clan as she could think of. Madge's parents next door agreed that their house should be included as part of the venue and to accommodate the guests, and everyone looked forward to a good afternoon and evening.

The train was unusually crowded as friends made their way to the wedding. The Castles couldn't use the firm's van: driving for pleasure was no longer allowed, and in any case the van would not accommodate many, so they all took the train.

As they spilled out of the train at Bryn Teg, the mood was already set for enjoyment. They were met by Delyth and Madge and led to the church where the ceremony was to take place. Maldwyn took Delyth's hand and walked with her, but he was uneasy, looking around as though expecting some trouble to emerge out of the quiet streets and threaten her.

When they went back to the house, Maldwyn sat beside his stepmother and took the opportunity of her mood, after sipping a few glasses of port, to ask why she had sent him away.

'I promised your Dad, Maldwyn, and it was the hardest thing I've ever done, believe me,' Winifred told him. 'I miss you, son.'

'Why?' he insisted.

'He was afraid you'd stay in the flower shop until old Mr Jolly died, then have to leave once his daughter took over, and drift into something else. He thought you'd make more of your life if you left home and had to look after yourself.' She touched his arm and smiled sadly, morbid with the unaccustomed effect of alcohol. 'I'm sorry, son.'

'I'm not. Dad was right. I've been so lucky working for Mrs Chapel. She's taught me more than I'd ever have learned from Mr Jolly. I'm well looked after by Mrs Denver and I've made some good friends.'

'I'm sorry,' she said again, not having taken his words in. 'Now's a good time to come back, mind. The Jollys' flower shop is for sale and perhaps you could get one of them mortgages?'

It was tempting. Living back home and close to Delyth seemed a perfect base on which to plan his future, but he knew he would miss St David's Well and the happy summers on the sands. He also knew he couldn't let Mrs Chapel down. She relied on him and he owed her a lot. He wondered how

Delyth would feel about leaving and coming to live there with him.

While everyone danced, he went to find Delyth. They sat alone in the back kitchen of Madge's house and talked. Without committing himself, he discussed owning his own shop, either in Bryn Teg or in St David's Well. Maldwyn held back from asking how she felt about working with him. He wasn't sure what would happen to his job when Mrs Chapel retired, and he needed to be secure before telling her how important she was to his plans.

The atmosphere – the crowd all intent on making it a day to remember – the unaccustomed drink and the fact that they were alone all contributed to a sensation of deepening love. Their talk became affectionate and the kiss when it came startled them both with its intensity. Maldwyn held her tight and knew that she was the one he loved and wanted to be with for the rest of his life. Delyth knew that the impossible had happened – he had forgotten Vera and was choosing her.

Then a screech of brakes outside, as a lorry pulled up to avoid a dog, brought Maldwyn's mind back to reality and he moved away from her. She was still in danger by associating with him. There had been no explanation of the attacks and whoever was responsible was still out there. He said goodbye to the new Mrs Trevor Gronow and left long before the party was over, using the excuse that Mrs Chapel was tired and needed to get home.

Delyth was devastated. So close and loving, sharing kisses that filled her body with warm desire, then walking away as though she meant nothing to him? Why had he done that? Was he afraid she would cling to him and demand what he couldn't give? Was he still thinking of Vera, who couldn't come today because she was feeling unwell? Perhaps he was hurrying back to make sure Vera was all right and had been amusing himself with her, affected by the romance of the moment, nothing more than that.

She freshened her make-up and forced herself to go into the front room and dance with one of her mother's friends to the recording of 'Begin the Beguine' played by Joe Loss's band. Later she joined enthusiastically in all the crazy party dances, like Hands, Knees and Bumps-a-Daisy and the Conga, in and out of neighbours' houses with the rest. No one would know how hurt she felt. The last thing she wanted was sympathy.

On Monday morning, Maldwyn picked up the van and went to the early-morning fruit and vegetable market to see what flowers he could find. There were very few. The weather was holding back deliveries and there wasn't much to deliver anyway. He settled for some rushes, which he planned to dye, and a few dried grasses. It would be paper flowers again to fill the window, and yet more painted fir cones fastened to yet more branches.

Whistling cheerfully, he went into the shop and called up, 'Fancy a cuppa, Mrs Chapel?' When her croaky voice answered, he ran up the stairs, knocked on her door and went in. 'What's up? Got a cold, have we?'

'I don't feel well enough to come down this morning, Maldwyn,' she said.

'Don't worry, I'll get the doctor, and while we're waiting I'll make you a hot drink. Pity we can't get a lemon, damn old Hitler, eh? Winifred swears by lemons. I'll dig in your pantry for a tin of soup later. That'll warm you, and you have to eat.'

He ran back downstairs, still whistling to hide his alarm. She seemed to have shrunk, and her face had lost its roundness. While he waited for the doctor to arrive he busied himself filling the window and running up and down asking her for suggestions, telling her what he was doing, to make sure she was drinking the hot tea he'd made and was warm enough.

While Maldwyn was looking after Mrs Chapel, Mrs Denver was attending to Vera. Maldwyn knew she was feeling ill, but privately presumed it was what many now called 'skiving'. He was unaware that Mrs Denver was up and down stairs, taking Aspros and hot drinks, using up all her milk ration, and most of her butter too, trying to coax the girl to take some nourishment.

Mrs Denver had her suspicions about Vera's condition and wondered vaguely whether Maldwyn was responsible, or if it was the unknown soldier Vera was dating. She also wondered whether Vera knew and if she should tell her.

220

She decided to wait awhile, in case her suspicions were wrong.

Delyth talked to Madge about the sudden change in Maldwyn, just when they seemed to be getting close. 'It was as though he'd just remembered something and moved away from me as though it was wrong. Vera, I expect,' she sighed. 'But it seemed so good – why did he act as though he really liked me then change so suddenly?'

'Go and see him. He might have an explanation. It could be to do with those threats. We can still go on Wednesday afternoon. There's no law that says we have to stop when the weather turns to ice and snow. And there's no reason we can't call at Mrs Denver's and ask to see Vera. Maldwyn is bound to be there.'

On Wednesday, wrapped warmly in thick coats, fur-lined boots, scarves, gloves and hats, they set off as soon as the shop closed at one o'clock. Delyth was still undecided on whether or not to go to Mrs Denver's. If Maldwyn didn't want to see her it could be embarrassing for both of them.

Mrs Denver told them that Vera was at work and Maldwyn was still at the flower shop. 'Seems poor Mrs Chapel isn't well and he's staying awhile to make sure she's all right,' she told them.

Maldwyn opened the door to them and they went inside. Delyth didn't know what to say, and Madge didn't know whether to go or stay. Maldwyn took them up to see Mrs Chapel, who was improving; she was sitting up beside a roaring fire, her face aglow and her eyes brighter. 'Visitors. There's lovely,' she exclaimed. The awkward few moments were eased by her obvious delight at seeing them. They sat drinking tea and talking about the wedding, and told her some stories about their customers that they knew would amuse her.

As they stood to go, there was a knock at the door and Mrs Chapel said, 'More visitors? I'll have to be ill more often!' Delyth noticed a frown crossing the old lady's face when the voices below were heard raised in anger. 'Oh dear, it sounds like my nephew, Gabriel,' she whispered conspiratorially. 'A bit of a grump, he is, between you and

221

me. Thank goodness Maldwyn's here. He'll sort him out for me.'

When the man walked in, Delyth had a feeling she had seen him before, but although she searched through her brain for the memory, it refused to come. It was something about the shoulders, uneven in height, making his head unbalanced and at an odd angle.

'Why wasn't Mam told you were ill?' he demanded. 'Maldwyn should have written.'

'He would have if I'd wanted him to. Now, Gabriel dear, it's nice to see you, but the doctor said I have to rest in the afternoons, didn't he Maldwyn?'

Gabriel stood, aggressively refusing to go, insisting he wanted to talk to his auntie alone. But eventually he was persuaded to leave. Outside, he stood beside an old Austin van, its back doors wide open, and looked up at the window with an angry stare.

When Delyth, Madge and Maldwyn left a few minutes later, he was still there. Ignoring him, Delyth glanced inside the van and saw a pair of cut-down wellingtons. Then she remembered. There was something about the way he held his head, tilting it slightly to one side. He was the man on the boat with the broken mast. She turned and looked at him, and he saw recognition and fear in her eyes. He smiled and slammed the door closed. As they walked away she knew, without turning around again, that he was still watching her, and she was afraid.

'It's him, I'm almost sure—' Then she stopped. Better to forget it, or she could be starting something she'd regret. Thoughts of the police, the questioning, giving evidence in a court, the possibility she had made a mistake, all this crowded in on her and she said nothing. She confided her fears to Madge as they were on their way home.

Delyth refused to leave the house apart from the hours she was in the clothing shop. As she walked to and from the shop she nervously waited for the sound or sight of a van, expecting to hear the revving of an engine and see a vehicle being aimed directly at her. If the street was empty she still imagined Mrs Chapel's nephew there, watching, waiting for a chance to harm her.

She wrote to Maldwyn, telling him of her belief that Gabriel had been the man in the boat involved with the theft of illegal food. But she tore it up before posting it. She could have been mistaken. Seen from above, the man was bound to look a little off balance, and it could also have been because of the way he was standing, looking around the bend in the shoreline as he made for the cave.

Anthony Kenneth Ward was an easy baby, and Eirlys coped very well with the addition to her family. She kept busy to stop her mind straying to the feeling of failure she felt. When Ken was in the house, she polished and scrubbed and everything was shining brightly – except her spirits.

One morning, while her father was at the allotment and the boys were in school, Ken asked her to explain, although he thought he knew.

'You saw me talking to Janet, didn't you?' he said, and his voice was gritty with tension. 'It wasn't arranged. She didn't come back to see me, she came back to arrange for the sale of the café and we met by accident. By *accident*!' he insisted angrily.

'Yes, I saw you,' she said, rubbing furiously at the sideboard with a polishing cloth.

Neither heard Morgan walk through in his stockinged feet, having left his muddy boots at the door. He stopped before entering the room, not wanting to listen but caught in a situation from which he couldn't escape. If he called to let them know he was there he couldn't prevent them knowing he'd heard enough.

'It's over, Eirlys,' Ken went on, and the words chilled Morgan and brought him almost to tears. He knew that sharing a house with himself and the three boys had added to the problems of their marriage. 'I want you and our baby.' Ken's voice was still harsh with suppressed emotion. 'But if you can't trust me ever again, well, I'm not going to live like this for the rest of my life.'

'What d'you mean?' She looked at him, loving him, the thought of losing him making her suspicions fade.

'I want to end it now. There's no point dragging it on.' Not

223

giving her a chance to respond, he turned and went out, bumping into a stricken Morgan in the doorway. Morgan stumbled into the living room, snatched the duster from Eirlys's hand and said, 'Go after him. Now!'

Hardly aware of seeing her father she ran out and, after a few more exchanges, Morgan saw them embrace. 'Stubborn girl, just like her mother,' he sighed. He went back to the allotment to give them time to talk.

'I feel so insecure,' Eirlys said to Ken.

'I can't help you. That's something you'll have to deal with yourself.'

'I love you; I want us to stay together.'

'Do you love me enough to forget Janet?'

She nodded. 'It's not much of a love if I can't, is it?'

He put his arms around her and they walked back to the house as Morgan scuttled off through the back gate. He was whistling cheerfully.

Alice went to visit her father every week, but he seemed less and less able to talk to her. She realised that he no longer knew who she was. He would jump in alarm when she leaned over and kissed his cheek, and when she said, 'Hello, Dadda,' he would repeat the words several times, as though they had some pleasing memory for him.

When she had a visit from one of the staff to tell her he had died, she was enveloped in sadness. Regret for the years he had lost since the injury he had suffered in the ring made his death more poignant. That blow had restricted his life to bare existence, and turned him into a stranger.

Eirlys and the baby went with her to collect his belongings, a small suitcase and a sad little bundle which they tucked in Anthony's pram. Insurance covered the funeral expenses and there was little more to do, no one to inform. She and Colin Potter had been alone in the world.

They went back to the two rooms Alice rented. Eirlys put the kettle on for tea while Alice unpacked the few belongings her father had left. 'The clothes will go to the Red Cross, they're all quite new. Besides those, I don't suppose there's much else. A few photographs, perhaps.' She slowly opened the bundle wrapped in a piece of blanket, and revealed a metal box that was firmly locked. It had her name printed on a label across the top. 'This was where he kept the newspaper cuttings of his fights. He was good when he was younger, but he went on too long, earning less and less, trying to make money for when he had to retire. I was always afraid for him, but everything was fine until the blow that ruined his life.'

'Will you open it?' Eirlys asked. 'There might be photographs to treasure.'

There was no key. Awkwardly, with a knife, then pliers, and finally a chisel and a hammer, they broke the box open and found it filled with newspaper cuttings, as Alice had expected, but among the fading descriptions of his fights were notes. Five-pound notes, one-pound notes and ten-shilling notes. There were also some coins in the thick paper envelopes used by banks.

'What on earth is all this?' Alice gasped.

'His life savings?'

'I didn't know he had any. Oh, Eirlys, we lived in an awful place, falling down it was. And all the time we could have moved to somewhere better.'

'He wanted you to have something after his time, something to remember him kindly by.'

'I do think of him kindly, he needn't have deprived himself for me.' She sobbed while Eirlys held her. She was sad for his lonely end, tucked away in the hospital, with only her weekly visits to break the monotony. 'I could have looked after him better if I'd known about this, found a place where we'd have been happier instead of the filth and misery of those rooms.'

'It was clearly his decision not to spend it. He loved you and this is his way of showing it,' Eirlys said.

'It's enough to buy a house, and we lived in those awful rooms behind a derelict shop.'

After Eirlys had gone, Alice took the money and went to see Marged and Huw.

'But that's wonderful,' Marged said, hugging her. 'What a wonderful thing for him to do. He must have been such a loving father, planning for you to find this after he'd gone.'

Huw went with her to see the bank manager and the money

was put in a deposit account, 'Until my husband comes home,' she told him with tightly crossed fingers. The money came to £200. 17s. 6d., an enormous amount. She didn't keep any of it; the money was for her and Eynon, after the war had been won.

She began to shiver. She hadn't heard from Eynon for several weeks, and with the death of her father she was even more afraid. If Eynon didn't come home she was completely on her own in the world.

'Tomorrow we'll hear from Eynon and Johnny, I'm sure of it,' Huw said, as though reading her thoughts. 'What a surprise this will be for that husband of yours, eh? Take on the whole of Hitler's army unaided he will, he'll be in such a hurry to get back home to you.'

'I'll write and tell him tonight,' Alice smiled. 'Ask him to think about where he wants to live.'

'Not too far from us I hope,' Marged said affectionately.

Vera was tearful and touchy, picking arguments with her colleagues and being barely civil to the kindly Mrs Denver. Her time-keeping was the cause for repeated complaints, as she found it so hard to get up in the mornings, even though she was often in bed hours before Maldwyn and Mrs Denver. She was no longer keen to go to dances or the pictures as she once had.

Mrs Denver knew she was writing to the boyfriend, but no letters had arrived in reply. Even worse, the letters written by Vera were returned marked ADDRESSEE UNKNOWN. She grieved for the girl and wanted to help, but she knew she would be accused of interfering if she tried to persuade her to talk. She must wait till Vera came to her.

The winter frost had a tight grip on everything. Snow fell, to the delight of children and the dismay of everyone else. Buses were cancelled, delivery men came part of the way on foot, men were out gritting the roads every day; children played in the snow and ice, running back to homes where fires were kept burning with logs gathered from the fields and woods outside the town; and every day the women continued the never-ending search for extra food.

226

Many people walked into work but Bernard Gregory managed to get around on a sleigh pulled by his pony, selling firewood to eager customers. Vegetables stayed in ground that was hard and impenetrable. Everything seemed to slow down, until St David's Well appeared to be sleeping.

Vera worried, keeping her fears to herself. The letters she had written to her lover had been returned. He had left her, and she was alone with the very thing her father had warned her of. She knew she was going to have a baby, and she had nowhere to go. Mrs Denver fussed over her and waited patiently to be told.

A letter came for Maldwyn, meanwhile, warning him to leave the town or his girlfriend would suffer. With little hope, he went to see the police. They assured him they would do anything they could, but at present, as he insisted he didn't have either an enemy or even a girlfriend, they had nothing to go on and would simply await further developments.

Charlie Grove walked with him as he was leaving. 'Call on me if you're worried. I'll do what I can.'

'I'm afraid for Delyth, not myself. The best way you can help is to tell anyone who's remotely interested that she's not important to me. That way she might be left alone when whoever this is catches up with me.'

Twelve

B y March, Vera could no longer pretend. Over breakfast, in hurried whispers when Mrs Denver was out of the room, Vera told Maldwyn she was expecting a baby.

'You're *what*?' Maldwyn gasped. More quietly, he asked who the father was. She faced him with a stubborn expression and said the father wasn't involved.

'But he has to be. You can't deal with this on your own.'

'Gone, he is, and I doubt if I'll see him again. What shall I do? I can't go home, our dad'll kill me. He's warned me and my sisters about this since we were old enough to understand. I knew more about temptation and having babies when I was ten than girls five years older. Fat lot of good it did me, eh?'

'You have to tell someone. Won't your mam help?'

She shook her head. 'Mam isn't really aware of what's going on any more. No, there'll be no help from the family, that's for sure.'

'Then you'll have to find the father. A soldier, wasn't he? There must be a way of reaching him. At least tell him, and give him the chance to do something. You can hardly blame him for clearing off if he isn't told.'

'The letters I wrote came back marked "Unknown". I doubt if the name or the address he gave me were true. No, Maldwyn, unless I find someone willing to marry me, I'm in a serious mess.'

He looked at her, his dark brown eyes troubled. A few months ago he would have been delighted at the prospect of marrying Vera Matthews, although whether he'd have been noble enough to take on a child he wasn't sure. Love didn't treat him kindly. First it had been Vera who wasn't interested; now his dreams were woven around Delyth but because of the

228

threats he couldn't even go near her. Vera mistook his sad expression for sympathy.

'Tell Mrs Denver,' he said after a thoughtful silence during which she had stared at him as though expecting him to miraculously solve her problem. 'At least she'll be able to advise you on what to do. Don't you have to see a doctor or something?'

He was out of his depth with this. An only child with no experience of babies, he was trying to help, but knew she needed someone knowledgeable to guide her, help her to do the best for herself and the baby. He stood up, wanting to get away from Vera and her problems. 'Mrs Denver is the one to tell, but if I can help, just ask.'

'Marry me?' she said, staring at him again.

He smiled nervously. 'I have to go. Good luck.'

At work that afternoon, Maldwyn noticed Arnold Elliot measuring their shopfront. Leaving the newspaper he was cutting for wrapping flowers, he went outside and asked what the man was doing.

'Your Mrs Chapel isn't going to be here much longer and when she retires I'll be buying the shop to extend mine,' he repeated. 'I just want her to know that I'm available with a good offer and not to ask anyone else.'

'But what makes you think she's going to retire? Your son isn't helping to persuade her, is he?' he asked suspiciously.

'Course not! I couldn't come in and see what you've done inside, could I?'

'No, I'm sorry but you can't. I don't want Mrs Chapel worrying about what will happen after her time.'

'Not well, is she?' Arnold said pointedly.

'What did he want?' Mrs Chapel asked when he went back inside.

'Oh, nothing, you know what he's like, always talking about buying your shop. I told him you'll be here for a long time yet. Now, what about a cuppa, eh?'

'Maldwyn, I have to go out this afternoon. Will you be all right for an hour?'

'Of course. Just let me bring up a few more things from the

229

cellar in case we have a rush and I'll be fine. Is there anything you want me to do while you're out?'

'No, dear. Just deal with customers and perhaps make a few more of those fir-cone arrangements. The season for them is finished but people will buy anything to add a bit of cheer, and apart from the daffs there isn't much else yet.'

'What about a few bunches of primroses and violets? Mrs Denver has told me where to find them growing wild. I thought I'd spend a few hours on Sunday picking them and bunching them to sell on Monday.'

'That'll be lovely. They always go well. I used to pick them for the Sunday school to give their children on Mothering Sunday, then they would take them home for their mothers; but I haven't managed it the last few years.'

'Perhaps I can do it for you?'

'Yes. You and Delyth could have an afternoon out.'

'Not Delyth, Mrs Chapel, just me. Delyth and I aren't very close friends.'

'Your mouth says you're not, but your face tells a different story.'

'Please, Mrs Chapel. If anyone asks, Delyth is not my girlfriend, right?'

'If you say so,' she replied with a frown. 'Is anything wrong?'

'Nothing wrong. I just wouldn't like anyone to have the impression that Delyth is important to me.'

Mrs Chapel went off in a taxi and he heard her asking to be taken to the station. She didn't return until after five thirty. Maldwyn was sitting in the back room waiting for her.

'Maldwyn, you didn't have to wait for me,' she said, sitting down near him. 'I've been into Cardiff to see my solicitor. Nothing serious – I just wanted him to reassure me about how I've written my will. I don't want there to be any confusion or arguments about my wishes after I'm gone.'

Thinking she was a little depressed, he said, 'Come on, Mrs Chapel, you've been ill but you're coming along nicely. The doctor says once the summer comes you'll be as fit as you ever were.'

'Oh, I'm not worried about my health, dear. I just wanted

to make sure everything will be done as I want. Now I can forget it and look forward to the summer, when we'll have the window filled with flowers and more flowers and not a painted twig in sight!'

'You are much better, and to celebrate I think I should treat you to lunch in a café tomorrow. What d'you say? You choose where we go and it'll be my treat.'

She thought for a moment then said, 'I'd like to go to the market café.'

'Mrs C! There are some nicer places than the market café.'

'You said I could choose. Well, it's the market café, and that nice young Beth Castle as was, Beth Gregory she is now of course. When are *you* going to think of getting married, Maldwyn?'

'Oh, not for a while. I haven't met Miss Right yet,' he joked, thinking of Delyth but unable to say so.

She looked at him shrewdly but said nothing.

The following day they closed the shop at twelve forty-five, fifteen minutes early, and walked to the market, where Beth found them a table and took their order. 'Vegetable soup and bread?' Maldwyn protested. 'Is that all you want?' He looked at the menu written on a blackboard and smiled. 'There isn't much else, is there? Rissoles, sausages, boiled potatoes and cold slice – that'll be luncheon meat, and that's more of a mystery than rissoles,' he whispered. The soup was warming and quite tasty, an excess of pepper making up for the limited ingredients.

Mrs Chapel looked around her at the groups of gossiping women. People passed and waved at her and she smiled back, happy to be there. 'I like this town,' she said. 'Do you?'

'I can't remember being happier than since I came here to work.' He looked at her and said, 'I did think of going back to Bryn Teg. There's an empty shop and I thought of starting my own business, but I gave up on the idea. I couldn't leave St David's Well.'

'Your own shop? Rich, are you? I'm obviously paying you too much,' she joked.

'My stepmother offered to help, and with a loan from the bank—'

'But you prefer living here, in St David's Well.'

'I don't think I'll ever move from here, whatever happens.'

'Good. Because after my days, the shop will be yours. Will you keep the name Chapel's Flowers?'

'What did you say?'

'I changed my will weeks ago. I knew the business would be in good hands. Yesterday I went to talk to my solicitor about my decision. I didn't want there to be any doubts about my state of mind or anything else. He assures me that everything is secure. The shop will be yours.'

'What about your sister's boy?'

'Gabriel hasn't shown any interest. In fact he hardly ever works, not legally anyway. He always seems to have money but there's no explanation of how he gets it. No, he isn't interested, and you are. Maldwyn, I'll be content if I know you'll take it on.'

'Thank you, but—'

'No buts, dear. Let's forget it until – well, let's forget it shall we?'

'Thank you,' he said again, staring at her as though at a stranger.

'You two look serious,' Beth said, coming to remove their dishes. 'Don't tell me the meal was so bad you don't know how to tell me!'

'The meal was one I'll never forget,' Maldwyn said seriously.

Beth frowned at him in amusement. 'That bad?'

Maldwyn stood up and slid the chair back for Mrs Chapel, and as they walked off Beth wondered if they had even heard her.

Delyth was approaching her nineteenth birthday. With Maldwyn avoiding her and her mother and stepfather barely aware of her existence, she thought seriously of joining the forces.

'We'll have to, sooner or later,' she said to Madge. 'The shop isn't exactly essential to the war effort, is it?'

'I wouldn't mind coming with you. It's a bit frightening though, not knowing where we'll go or what we'll have to do. What if we're sent overseas?'

232

'It can't be far enough for me,' Delyth said.

'He hasn't written then?' Madge guessed her friend was thinking about Maldwyn.

'He seemed so attracted, then without warning he pulled away from me and I haven't heard a word since.'

'Let's go to St David's Well. We can walk past the shop, or even go and see Vera at Mrs Denver's. Then, if we accidentally bump into him, it will be up to him how he treats you. At least you'll know for sure if he makes it clear he isn't interested.'

'Will you write to Charlie?'

Madge didn't tell her she already had, and had arranged to see him before suggesting Delyth went with her. 'I'll ask him. He'll meet us if he isn't working.'

The March day was dry and coldly bright. From the train they saw the countryside slowly waking up to spring. In a field where they normally saw swaying corn, they were surprised to see scores of tents, and soldiers busily attending to vehicles parked on the periphery of the once-quiet field.

Madge shivered. 'Can you imagine us in the middle of something like that?'

'Better than the boring shop and evenings feeling in the way while Mam whispers "sweet nothings" to Uncle Trev!'

'Don't you call him Dad?' Madge teased.

'That'll be the day!'

Leaving the newly sprouted Army camp behind, they headed south, then turned west to make their way through the coastal strip of small towns and villages before getting out in the centre of St David's Well. Perhaps later they would make their way to the beach, but first there was Charlie to meet, and hopefully an encounter with Maldwyn.

Vera was not at home, but Mrs Denver told them where to find Maldwyn. 'Up in the woods, he is. Gathering wild flowers for Mrs Chapel's shop.' She gave them directions, and after some hesitation they decided to try to find him. They set off for Dallow Woods, not far from the town, and found him with a basket filled with primroses, blue and white violets, and small sprigs of hazel with their tiny catkins ready to grow. He had also gathered a few branches of horse chestnut with their sticky buds. These would open slowly and give a wonderful display of rich green leaves, something he knew Mrs Chapel would enjoy.

He seemed uneasy when he saw them, and looked around as though being watched.

'Expecting someone?' Delyth asked. 'We'll clear off if we're intruding.'

'No, of course not.'

'You don't seem very pleased to see us.'

'I still worry about that lorry, and you being pushed into the hedge. While you're with me I'm always afraid of something similar happening.'

'You don't have to worry about me.'

'But I do. Until I find the person who played those tricks I won't feel happy about being with you.'

'Is that why you went off so hurriedly on the day of the wedding?'

He went on picking flowers, tying them in bunches of fifteen, dropping them carelessly into his basket, wondering whether it was safe to tell her about the letter and other incidents. He told her a little, but not of the warnings aimed at her. 'So I want you to stay away from me, make people think you and I are nothing more than casual friends, until the man is caught . . . I like you. I like you a lot, and once this is over I hope you and I—' Madge and Charlie approached and he didn't finish, but the look in his dark eyes behind the heavy spectacles told her more clearly than words what he had been about to say.

Maldwyn had to go back to the shop and put his bunches in water, so, persuading him he was worrying about nothing, they arranged to meet at the beach where they hoped to find a café open. When he arrived, he found Madge and Charlie but no sign of Delyth.

'She just disappeared,' a frantic Madge told him. 'We went along the cliff path, as it was such a nice day, and Charlie and I went to look down at some birds we thought were plovers. When we came back to where she'd been standing she was gone.'

*   *   *

234

It wasn't Mrs Denver whom Vera told of her situation. She went to talk to Marged. Vera knew she would have a sympathetic hearing and some sound advice.

'The first thing you must do is tell your family,' Marged said when the problem was explained.

'No! And that's for definite!' Vera replied.

'All right, we'll leave that for the moment, but I think you'll have to face it very soon. Now, what about your young man? You have tried to find him?'

'No luck there. I've written time and again but there's no one of that name at the address he gave me. He told me false, and I'll never see him again,' Vera said, trying to hold back tears.

Marged comforted the girl and gently tried again to persuade her to go home.

When Vera returned to Mrs Denver's the police were there. At first she thought something had happened to Mrs Denver, and immediately her thoughts were for herself. How would she manage with a child and no place to live? She hadn't told her kind landlady about her condition but knew she'd be able to persuade her to let her stay.

Once she learned that Delyth was missing and people were searching for her below the cliffs, Vera forgot her own worries and asked how she could help. With other volunteers she walked through the woods where the four friends had gone to pick wild flowers earlier that day, wondering if Delyth had perhaps lost something and gone back to retrieve it. It was a theory no one believed, but everything had to be checked, however unlikely. The police enquired at the station and at her home in Bryn Teg, but no one had seen her since that morning when she had left with Madge. Police, coastguards, walkers, owners of small boats and many townspeople including Huw and Bleddyn Castle and Peter Gregory, searched the most likely, the possible, the unlikely and the downright stupid places, but without success.

When darkness fell on that bright spring day, no trace of Delyth had been found.

Delyth was not far away. She was locked in a dark place

smelling of the sea and stale fish and that, together with the wooden structure, told her she was on a boat.

She had been grabbed, with a hand covering her mouth to prevent her from making the smallest sound, dragged roughly down to the water's edge and pushed into the small niche where black-market goods had been found. Impatiently pushed and slapped, she had then been tied and gagged.

Afterwards she wondered how the man had managed to tie and gag her without apparent difficulty. She was so scared and confused she hadn't made any effort to fight, or so it seemed to her in the hours following, when she went over the sequence of events that were so confused and eventually reduced to a blur.

While her friends went further afield looking for her she was made to sit on a cold, rough surface, and she felt water slowly lapping around her feet. It was painfully cold but she couldn't move to warm herself. She had been gagged and tied then pushed ahead of the man, who hit her occasionally, and when she fell over in about a foot of water, spluttering and helpless, had hauled her up roughly and hurried her on. Still with her hands tied, the man close behind her, she was forced to climb a ladder, something she did willingly, afraid of the water that had become deeper and now reached to her thighs.

Later, much later, when the town was dark, she was carried over ground that was uneven and smelled of the sea. She knew she was on a beach and she struggled, convinced she was going to be thrown in to drown.

She cried softly, angry with herself for not struggling and making herself heard. Surely there had been time between the first sounds, the intimation of danger, to the moment that huge hand slapped across her mouth, for her to call for Maldwyn?

Treated like a parcel, she was dropped and lifted, then dropped again and ended up alone in this boat. She had dozed a little and awoken to the revival of fear.

The boat was stirring slightly, lifting up and gently dropping back. She listened for the sound of someone coming. 'Maldwyn,' she whispered against the gag that was still tight across her mouth. 'Maldwyn, please come and find me.'

The movement of the boat was caused by the tide coming in and gradually floating the craft. Her fear increased as she wondered if the boat had been holed, and she was going to feel the water rising until she died. But as the hours passed and she began to feel stiff and sore, she realised that drowning was not going to be her fate. Perhaps starvation was.

She had a woollen covering of some kind tucked around her, but it wasn't enough to keep away the chill. The wood of the boat was wet and the cold was eating into her bones. Panic, as she imagined being left there until death came, made breathing difficult and the gag seemed to be choking her. She tried to calm down, reciting poetry, thinking of Maldwyn and of her mother, but she found no comfort. She was going to die.

The searchers gave up around midnight. They gathered in various houses, planning a more thorough search the following day. At the police station, Maldwyn was once again a suspect. He went over everything that had happened, starting with the near-miss with the lorry when he and Delyth were together. He showed them the letter warning him to get out of the shop, and they took samples of his handwriting, asking him to copy the note several times.

When he suggested that Arnold Elliot might be doing these things in order to buy Chapel's flowers, they laughed. Mr Elliot was a respected businessman and he didn't need to resort to such behaviour. But they interviewed him anyway.

For Maldwyn the questions and analysis were a frightening waste of time. Every minute they sat here asking stupid questions added to the time before Delyth was found. 'How could you think these things were down to me?' he shouted in frustration. '*I* was the one the lorry was aimed at!'

'That could have been a near-accident and nothing to do with the rest of it,' a police inspector said, watching his reaction to the suggestion. 'That could have given you the idea; the rest could certainly have been down to you!'

'Please, just find her,' he pleaded. 'She could be in real danger. Help her, please!'

'There are plenty of people searching, and as soon as it's light others will join in. What you can do is admit your part in it before you face more serious charges.'

*   *   *

237

The sea moved gently under the boat. Exhaustion overcame Delyth and she dozed again. A sound woke her and she tried to free her hands, crying in frustration at her helplessness. The boat moved differently, tilting wildly. Someone was on board. It was dark. It might be a fisherman checking his nets. Making as much noise as she could, achieving little more than mewing like a small kitten, she looked towards the door of the tiny cabin.

She heard voices, and the sound of cans and metal objects being moved around. Someone had come, and was searching for her. Then the door opened and the flickering light of a torch span around the cabin, but no one entered. As the door closed again, she tried to move the boat, lifting her body and dropping it, trying to make a noise, but the voices faded, the boat moved jerkily and then was still.

Hours later, when she guessed it was the middle of the night, the sounds were repeated. Again she stared in the direction of the door and saw, in the light of a small lantern, not Maldwyn, but a strange man with a scarf covering the bottom of his face. He unbound her mouth and her hands, tying one wrist to a ring on the boat's side first. She screamed and shouted and begged him to let her go but he told her they were too far off shore for anyone to hear them and, taking out food and a flask, he put them beside her.

At first she refused to eat. 'I'm not eating anything you bring. I insist you take me home,' she said, trying to be strong, ashamed at the wavering fear in her voice.

'Up to you, Delyth Owen, but I'll be tying your hands again when I leave and you'll be looking at it, smelling it, wanting it and unable to reach it. Like that, would you? Hungry, seeing the food and not being able to touch it?'

She reeled off a list of questions, asking what he wanted, why she had been brought there, promising all the money she could raise if that was what he wanted, but he just grunted and gave one flat reply, 'Maldwyn knows.'

He waited while she ate, then retied her hands, leaving the extra rope on her wrist ready, she presumed, for the next time he came.

She was filled with ever deeper despair now. His organisation of food and drink suggested he intended to keep her there for a long time. No one knew where to find her. She could be here until she died. Then an extra panic added to her misery. What if he had an accident? Died, even? Then she would die too. She was completely dependent on just one man. No one else would find her if he didn't return, and on a whim he might decide just that.

She struggled and tried to ease her hands out of the rope: wet, dirty, smelly rope, but strong. Too strong for her to loosen, even if she could get her teeth to it. She wished she hadn't been gagged, and tried to push it down by rubbing the back of her head against the side of the boat; after a while she realised it was less tight. More wriggling and it dropped below her chin; she cried with relief at the small victory.

The police let Maldwyn go and before he went to the beach, where he still hoped to find a clue to Delyth's capture, he went to see if Mrs Chapel was all right. She was sitting in a chair, talking to three or four friends, all waiting for news of Delyth being found safe and well. The news of her disappearance had spread through the town and everyone was anxious for more details.

He told them what had happened and, after swallowing a slice of bread and jam and a cup of tea Mrs Chapel had prepared for him, he stood to leave.

'Will you be all right, Mrs Chapel? Is there anything you need before I go?'

'Well, I can't find my shawl. You know I like it around my knees. If you can find it, or get me something else, I'd be grateful.'

He ran up to her flat and looked for her favourite blanket, made from crocheted squares, but, impatient to be off, he didn't search for it too diligently. He ran back down to the shop carrying another blanket, which he wrapped around her. 'Now don't try to do everything, mind. I'll see to the orders when I get back. Just as soon as Delyth is found.'

'Don't worry about the shop, Maldwyn. Just find her.'

*　　*　　*

Huw was finishing the inspection of Castle's Café. It was approaching the time when they would start painting and freshening things ready for the new season. He stepped out of the café on to the cliff path and as he locked the door he looked around him, wondering where the missing girl might be. He decided to walk along the path, just in case there was a sign of her. She might have fallen and been knocked unconscious, and now be trying to get back to the path. He knew the police and the other services would have checked thoroughly, but in the heart of every searcher was the hope that he would be the one to find her.

He stood for a while at the place where she had disappeared, then went back and took a different path, up to the top of the promontory. There he walked across to a small bay further along. There was no beach. The sea was never less than a couple of feet deep, the cliffs were sheer and no one went there.

He stood for a while, listening, calling her name and feeling a bit foolish doing so, but imagining the thrill of hearing her answering. Out to sea he could make out the defences put there against the threat of invasion. This part of the coast was not a likely place for a landing, although it had been a look-out point for the Home Guard and their hut was still here. There were two boats anchored, one way out beyond the breakers and not far from the barrier. They didn't usually get that close. The Army was likely to blow them out of the water if they drifted within reach of the barrier, suspicious of messages being passed between spies and the enemy.

The sea was quiet, moving against the rocks below with little excitement, no foaming white protest at the restriction of the cliff face. He looked at the two boats; one was quite still on a glassy sea, its almost perfect silhouette mirrored in the water; the other was moving, disturbing the calm of the sea, and he idly wondered why.

Delyth was cold and very hungry. The shawl that the man had placed around her had slipped during her struggles to move the boat in the hope of attracting attention. She had no idea of the time. The man wouldn't come until darkness had fallen, and the hours stretched painfully and miserably before her. If only Maldwyn would guess where she was and come for her. But she knew there was no reason why he or anyone else should look for her in a boat right out on the sea.

When Maldwyn met up with Huw and several others, Madge was with them. She had been unable to leave until her friend was found. They went over the same ground, moving every bush and crawling through the grass and the brittle stalks of last year's wild flowers in the hope of finding some clue. Then they went into one of the cafés not far from the beach and comforted themselves with hot drinks and sandwiches. There they were joined by Mrs Chapel's nephew, Gabriel.

'My aunt told me your girlfriend is lost. Want any help looking for her?'

Maldwyn stared at him and when Madge had gone to 'powder her nose' he asked, 'You don't know anything about all this, do you?'

'About your girlfriend running off? No, of course not. But I do know about you trying to steal my auntie's shop from me.'

'That's nonsense. I did nothing to persuade her. She told me you weren't interested.'

'I want my auntie's shop. I'm entitled. You're not.'

'Are you responsible for Delyth's disappearance?'

'No, you are. Stealing my inheritance, being nice to her until she gave you what's rightfully mine.'

'You're wrong! She didn't think you were interested,' he repeated. 'Please, tell me where to find Delyth. This is all a mistake!'

'No mistake. This is down to you stealing what's mine. I want the shop so I can sell it. Why should you have it?'

'If you know something, you have to tell me. What d'you want me to do? I'll do anything.' As realisation came he gasped, 'It was you, wasn't it? The lorry, everything. Frightening her, warning me to get out. It's the shop, and you all along.'

'All you have to do is write to that solicitor and tell them you won't accept the shop, and want me to have it. That might refresh my memory, help me remember where I've taken her.'

Maldwyn turned and called to the policemen who were outside with the others. As he began to shout, Gabriel grabbed his arm and whispered warningly, 'Don't. My memory might take days to come back if the police upset me with a lot of questions. Cold she'll be, and with no food. Pity for her.'

'Where is she? I'll kill you for this!'

'Talk to the solicitor, sign the shop over to me and she'll turn up, unharmed. If you don't hang about too long, that is.'

'Who was that?' Madge asked as Gabriel moved away. 'He looks familiar.'

'Mrs Chapel's nephew and –' he almost blurted out the truth but he realised that it would put Delyth in more danger – 'and he wants to help us search,' he finished.

Breaking a promise seemed unimportant now, so Madge said, 'I remember Delyth saying he might be the man on that odd little boat we saw from the cliffs. Something about the way he stood with his head to one side – you know how observant she is; her artist's eye, I suppose. She remembered him wearing cut-down wellingtons and saw some in that man's van. Probably a coincidence, mind. She wasn't sure.'

Maldwyn went with the others to search some fields further away. All the time Gabriel stayed near him, warning him against telling anyone what he'd learned. He wondered if Gabriel were telling the truth about holding Delyth, or just taking advantage of the situation to get the shop. He knew this was something the police should handle, but he daren't risk telling them in case Gabriel *was* holding Delyth.

At four o'clock they stopped for a rest and a conference.

'Time passes so fast sometimes, doesn't it?' Gabriel said.

Maldwyn turned to him and nodded. 'All right. I'll telephone the solicitor, and tomorrow I'll go and sign anything you want.'

At the telephone box, Gabriel listened to both sides of the conversation and nodded. 'Tomorrow, when you've signed the shop to me, and explained to my dear aunt how excited I am at learning the flower trade, I'll tell you where to find her.'

'Please, don't leave her for another night.'

242

Gabriel smiled. 'No tricks mind. I'm the only one who knows where she is, remember. I'll meet you at the flower shop tomorrow morning at nine and we'll go together to the solicitor, right?'

It was as Gabriel ran across the road near the promenade that the Castles' van hit him. He lay unmoving on the road and anxiously Huw waited while someone telephoned for an ambulance. Gabriel was not hurt but he remained on the ground, his eyes closed. Maldwyn ran up, put his head close to the man's ear and begged him to tell where he had hidden Delyth. Feigning unconsciousness, Gabriel stifled his amusement at the irony of the ill-timed accident.

Delyth watched the light fade and the night close in. She was extremely cold, unable to exercise her stiff and painful limbs. She was thirsty and hungry but no one came. She was unaware that her worst fears had materialised and the only man who knew where she was wouldn't tell anyone and couldn't come himself.

Madge was staying in Sidney Street, where she and Delyth had stayed before, but she spent the evening with Marged and Huw. Maldwyn was there too, and they went over and over what had happened, trying in vain to think of an explanation. Maldwyn said very little. He was imagining Delyth lying somewhere without food or comfort, alone and afraid. And it was all his fault. If he hadn't asked Mrs Chapel for a job, none of this would have happened. He counted the long hours that would have to pass before he could sign the forms that would hand over the shop to Gabriel, and even then everything would depend on Gabriel being well enough to keep their appointment. He prayed to the fates not to let Gabriel be badly hurt or change his mind about freeing her.

When Madge's words entered his mind he didn't react at first.

'A boat, did you say, Madge?' He turned to Huw. 'Have the police searched the boats in the harbour?'

'Of course they have. And all those around the beach.' To take Maldwyn's mind off Delyth, Huw went on, 'Funny thing, mind, there's an old abandoned boat out in the next bay and this morning I watched it moving, yet the sea was calm. I bet there's a couple of big fish out there. What say we go out one day and see what we can catch, eh Bleddyn?'

Bleddyn and Maldwyn had the same thought at the same time. They leaped up and grabbed their coats. 'Come on. It's worth checking!'

Bleddyn had once taken trippers for boat rides around the bay and along the coast, but the war had stopped all that. His boat was in a stable, propped up on trestles until he could use it on the beach once more. He led the others to a shed and pulled out a small rowing boat, which they dragged down over the shingles of the pebbly beach some distance from their destination. Bleddyn began to row strongly, cursing the lack of petrol for the engine that would have made their journey faster.

As they came around the promontory that protected the cove, he was tiring. 'Out of training for this, I am,' he complained, but he wouldn't let Maldwyn take over. Inexperience would have slowed them more than his aching muscles.

Delyth was sleeping, her breathing shallow. She heard talking, and felt the movement of someone coming aboard, but didn't move. The door opened and all she was thinking about was that if the man was bringing food, the effort of eating would be more than she could manage.

'Delyth?'

She didn't reply. She must be dreaming. She'd heard him call her name so often in the past hours and every time she'd responded the silence had returned to mock her.

'Delyth, are you there?' The lantern beam shone on her face and she closed her eyes against the glare. 'Maldwyn?' she whispered. 'Is it really you?'

'Yes, it's me, lovely girl, it's me.'

He wouldn't let Bleddyn help him. He untied her, sobbing unmanfully at the stubborn knots and the swollen rope, and lifted her, talking soothingly all the time, promising her that it was all over and she was safe. He carried her to the side of the

244

boat where he reluctantly handed her to Bleddyn, just briefly, before getting in and holding her tight until they reached the shore just below Castle's Café.

'I'm never letting you go again,' he murmured. 'I love you and I want us to be together for always.'

She was too weak to reply, but she touched his face and snuggled closer, and that was enough. Bleddyn went on rowing, whistling and pretending he couldn't hear.

Gabriel was insisting he had to get out of the hospital. His head was aching and he had a few bruises but nothing more; he'd be fine, he insisted. But the doctor refused to let him leave until the morning.

He woke to see two policemen sitting beside his bed.

'Get the man who knocked me down?' he asked.

'Yes, and I'll pat him on the back when I meet him,' Charlie Grove said grimly, raising his arm to show the handcuffs he had ready to clip in place.

There was an air of celebration in the town as the news broke. Ken and Eirlys walked up to the flower shop and congratulated Maldwyn.

'We hear an engagement will soon be announced,' Eirlys said. She took Ken's hand. 'I hope you'll be as happy as we are now.' Their contentment was clear to see. Whatever rumours and gossip they had inspired, it looked as though it was all behind them.

On a ship heading out of Dover, Janet sat in a cabin with a dozen other girls. She was going out to be a part of a travelling concert party. She opened her kit bag and took out Ken's letters. Other girls watched, but no one made a comment as she tore them up as small as she could and threw them into a bin. It was time to move on.

Mrs Chapel sorted everything out with the solicitor, and Maldwyn and Delyth announced their engagement a few days later. Beth and Peter insisted they have a party and, with the weather promising a good day, half the town made its way to the early, unofficial opening of Castle's Café, the venue for so many of the town's events.

Vera wasn't there. She had left the factory once her condition was known, and after an exchange of letters between herself and her father she had gone home.

Madge came, accompanied by Charlie Grove, and from the way they behaved Delyth thought another engagement was likely soon. She held Maldwyn's hand and looked around her at the slowly wakening seaside town. A few visitors were already trickling in, ignoring the government's pleas to holiday at home. St David's Well Bay would always be an attraction for families, a friendly place where people were sure of a welcome. It would take more than a war to persuade people otherwise.

'Day trippers we were, Maldwyn, you, me and Madge, but now we're locals. Any regrets?'

'Absolutely none, lovely girl.'